BILLY BOY

THE SUNDAY SOLDIER OF THE 17TH MAINE

Jean Mary Flahive

Jean Mary Flahive

Other books from Islandport Press

Contentment Cove
by Miriam Colwell

Stealing History
by William D. Andrews

Shoutin' into the Fog
by Thomas Hanna

down the road a piece: A Storyteller's Guide to Maine, and
A Moose and a Lobster Walk into a Bar
by John McDonald

Windswept, Mary Peters, and *Silas Crockett*
by Mary Ellen Chase

Nine Mile Bridge
by Helen Hamlin

In Maine
by John N. Cole

The Story of Mount Desert Island
by Samuel Eliot Morison

The Cows Are Out! Two Decades on a Maine Dairy Farm
by Trudy Chambers Price

Hauling by Hand: The Life and Times of a Maine Island
by Dean Lawrence Lunt

These and other Maine books are available at:
www.islandportpress.com.

BILLY BOY

THE SUNDAY SOLDIER OF
THE 17TH MAINE

Jean Mary Flahive

ISLANDPORT PRESS

FRENCHBORO • NEW GLOUCESTER • MAINE

Islandport Press
P.O. Box 10
Yarmouth, Maine 04096
www.islandportpress.com
207.688.6290

Islandport Press edition September 2007

ISBN: 978-1-934031-13-1
Library of Congress Card Number: 2007934609

Book cover design by Karen F. Hoots, Hoots Design
Book design by Michelle A. Lunt, Islandport Press, Inc.

To Billy Laird
who sleeps beside the Little River
and to Bill
for finding him

Sunday Soldier
(Civil War slang for a soldier of little merit)

A sudden death, a striking call
A warning voice—which speaks to all
To all to be prepared to die,
And meet our God who dwells on high
To meet our friends now gone before

—*Epitaph on the gravestone of William H. Laird*

Acknowledgments

I first want to thank the handful of strangers who answered my queries and helped enormously with the many technical questions I asked about life in 1862: the National Railroad Historical Society folks for their information on the rail lines and stations; the Sandy Spring Museum staff in Sandy Spring, Maryland, for providing a historic glimpse of their community and the early Quaker settlers, also referenced in the Chronicles of Sandy Spring Friends Meeting and Environs; the director of reference services, Maryland State Archives; Maine State Archives, the archivists at the National Archives and Records Administration; and the William Still Foundation, particularly descendants Derrick and Clem, for giving me insight into their remarkable ancestor, William Still, and whose book, *The Underground Railroad*, was the source for Elijah's interview.

A very special thanks to David Madden, novelist and Louisiana State University professor, for believing in me when I needed it most; Emily Staat, David's assistant; Betsy Dorr for her insight on people with developmental disabilities; Jean Wilhelm, retired Goucher College professor, for her unflagging support; my literary mentor, Nancy Heiser, who read my first draft and inspired me to continue; Elizabeth Pierson, for her excellent copy editing of a very messy manuscript; Laurel Robinson, copy editor on a later draft; Fathers John Phelps and Paul Sullivan, my "Reverends Snow"; Pauli Caruncho, for cheering me on; Robert Stillings of Berwick for helping me research the historical facts and taking me to William Laird's grave; Robert's late brother Richard Stillings, who chronicled the veterans of Berwick, Maine; my sister, Judith Thyng, for painstakingly reading my early drafts, page by page; my stepson Billy and the late J.D. Ferguson, for helping me choose the title of this book; to my loving, supportive husband Bill, who, upon hearing about William Laird, knew he had found the story that would become my first book; and finally, to my late mother, Mary, whose spirit was in every word.

To the good people of Berwick, Maine: I have taken liberties beyond what we know of the facts about William Laird. I hope you will accept this story as just that.

Prologue

July 13, 1863

President Lincoln escorted the young mother and her child into the Grand Hallway, politely bade them farewell, and then beckoned John Nicolay to follow him into the Oval Office, smiling as he watched his loyal secretary leap from his swivel chair and scoop several papers into his hand.

"Nicolay," said Lincoln as he riffled through the mass of papers scattered on his desk, "I was reading some correspondence before the last visitor arrived. There was another letter from a mother asking for a pardon for her son. Oh, yes, here it is."

Picking up the letter, Lincoln placed his short-shanked gold spectacles low on his nose and began reading. "The lad is only twenty. From her description of him, he sounds quite ingenuous, simpleminded. Hmmm . . ."

Lincoln finished the letter in silence, folded it, and looked at his secretary. "His name is Billy Laird. A private in the Seventeenth Maine Regiment. The mother says he mustered to be with his friends, without a sense of what he was doing."

Nicolay dropped his handful of papers onto the president's desk and leafed meticulously through the stack, carefully pulling out a half-torn sheet. "And that is echoed by one of the private's friends, Corporal Harry Warren," said Nicolay. "His passionate plea caught my attention. I took the liberty of checking with the War Department about Warren's record. From the regiment reports, he received a promotion on May 8,

Billy Boy

1863, as well as the Kearney Medal of Honor following his acts of valor at Chancellorsville."

"Tell me more of what you learned about this soldier, this friend of Billy Laird," said Lincoln as he leaned back in his chair, steepled his fingers, and rested his forearms on his chest.

"Apparently when the Federals were pulling back under heavy fire, a shell exploded beneath a caisson, wounding several men. There was heavy cross fire of artillery and musketry up and down the plank road, but Warren ran to the caisson and dragged the wounded to cover, firing and reloading each of their muskets."

Lincoln lowered his head and sighed. "Undaunted bravery," he said in a low tone. "You have this letter from Warren?"

Nicolay held the torn paper in his hand and cleared his throat. "It is dated June twenty-third, 1863.

Dear President Lincoln:

I'm a soldier who's honored to serve in the Army of the Potomac. I don't know if I've a right to ask you this, sir, but I hear talk that you sometimes pardon a soldier who has violated the Articles of War. Well, Mr. President, my friend, Private Billy Laird, is facing a court-martial back in Maine for desertion. My superior officer said that Billy is almost certain to face a firing squad.

Mr. President, Billy Laird never belonged in this great army. I've known Billy most all my life and I'm going to be plain honest with you about him: Billy never learned to read or write or understand even the simplest things, like playing checkers. I know he only mustered in the army to be with me, most likely because I've always watched out for him, protected him. Now, what he has done falls heavy on my shoulders. In my heart I believe that Billy would still be at my side, carrying his musket, had he not been sent to another unit.

Mr. President, if God permitted, I would change places with my friend. But failing that, I pledge to fight under our flag as if two souls breathed in me. His picket duty is my duty. His musket is my musket. He stands before the enemy as I stand.

Billy is no stranger to battle. He's struggled his whole life to be like the rest of us, and he just can't understand why God chose him to be different. But I believe God also chose me to watch over Billy and to fight his battles. And in that, I will not fail my friend, or you, Mr. President.

Your humble servant,
Corporal Harry Warren
17th Regiment, Company G, Maine Volunteers

Deep lines cut across Lincoln's brow, and a heavy sadness fell across his face. He raised himself slowly from his chair and pushed it aside with his foot. Hands fisted behind his back, he walked to the long-paned window, gazing out at the summer garden. He spoke haltingly in a near whisper.

"Sleep eludes me on many nights, Nicolay. In my mind's eye I see so many boys—young boys, lying dead or wounded in trampled fields stained red with blood. I hear their mournful wails and I bear a mother's agony. I am haunted by such images . . ."

Lincoln stared silently for several moments and slowly turned back to his desk, glancing at Nicolay and the letter he held in his hand.

"It seems by his valiant actions our young corporal honors his pledge." Lincoln paused and looked over his spectacles. "There are mitigating circumstances here, and I find no justice served in executing Billy Laird. What do we know of his trial?"

"The War Department reports he was tried over a week ago and found guilty. He's being held at Fort Preble in Maine and is to be executed in three days' time, on July fifteenth," said Nicolay.

With a shake of his head and a sigh, Lincoln said, "Then we must move quickly. Have the commander of Fort Preble telegraphed at once."

He reached into a pigeonhole in his desk and withdrew a slip of paper. Dipping his pen in the inkwell, he scratched several lines and handed the note to his secretary. "Take this to the War Department. It should be enough to grant a pardon on such short notice."

"A compassionate act, Mr. President."

Lincoln looked over his spectacles, his eyes calm, his voice unwavering.

"See that this young boy goes home—where he belongs."

Chapter 1

The hot sun beat down on Billy's shoulders as he turned the grass in large forkfuls and made his way across the rocky pasture. He was mad clear through. Mad at his pa, mostly. Harry Warren and his other friends had wanted him to go swimming at Frog Pond, but Pa said he had to finish turning the hay. Said the grass was needing to dry before gathering it for the barn. Haying season in New England was short, after all—shorter than ever on their Maine farm, his Pa reminded him—and there was no time for tarrying.

Sweat poured down Billy's neck. As he tossed hay in the muggy, late-July air, he thought of his friends, most of them nearly twenty years old like him, splashing in the deep, cool water. He paused, pulled out his handkerchief, and wiped his dusty face.

"Ain't fair I didn't get to go swimmin'," he mumbled to himself. Then he remembered that Harry had told him they were all meeting up at the store after their swim. There was some big news, Harry had said, and now Billy was going to miss out on that, too.

Shielding his eyes from the glare of the sun, Billy gazed at the graying rows of unturned grass. Tossing his pitchfork against the boulder, Billy defiantly crossed the field to the road. His mood was stormy as he kicked up the yellow dust with his boots, and he sneezed when it settled in his sandy brown hair.

When he reached the bridge over Little River, Billy took off his boots and rolled his trousers high up on his long legs, choosing to wade across the shallow stream. He'd get a tanning for sure, going to Blaisdell's Store before all the hay was turned, but he didn't care.

He never left the farm much anymore, what with the teasing and all. And only now, figuring that Harry would be there, was he willing to go to Blaisdell's alone. Fellas in town most always poked fun, calling him names. Doc Stillings said Billy's mind just worked a little slower, but that didn't give folks cause to be hurtful. Even Mr. Blaisdell yanked all the coins from his hand one time, counting each one, loud as a braying mule. Folks in the store were laughing because Billy couldn't make change. Leastways Harry changed that. He'd sooner fight anyone who poked fun at Billy. Back on dry ground, Billy jingled the coins in his pocket. He reckoned there was enough to buy some candied ginger. After Mr. Blaisdell's poking fun, Harry showed Billy how many pennies he needed to buy the candy. He went and took one of Billy's hands and laid a penny on each finger. Said Billy would have enough to buy him a whole bag.

When Billy reached the top of Pine Hill he stopped to catch his breath. Scattered farms worked the hillsides, and in the valley below, he could see the small villages of Berwick, Maine, and Somersworth, New Hampshire, separated by the Salmon Falls River. A gray cluster of woolen and cotton mills flanked the riverbanks.

Blaisdell's Store, a large white clapboard building on the corner of Milk and Berwick streets, was the local gathering place in Berwick. Even with his pocket full of change, Billy felt uneasy as he went into the store to wait for Harry. Inside he smelled the store's familiar but peculiar aromatic blend of salt codfish, West India spices, and tobacco. He stood quietly to the

Map of Berwick, circa 1872 from "The Old Maps York County, Maine in 1972." *Courtesy of Maine Historical Society Collection.*

side in the cluttered old establishment, nervously fingering the colorful bolts of cloth, watching curiously as Mr. Blaisdell scribbled several lines on a square of slate and set it prominently in the storefront window. Then Mr. Blaisdell unrolled a large parchment on the countertop and smoothed it with the palm of his hand before he nailed it to the rafter above the unfired woodstove. Billy was glad Mr. Blaisdell never once glanced his way.

He sighed, wishing Harry would hurry along. When Mr. Blaisdell at last disappeared behind the stacks of canned goods, Billy hurried across the floor and glanced up at the poster, frustrated that he could not read its bold print. It reminded him of the day Miss Dame had walked him home from the schoolhouse and talked to his folks. He was just eight, but he never went back to school again. Ma said there were things enough to learn at the farm. That's when Pa started teaching him to work the horses. Pa said he had a way with animals. Like that time at the Hall farm, when Mr. Hall wanted to shoot a year-old colt—said he was born mean, always biting and kicking. But Billy walked right up to the frightened colt, stroked his neck, talked nice, and sure enough, the little fella calmed down. Even followed Billy clear across the pen, right over his shoulder. Mr. Hall said he'd never seen anyone soothe a horse like Billy had done.

Billy studied the ink drawing at the top of the paper, a bald eagle with its talons gripping a long white banner. Creases furrowed his brow as he ran his finger along the eagle's outstretched wings. Suddenly shouts erupted outside, and he spun around to see Harry, Leighton Tasker, and Josh Ricker pointing wildly at the slate in the storefront window. Seconds later, Harry and Josh rushed through the door, feverishly glancing around the store.

"It's over there—tacked on the beam!" Josh shouted. He and Harry raced across the store, and behind them biscuit crates toppled as the ungainly Leighton lumbered over the uneven floor, his immense size filling the narrow aisles.

"Hey, Billy." Harry grinned and, taking a deep breath, turned an anxious glance to the poster as he ran his fingers through his damp black hair. His gray eyes flashed in excitement. "Says here we get a hundred and sixty acres of land after the war! Free!"

"And seventy-five dollars!" shouted Josh as he ducked his small, wiry body under Harry's arm and scooted in front of him. "Don't that beat all."

Billy tugged at Harry's shirtsleeve. "What's it mean?"

"It's a recruiting poster, Billy. That's the news we've been waiting for. Army's forming the Seventeenth Maine Regiment, and they're looking for able-bodied men right here in Berwick. You know, for the war."

"War? We're fightin' a war here—in Berwick?"

"Billy, this here's President Lincoln's war. Fighting's going on down south mostly. The whole country's been at war for over a year now—since last April. Us Northern folks against them Southerners—you know, them boys I call Johnnies."

"Why are we fightin' them Johnnies?" Billy asked.

Reaching up to place both hands on Billy's tall, thin shoulders, Harry said, "President Lincoln says we got to keep this country together and free the slaves, and well, down south, some folks don't think the coloreds got a right to be free."

Billy nodded. He remembered Reverend Snow talked about the slaves not being free and all.

"So, Billy Boy, Leighton and Josh and I are thinking about going in the army."

"All of you?"

"Look at this! We're gonna get us a bounty of two hundred and sixty dollars just for signing up," said Josh. "Says a recruiting officer's gonna be in town come Monday."

"I'm goin' with you."

Harry shook his head slowly. "Aw, Billy, me and Leighton and Josh are gonna do the fighting. You need to stay here—take care of things for us."

"Ain't fair!"

"I ain't much for fightin'," Leighton said, placing his hands on his hips. "Thing is, my folks need this money. Believe you me, I'd rather pitch manure all day than go off to this here war."

"Leastways you won't smell as bad," said Josh as he turned and punched Leighton playfully in his soft, round belly.

"You puny little bugger!" Grabbing Josh by his rope belt, Leighton swooped him off the floor and threatened to toss him onto the crates of salt codfish. Laughter exploded as Josh hollered for mercy, his arms and legs shadowboxing the air, each swing missing his big friend.

"Like as not, I'm goin' too," said Billy, crossing his arms and ignoring the tussle and merriment.

"Well, I ain't real sure the army will let you muster, being how you—well, I mean, the learning and all," Harry said gently. "Remember all the trouble you had at the schoolhouse, with Miss Dame . . ."

"I been rememberin'." Billy's black mood returned and fear pulsed through him as he thought of being separated from Harry. What would he do without his friend? The taunts, the name-calling, the loneliness; he didn't want to face all that again on his own.

"Just wantin' to be with you is all."

"Your folks would be mighty worried."

"I'm nineteen, same as you!"

Leighton lowered Josh to the floor and glanced at Billy. "Hey, you got any of that ginger candy on you?"

"Been waitin' . . ."

"Let me see what you got for coins," said Harry.

Reaching into his trouser pocket, Billy pulled out a fistful of pennies. Suddenly feeling unsure of himself, he dropped them into Harry's palm. "Enough?"

"You betcha," said Harry. "Did you use your fingers like I showed you?"

Billy nodded.

"Still ain't ready to talk to that ol' sourpuss, eh? All right then, I'll get it for you this time." Calling out to Mr. Blaisdell, Harry turned and walked to the front of the store.

Billy spun around and stared at Leighton as he ran his finger back and forth along the recruiting poster. As tall as Billy was, he felt small against his giant friend. "What's it say?"

"Says here we gotta muster for three years—unless sooner discharged."

"I ain't understandin'."

"Oh, if I was to be wounded or get real sick, then I get to come on home before the three years is up, in 'sixty-five."

"Likely be home in a fortnight," Josh said with a wink. "Ain't no graycoat gonna miss your fat ol' body."

"Scratch your fleas!"

"Go jump in a cow flap!"

"You fellas still at it?" said Harry as he approached and tossed a small bag to Billy.

Seizing the bag in midair, Billy pulled out a flat, honey-colored candy, popped it in his mouth, and licked the sugary coating from his fingers.

"It's for three years, you know, Harry," said Billy.

"That's right. And when I get back I'm gonna get me a nice little spread with all them free acres so's me and Mary Rogers can settle down."

"I can fire a musket," said Billy, reaching into the bag without an upward glance.

"Aw, Billy," Harry said. "War ain't like firing your musket at a deer. Gonna be aiming at fellas just like us." Suddenly his voice rose. "Hey, you finish all that haying this afternoon?"

"Well, not all, I reckon," Billy said in a half-whisper. "Ain't fair I didn't get to go swimmin'."

"Your pa's gonna take a fit if you didn't turn all the hay. You best go on now so you don't get yourself in trouble."

"All right then. But like as not, I'm musterin', same as you."

"We'll go swimming again right soon, Billy Boy." Leighton pushed his hand into the paper bag and pulled out a piece of candy.

Billy raised a worried eyebrow, peered into the bag, and smiled in relief at the candy still settled at the bottom. He quickly rolled up the bag and stuffed it into his shirt pocket. Harry was right, he figured—if he left now, maybe there was time enough to finish turning the hay. Then he thought about his friends staying in town, laughing and joshing about the war and all, and he hesitated, shifted the weight on his feet, and stared vacantly at the floor.

After an awkward silence, Harry leaned in close to Billy, ruffled his hair, and said quietly, "I ain't got no right to stop you from joining up. Go on and talk to your pa. If he lets you muster, tell him Harry won't let nothing happen to you."

Soothed by those words, Billy darted a smile at his friends. Harry wouldn't let him down after all. "And I'm gonna buy me a whole bag of ginger candy with all that money when I get back. Ma says I got me an awful sweet tooth."

The sun lowered over the hills as Billy ran down Cranberry Meadow Road and started up the easy slope to the boulder to pick up the pitchfork. He circled the lichen-covered outcrop several times. The fork wasn't there. There'd be a tanning for sure. Worried, he started out across the darkening field, suddenly stopping in his tracks. All the hay was turned. Had his pa been here? His heart pounded against his chest. In the gathering shadows of the pines edging the field he spotted a grayish silhouette tossing a forkful of dry grass. He squinted. Jamie? Jamie's gone and done my chores? Billy raced down the hill, relief splitting a grin across his face.

"You turned the hay!"

Laughing, Billy scooped his ten-year-old brother up off the ground and lifted him onto his shoulders. He felt Jamie's small hand slide down the front of his cotton shirt and reach into the pocket.

"I seen you run off," Jamie said. "You got candy in here?" He opened the crumpled bag and pinched his nose. "This is nasty-tasting, Billy. Ain't you ever gonna buy them licorice strings?" Leaning over, Jamie stuffed the bag back into the pocket.

"I like this ginger candy." Billy eased Jamie back to the ground and watched as the sandy-haired child picked up the pitchfork and combed bits and pieces of grass from its muddied prongs. Small as Jamie was, Ma said he looked just like Billy. And Ma was always telling folks her boys' eyes were blue as a robin's egg. Billy took a deep breath and let it out slowly as it dawned on him that running off to war would mean leaving Jamie behind. He loved his little brother. Pa said Jamie was smart as a whip. For dang sure, folks had no cause to laugh at Jamie.

Billy and Jamie headed back across the pasture, the rocky landscape turning a dark purple in the dimming light. Maybe Ma would let them play a game of checkers before supper.

"You wantin' to play checkers when we get home?" Billy asked.

"Reckon."

"Can I use them black checkers this time?"

"You know them black ones is mine."

"Ain't never won a game is all. It's them dang red checkers, I'm thinkin'."

Jamie let out a laugh.

Chapter 2

T he bells were pealing as Billy stood on the steps of the
Congregational Church, waiting for his friends. He
squinted in the sunlight and smiled when he spotted Jamie
swinging wildly on the branch of a bending birch. Behind Billy,
standing beside Pa, was Stuart Marston, stirring a group of
men with talk of war.

Suddenly, from the bottom of the steps, Henry Kinsley
grumbled and raised a pointed finger. "You may think yourself a
ready speaker, Stuart, but this danged rebellion won't get all
my sons—not all five, by God! I can't run the largest dairy
farm in York County myself."

Marston replied, "President Lincoln asked for three hundred
thousand volunteers to help keep this country together. If the
Federal army can't meet its quota, this town's obliged to give
up her sons." Marston placed his hands on his hips, shook his
head, and stared at his cracked kip boots. "My Charlie's signing
up tomorrow. And he's the only boy I got. No matter if it's one
or five, reckon we got to let our boys choose their own way."

Billy liked Mr. Marston, but he didn't much like Mr.
Kinsley. Pa said Kinsley was a hard man to do business with,
always wanting to trade one of his dairy calves for a load of Pa's
timber, even though Pa said calves didn't pay the taxes. Mr.
Kinsley and his boys would ride up the lane with their empty
wood sled, and the boys would take out their axes and fell the
tall pines while Mr. Kinsley strutted around the farmyard like a
rooster. Billy winced as Mr. Kinsley shot a look at him, and
then Kinsley turned to Pa.

11

"And what about you, John? We let them send our sons off to war?"

John Laird pressed his Bible against his chest, his bony fingers fidgeting with the worn leather. His thick, graying brown hair framed his angular face. "Reckon we got us a duty. Our grandfathers fought on this very soil to preserve our Constitution, and I ain't about to walk over yonder, stand by Ephraim Laird's grave, and tell him we ain't fighting to keep it."

"Suppose you call it our duty to free them slaves down south?" Kinsley muttered under his breath before spitting a wad of tobacco on the ground.

Billy saw Pa's jaw tighten. Sure enough, Pa was minding his temper.

"No man's got a right to own another, Henry. We're all God's children."

"You talk mighty big," Kinsley said angrily, "but folks know you ain't sending your simpleton off to war."

The insult was familiar to Billy; he knew it was directed at him. He felt the heat rise in his cheeks and even his ears prickled hot. Heads turned in his direction. His eyes downcast, he stared awkwardly at the whitewashed steps, wishing he could disappear into the cracked and splintered wood.

"You got no cause to talk like that, Henry." The firmness in John Laird's face crumbled. He turned and stomped up the steps. Billy hurried after him.

Billy slid into the family pew. Pa bowed his head in silent prayer. Billy angled his long legs out of the way as Ma joined them, offering her a faint smile. He warmed to her soft blue eyes. Her plaited hair reminded him of the color of honey, and Pa always said her cheeks were the pink of roses. Ma smoothed the folds of her plain linen dress, reached over and squeezed his hand, and closed her eyes. The church was filling with people. Jamie stumbled into the pew, all in a rush, his Sunday clothes soiled with dirt and grass. Billy started to laugh, but Pa looked up with a stern face.

With a deep sigh Billy settled back into the bench and glanced across the aisle, searching for his friends. Harry's folks sat in their customary pew, but there was an empty space beside them. He wondered why Harry wasn't in church. Restless, he squirmed and looked over his shoulder, studying the rows behind him. Mabel Tasker smiled at him and nodded her head. He smiled back, but noticed that her son was nowhere to be seen. Leighton always sat next to his ma; where could he be? A nudge from Billy's own ma interrupted him. He turned around as Reverend Snow approached the pulpit and looked out at the congregation over his half-rim spectacles.

Billy was fond of the kindly old reverend with his round cheeks and tufts of wavy white hair. The reverend was a seafarer's son, and had told Billy a frightening tale from his childhood. When he was just a boy, his pa had taken him on his first trip out of Portsmouth Harbor. Not two days out to sea, a gale blew their small sailing vessel off course. Trying to tighten the riggings against the rough swells, his pa had slipped on the deck and hurt his back. The reverend had been forced to take the helm, young as he was. It was another two days before another fishing ship spotted them and pulled their vessel into Gloucester. The reverend always told folks how he had received the Lord after that. Said he'd felt the hand of God steering the bow headfirst into those swollen waves.

The tapping of drumbeats shook Billy from his thoughts. *Rat-a-tap-tap.* He shook his head. Where was that coming from? *Rat-a-tap-tap.* There it was again, along with music from a fife.

The rhythmic sound grew louder. *Rat-a-tap-tap*. Billy spun his head to the back of the room. The church doors opened and the tramping of marching feet mingled with the fife and drum. Around him, the congregation turned in their pews, whispering, wondering.

A parade of men, older men like Pa—Rufus Emery the shoemaker, the wheelwright Josephus White, Clarence Hasty the blacksmith, and many of the farmers—marched in measured steps down the center aisle to a pew left empty in front of the pulpit. The cadence of fife and drum filled the church.

Suddenly a line of boys tramped down the aisle behind the older men. The congregation erupted with shouts of enthusiasm. Billy's eyes widened in bewilderment as the young men filed by. Leighton. And Harry! Josh. And Charlie Marston—and Jeb Hall. And then he saw the Kinsley fellas and . . . and . . .

Billy's pulse raced. Reverend Snow stepped down from the pulpit and warmly greeted the late arrivals, smiling and shaking their hands. Then, raising a robed arm to the drummer and fife player at the church door, the reverend returned to the pulpit. A hush fell over the room.

"In the words of Isaiah thirteen, verse four," the reverend began in a resounding voice, " 'The noise of the multitude in the mountains, like as of a people; a tumultuous noise of the kingdoms of nations gathered together: the Lord of hosts mustereth the host of battle!' "

Billy stared in wonderment as arms rose from the front rows, fists clenched, beating the air. The congregation once again erupted in cheers.

Ma stretched her slender frame over Billy, and pinched Pa's shirtsleeve. "This is the Sabbath!" she whispered.

"Reckon we need to get used to this," Pa said.

"Pa," Billy whispered. "I ain't understandin'."

"Me neither," echoed Jamie.

Pa leaned close to Billy's ear. "These fellas plan on signing with the recruiting officer tomorrow and going off to war."

"Pa, they're my friends; I'm wantin'—"

"Shhh . . . listen, son."

Reverend Snow waved his hand to quiet the crowd, then continued solemnly. "My good friends, there are purposes under heaven that we are helpless to control. This is a time of God's calling, when no man has a choice, however gentle and peace-loving he may be. 'I have seen the travail, which God has given to the sons of men to be exercised in it.' We have heard the call to war—a mighty call for our sons."

The reverend glanced down at the men sitting in the front pews. "A time of war. Oh, Lord, give us the wisdom to understand all things that are done under heaven."

Billy fidgeted, arched his back, fighting the urge to run over and sit beside Harry. Why hadn't his friends asked him to join them? He struggled to listen, catching the end of the reverend's words. " 'Therefore, my sons, take unto you the whole armor of God, that ye may be able to withstand in the evil of the day, and having done all, to stand!' Our brave and courageous fledgling soldiers, deliver unto us a time of peace."

In the immediate silence that followed, Billy leaned forward, craned his neck, and saw the big grins on his friends' faces. He tried to catch Harry's eye, but the organist banged her fingers on the keys and in seconds the congregation was on its feet, singing "America." Then Reverend Snow stepped down from the pulpit, embracing the boys, patting the shoulders of the older men.

Billy felt very alone. Yesterday Harry had tried to talk him out of mustering. Then Mr. Kinsley had talked hurtful in front of folks. *Ain't fair. I can fire a musket same as anyone.* He should be sitting in the front row too. He listened, stone-faced, to the rest of the service.

In the soft glow of the lantern, the evening meal passed in near silence. Billy shuffled in his chair and glanced at his little brother pushing carrots around his plate.

"Ma's gonna make you sit here all night if you don't eat them carrots, Jamie."

"Don't care. Besides, I seen you hide them turnips in your pocket."

"Not by a darned sight!"

"Hush, the both of you," snapped Ma. "I'm in no mood to listen to your fighting."

"Pa?"

"What is it, son?"

"I can fire a musket same as Harry."

Pa's jaw tightened, his brow wrinkled. "I know dang well what you're thinking. And you ain't never fired your rifle at another fella before," he said sharply.

Billy stared at the half-eaten food on his plate. Pa was right smart, figuring out what he was going to ask.

"You think you can fire at a fella when you can't even shoot a bad colt?" Pa slammed his fork on the table.

"Weren't no need of shootin' the colt. I soothed her down good."

"Well, let me tell you something, Billy. You ain't soothing any Reb soldier down. They're gonna be shooting at you. And you got to fire that ol' muzzleloader, load another ball just as fast as you can spit, and fire again—right at them."

"My friends—"

"War ain't about being with friends, son."

"Just wantin' to be like Harry."

"You goin' to war, Billy?" asked Jamie. He pushed out his lower lip.

"Billy ain't going anywhere but to do his evening chores," interrupted Ma. "Go on, the both of you."

"Jamie ain't eatin' his carrots, Ma."

"Billeeee!"

"I'll mind what your brother's eating."

It was a clear night, and without the cover of clouds the summer air was cool. Leaning over the rail fence, Billy scanned the sky in search of the North Star. For weeks Pa had been showing him how to find it. Said it was like a signpost, and that their farm sat right under it. Billy looked hard, but couldn't find the star. It was hard, what with the stars all looking the same. He was getting a crick in his neck.

He unhitched the gate and ran to the middle of the pasture. Determined, he lay down on the ground on his back, his hands behind his head. It was easier to look up this way. Now, what had Pa told him to look for first? A cluster of stars that looked like a large ladle in a kettle of stew. Said it was called the Big Dipper. He thought he saw something. He sat up and leaned on his elbows. *It does* look like a ladle! And a plum big one! That's it—the Big Dipper. His heart pounding, he traced his finger across the starry bowl.

I see it, Pa, I see it. He had never found the North Star by himself before, and the small victory made him think that maybe he wasn't a simpleton after all. Billy glanced across the darkened field. The yellow light from the kerosene lamp cast a warm glow in the farmhouse window, and he could see the shadowy silhouette of his brother pressed against the glass, searching for him. *Things don't work out at war, I'll just come home is all. Got me a signpost now.*

Billy jumped to his feet and ran through the blackness, toward the light across the pasture.

Chapter 3

Billy awoke with the sun, but he was still tired. All night he had tossed and turned, wrestling with his decision of whether or not to follow his friends. Pa said he had never fired a musket at another fella, and it didn't seem right, shooting at someone. But Harry, Leighton, and Josh had all acted so excited reading that recruiting sign in Blaisdell's Store. And then with all the goings-on at church yesterday, even Reverend Snow had been riled up about it. His mind was made up.

He let out a big yawn as he thought about his day's work ahead, what with the hay still to be gathered and stored in the barn. He picked his trousers and blue cotton shirt off the floor and struggled to squeeze his feet into his boots, which he always left half-laced. With care he smoothed the worn bed-clothes and placed the quilt Ma had made especially for him when he was a boy neatly over his bed.

He clambered down the narrow staircase that emptied into the mudroom off the kitchen. The sweet smell of smoky bacon and boiled coffee stirred hunger in his belly, but there was no time to eat, and for sure he didn't want Ma asking about his business. Billy yanked his jacket off the wall peg and moved quietly toward the back door.

"Billy?" Ma stepped into the entryway, wiping her hands against her apron. "Where you off to without your breakfast?"

"Ain't hungry now, Ma," he said, hating to tell a lie, feeling the heat rise in his cheeks. He stepped across the floor and, as was his custom, leaned over and kissed her on top of her head.

"Well, then, go and get started on your work. There's a lot
of hay to be loaded. I'll keep something warm for you for
when you do get hungry."

"Yes, Ma."

Billy raced across the farmyard and headed to the far pasture. He followed the granite stone wall built by his grandfather to the edge of the woods, emerging at last onto Cranberry
Meadow Road. Sugar maples lined the winding lane. Last
spring Pa had tapped all those maples. Then Billy and Jamie had
lugged the heavy buckets of sap to the sugaring house and
watched over a blazing log fire while the sap boiled down to
rich amber syrup. Billy smiled, remembering the morning they
had trudged through a fresh snowfall, buckets sloshing with the
watery sap. All of a sudden his little brother had stopped, set
his bucket down, and grabbed a fistful of snow, packing it into a
firm ball. Jamie dunked the snowball into the sap bucket. A
sigh rose inside Billy's chest as he thought about sitting on a
bare log with his brother, eating handfuls of sweetened, sticky
snowballs.

The morning sky threatened rain by the time Billy reached
the Berwick town hall. Pa would be fretting about the rain
spoiling the dried hay, he thought. He'll likely pull the hay cart
onto the field looking for me, long before the afternoon. He
rubbed his sweaty palms down the side of his trousers, ran his
fingers through his uncombed hair, and opened the door.

Smoke from pipe tobacco and rolled cigarettes stung his
eyes and raucous voices bounced off the high tin ceiling and
jarred his ears. Sitting at a small desk smack in the middle of
the crowded hallway was Frances Porter, the town clerk, laughing with the blacksmith. Around her, clusters of men leaned
against the wall in lively conversation. Rows of chairs were

20

filled with familiar faces; newspapers lay scattered across the
floor. Billy spotted one of the Kinsley boys, averted his gaze,
and approached the stout town clerk, a shy smile across his
face.

"You here to see the recruiting officer?" Miss Porter asked,
cheerfully turning away from the blacksmith who walked over
to an empty chair and sat down.

"Yes, ma'am."

"Have a seat, young man," she said, pointing to the back of
the hallway. "We've had such a rush of boys already. It's going
to be a little while. You'll need to wait your turn, but I'll let
you know. You John Laird's boy?"

Billy nodded and stepped away from the desk, sneaking a
glance at the half-open door to the recruiting office. He swallowed hard, tore at an already jagged fingernail, and walked to
the last row of chairs. Hoping not to be noticed, he crossed his
arms over his chest, stretched his legs, and closed his tired
eyes.

A finger tapped his shoulder. He raised his head, which felt
a little foggy. Frances Porter was looking down at him.

"You can go in now. I hope I didn't startle you," she said.
"You've been asleep for some time."

"Yes, ma'am," he said, rubbing his eyes. In the chair next to
him an older man jabbed him in the ribs.

"You'll be in a heap of trouble if the army catches you dozing on picket duty," he said with a smirk.

"Picket duty?"

"Oh, an innocent you are."

Billy said nothing, and walked timidly across the hall. He
hesitated at the doorjamb, his gaze fixed on the grooves in the
hobnailed floor.

21

"Don't stop there," a firm voice said.

Billy stepped warily into the room and stared at the officer in the crisp blue uniform sitting behind a desk, his thick, dark beard falling below a high-buttoned collar, his brown eyes narrow and penetrating. Billy recognized the oak desk as one from the schoolhouse and quietly wondered if his own pocketknife had marred its scarred surface. An American flag hung limply on a wooden shaft in the far corner of the bare room, providing the only color against the dull gray walls.

Billy spoke first. "You the recruitin' officer?"

The uniformed man nodded. "Lieutenant Colonel Merrill. How old are you, son?" He scrutinized Billy from head to toe.

"Gonna be twenty come December."

"Fair enough. Enlistment's for three years. Are you aware of that?"

"Yes, sir."

"You a drinking man?"

"No."

"Ever been in trouble?"

Billy hesitated, shifted nervously on his feet. "Well, yes, sir, I reckon I have."

A frown crossed the officer's face. "What kind of trouble?"

"Well, last time when I didn't finish up all my chores, Pa—"

"Chores?" The officer's bushy eyebrows arched his face into a frown. "That the most trouble you've been in? Not finishing your chores?"

Billy turned away from the officer's stern gaze and stared vacantly at the American flag. He felt a lump in his throat. "Just forgot is all," he said, wondering if he should leave.

Lieutenant Colonel Merrill rubbed a hand along his beard, and then a faint smile crossed his face. "Farm boy, eh?"

22

"Yes."

"This won't be like the farm. You think you can perform the duties of a soldier?"

Billy frowned with uncertainty.

"Duties, young man. Can you handle them?"

"You mean like doing chores and all?"

Lieutenant Colonel Merrill mumbled under his breath and then picked up a piece of paper from the desk. "I guess you could say duty is like doing chores. Only you have to finish your chores in the army."

"Oh, yes, sir." Billy bit down on his lower lip. "Then you ain't sore at me? Am I gonna—"

The officer waved an impatient hand as he cut Billy off in midsentence. "What's your name?"

"Billy Laird."

"Full name."

"William H. Laird."

"Well, William H. Laird, you can expect to leave for Camp King on August seventh. Here are the terms of the enlistment."

Billy leaped down the town hall steps two at a time. The sky was a dark gray, the winds gusting, swirling dust and dirt in the crowded street. He hoped there was time to finish gathering hay before the rain came. Someone shouted his name. It was Harry, waving to him from the porch of Blaisdell's Store, beckoning him over. Beside him, Mary Rogers held onto her hat and smiled.

"Harry!" Billy yelled back as he ran into the street, darting out of the way of a wagon with empty milk tins rattling in the tailboard.

"Hey, Billy."

Billy stumbled on the stairs, laughed at his own clumsiness, and brushed the dirt from his trousers. He grinned at Mary, beguiled as the wind lifted ringlets of her auburn hair from under her bonnet. "You sure look pretty today, Mary."

"Why, that's mighty nice of you, Billy."

"Can I tell him?" Harry asked excitedly as he turned to Mary. She blushed and lowered her eyelids, nodding slowly.

"Mary said she'd wait for me—you know, after the war."

"Wait for what?"

"We're going to get married!"

"When Harry gets back; three years, most like," Mary said softly. Dust and dirt spewed from the windswept street. She placed a hand over her mouth and coughed. "I'll be going now, Harry. Why don't you stay and talk with Billy for a while." Mary turned around, the wind fanning her calico skirt around her ankles as she hurried down the steps. "Billy, tell your brother that I'll be his teacher come the fall term," she said without looking back.

"Yes, ma'am."

Harry laughed and shook his head. "Been angling for Mary's attention since she first come to Sunday school all them years ago. Remember how I told her I'd lost my Bible just so she would share hers with me? Walked her home in the rain, and when I offered up my jacket, my Bible plum fell out of the pocket! Been on a chase for near six years. I'm thinking this here war helped me out this time, what with me leaving and all."

Suddenly he glanced at the white clapboard building across the street and turned back to Billy. "Where were you just now?"

24

"Town hall."

"You enlisted?"

"Same as you."

"Your pa's letting you do this?"

Billy scuffed his boots across the plank steps, and then raised his face to the storm clouds rolling black across the skies.

"Billy—you ain't told your pa, have you?"

"Wanted to be with you and Leighton and Josh and—"

"Billy . . ." Harry ran his fingers through his hair.

"You sore at me?"

"Look, I ain't sore at you. It's just that you went off and done this . . ."

The sky rumbled and clapped with thunder. Finally the clouds burst, and in an instant Main Street turned to mud. Billy slapped a hand over his mouth. *The hay!*

"I'm needin' to go!"

He raced down the greasy steps, his heart pounding as he stumbled through the drenching rain.

Chores.

Duty.

You have to finish your chores in the army.

"Sit over there, son," Pa said sharply, pointing to a row of chairs in the empty hallway. Billy nodded glumly and chose a seat that offered a clear view of the office. He could see Lieutenant Colonel Merrill still at his desk, dropping a stack of papers into a satchel. He glanced quickly around the hallway and noticed that Frances Porter's desk was no longer there.

Billy hoped Pa wouldn't tell the officer about how he had spoiled the hay. When he got back to the pasture he had seen the rutted tracks of the hay cart in the sodden field, where, heavy with rain, haystacks lay flattened. Billy ran to the barn only to find Pa, Jamie, and Ma piling what little hay they had saved into the loft. Ma turned away when she saw him. He was sure Pa would scold him good, maybe even tan him right there, but he hadn't raised a hand. Just told him to get in the wagon. Said one of the Kinsley boys had been by. He'd seen Billy at the recruiting office.

Billy watched Pa pull off his cap and step into the office, his muddied boots heavy across the floor. Resting his elbows on his knees, his chin cupped in his hands, Billy leaned forward and listened.

"Name's John Laird. Understand my son come by and signed up this morning."

"Hmm—yes, here it is. William H. Laird?"

Billy saw his father nod his head, sit down, and pick at wisps of straw embedded in his overalls. "Mind you, I support the war we're fighting. My son, Billy, though—well, he can't read or nothing."

Lieutenant Colonel Merrill laughed. "We have many soldiers who don't know how to read—or write."

"Billy ain't ever gonna read. He can't learn simple things. Well, sir, his mind just don't work the way most folks' do."

"Mr. Laird," Merrill replied firmly, "your son is over eighteen and has willingly volunteered. He'll report for training in two weeks, same as the others. In any event, his name is on the draft list. If we don't meet our quota here, your son will be in the army regardless."

"You mean he's gonna get signed up no matter what?"

"It's entirely possible. No doubt before this war is over."

It was quiet for a moment. Billy chewed nervously on his thumbnail.

"Of course, Mr. Laird, you have the option of hiring a substitute."

"A substitute?"

"You pay someone else to take your son's place. I hear that's going now for up to three hundred dollars."

Billy heard Pa let out a huge sigh. "I'm just a farmer. Only money I know is in the fields I harvest, the woods I hunt. Most ends up on our table. Sell just enough crops and lumber to pay my taxes."

"I know it's a great deal of money, Mr. Laird."

"It's just that he ain't like the rest of us. Do you understand what I'm trying to tell you?"

"The army needs soldiers, not excuses." The officer stood and scraped his chair across the floor. "A good soldier needs to have courage and to follow orders. And, I might add, none of that requires reading."

Pa slapped his cap hard over his knee, over and over again. "Billy don't know how to manage alone."

Billy could barely hear him now. *What if Pa's telling him about the hay?* His heart pounded against his chest. The officer had told him he had to finish his chores, and right off he went and ruined the hay.

"He'll belong to a company with very capable officers. Colonel Roberts is an outstanding man. Your son will be fine— and he won't be alone." The straps of his satchel buckled into place, the officer pushed away from the desk.

Pa moved slowly from the chair, glanced into the hallway at Billy, and then hesitated at the door, his fingers fidgeting with the rim of his tattered cap.

27

"Seems to me every man's alone on the battlefield when there's a loaded rifle pointed right at you! And Billy, why, he—" Stopping in midsentence, Pa put on his cap and stormed out of the office.

Billy leaped from his chair. "Pa? What happened, Pa? Is he sore at me? You tell him about the hay?"

Without so much as a glance at Billy, Pa hurried past, pushed open the door, and stepped out into the dark, his shoulders hunched against the rain.

Frightened, Billy hurried after him, shouting, stumbling in the muddied street.

Finally, Pa stopped, wiped the rain from his face, and waited.

"Pa?"

Pa stared long and hard. Billy shivered but said nothing.

Suddenly Pa reached over and placed an arm around Billy's shoulders. His voice cracked with emotion.

"Let's go home, son."

"Pa?"

"Billy, I didn't tell him about the hay."

Chapter 4

Billy nudged his way through the railroad car as the train
pulled slowly away from the station. The noise around him
was deafening. Men pushed and shoved, their bodies reeking of
sweat and tobacco. Harry and Leighton were at the window,
their bodies leaning halfway out. Desperate for a glimpse of his
family, Billy wormed his way between them. Propping his
elbows on the sill, he looked out across the crowded platform.
So many folks saying good-bye. Children jumped at the windows
and ran beside the slow-moving train. American flags and
ladies' handkerchiefs waved and fluttered wildly in the air.

Craning his neck, Billy leaned farther out the window. A
whistle shrieked. Where were his folks? Against the ringing of
church bells, a brass band played a lively tune. The sights and
sounds raised a lump in his throat. *I see 'em!* They were beside
the band. When he saw Jamie's head buried in the folds of Ma's
skirt, he had to wipe his eyes with the back of his hand. Pa
waved at him. Billy watched Pa lift Jamie over his shoulders
and point in his direction. Then Jamie raised both hands over
his head, crossed them in the air, back and forth. He warmed
to Ma's smile and gazed at the bouquet of Sweet William
clutched against her chest. Overwhelmed with sadness, he
buried his face in his arms.

Billy lingered at the window as the train inched its way
through Somersworth before turning inland, away from the
Salmon Falls River. He remembered the many times he had run
across the pasture into the woods to Little River, wandering
along its pine-needled banks until it emptied into Salmon Falls.

In late spring he fished for trout with Pa. Harry tugged at his shirt, pulling him back into his seat. Billy sat down and glanced around the packed car. It was strangely quiet. Curiously he watched Harry finger a pink ribbon, fold and place it carefully inside his Bible. Josh curled up on the hard wooden bench and leaned his small frame against Leighton. Across the aisle, Charlie sat with his arms crossed, his face unflinching. And Jeb Hall, eyes all puffy and red, sat beside him.

Billy pressed his back into the bench and glanced around the car. It was hard to figure out all the feelings going on inside him. One moment he was sad, and then, before he knew it, he was excited again. He liked being with Harry and his friends. This time it was just like church, sitting right up in the front pew.

The train whistled its final stop—Portland. Grabbing his pack, Billy leaped down the platform steps, relieved to breathe deeply of the salt-scented air. Gulls screeched and hovered overhead as he walked beside his friends over the long bridge across the bay to the endless rows of cone-shaped tents that dotted the fields.

"Is that the army?" Billy asked, wiping sweat from his brow and pointing to the other side of the inlet.

Harry chuckled. "Yeah, it's Camp King all right. Only it's just a training bivouac for the Seventeenth Maine, Billy."

"Bivouac?"

"It means we're going to camp here."

Billy stopped in the middle of the bridge and looked back over his shoulder. In the distance he spotted the railway depot, red brick against the light blue sky. His spirits soared. "This ain't so far from home."

Leighton threw his arm around Billy's shoulders and laughed. "Billy Boy, we ain't fightin' the rebellion in Portland, Maine. The army's learnin' us to be soldiers here, but we're gonna be a long way from home afore long."

Billy buttoned his trousers, tucked in his shirt, and politely nodded at the army surgeon as he moved through the line of new recruits in the broiling sun. With little scheduled for the rest of the day, Billy and his friends scouted the encampment until the dinner call sounded from the frame cookhouse. Shadowing Harry's footsteps, Billy followed him through the long meal line, averting his eyes from those of strangers gathering for their first meal in the army. Under the cool shade of an oak, he settled on the grass with his friends and Jeb and Charlie and reached for the fork tucked in his shirt pocket. He stared curiously at the rations in his tin tray, turning up his nose at the grayish meat, poking the cracker.

Leighton emitted a low moan as he forked a hunk of meat. "Nothin' but some fatty boiled beef and tasteless hardtack. This ain't fightin' food."

"We ain't fighting yet," said Josh, sopping his cracker in the watery gravy.

Harry laughed. "We may be eating field mice before this is over. Best enjoy what you got right now."

"Well, what I got ain't enough," Leighton grumped.

Billy sat quietly, the food on his tray untouched. "You gonna eat any of that dismal grub, Billy Boy?" asked Leighton.

Billy shook his head. "Reckon I ain't much hungry." He held out his tray. Leighton reached over, stabbed the boiled beef, and shoved it into his mouth.

"I'll likely starve to death before I see a bullet," Leighton said.

"Wager you'll take a bullet sooner. Take you more'n a fortnight to starve with all that fat you got on you," said Josh.

Harry jumped to his feet. "Enough of this fool talk! Ain't nobody here gonna take a bullet. Besides, we got to figure out where we're sleeping tonight." He glanced at Billy. "If you ain't gonna eat, then come with me."

Captain Martin introduced himself as the officer of the day and, when Harry asked for bedding for himself and the five others, he checked his log and tossed three wool blankets on the table.

Billy stared at the small stack. He glanced at Harry.

"May we have three more blankets, sir?" Harry asked, a perplexed look on his face.

Captain Martin smirked. "Privates don't ask questions." He dismissed them both with a wave of his hand.

"Harry," Billy asked as he followed him across the field, "you thinkin' 'bout how we gonna stay warm at night?"

"Sleep in everything but your boots," he chuckled. "Good thing it's August and not November. Looks like the army ain't interested in giving us lowly privates proper bedding."

Billy stood on the edge of the bank and looked out over the mudflats below. A rivulet ran through the center of the marsh. "Smell the sea, Harry?"

"Tide's out. That's the Fore River below us. Flows into Casco Bay over there. When the tide comes in, she fills right up and covers all that mud."

"This here tent's eighteen feet wide," hollered Charlie from inside the white canvas. "Just paced it out." He blew a low whistle as he walked over to the campfire and sat down. "Some fella said we'll be sleeping twelve men to a tent when we're in the field. Said there's only one way to fit everyone—everyone's got to point his feet to the center."

Billy smiled. He liked Charlie. He was older than the others, but he was friendly and all, and right smart.

"Well, I'm pointin' these big feet to bed." Leighton stared at the blankets still folded on the ground, reached over, and flung one over this shoulder. "Guess we got to partner up. So who's gonna share a blanket with me? You, Harry?"

"Sorry, Leighton," he answered. "Josh, you being the smallest, you go on and sleep with Leighton."

"Not by a darned sight!" Josh placed his hands on his hips. "Leighton, you're my best friend and all, but like as not your big ol' body's gonna roll over and squash me dead."

"Why don't I just squash you dead right now."

"I'm sleeping with Jeb."

"I'll share with you, Leighton," Billy said.

Leighton laughed and let out a huge sigh. "You're all right, Billy—better'n the whole lot of 'em."

Billy stood in front of the fire and watched a heavy mist creep through the camp. Drizzle seeped through his clothes, chilling him. Finally he ducked into the tent and found Leighton on his knees spreading the blanket across a floor of hay before he crashed his bulky frame down on top of it. Billy sat down beside him, pulled off his boots, and rested his chin on his knees.

"Leighton?" he asked quietly.

"Yeah?"

"You scared of fightin'?"

"Naw." He heard Leighton yawn. "Wrestled too many ornery bulls to be scared of a few Johnnies."

"You thinkin' I'll be a good soldier?"

Billy Boy

"Don't rightly know if *I'll* be a good one." Leighton yawned again, rolled on his side.

"We gonna die? Harry says we won't take a bullet—"

"Truth is, we ain't all comin' back, Billy Boy."

Leighton's words frightened Billy. Staring into the darkness, he hesitated for several moments.

"If I don't like it and all, can I go home? I can find my way."

"Ain't none of us goin' home for a long time. We do what the army says now."

"Leighton?"

"Billy, you ask me one more question and I'm gonna throw you outta this tent. Now lie down and get some sleep."

Billy ran his fingers through his hair and moved to the edge of the blanket. "Sure enough, you take up the whole dang thing." Rocking his thin body, his arms clasped around his knees, Billy thought about home. Already he sorely missed Jamie. Sometimes Jamie sneaked across the hall and crawled beneath Billy's covers, snuggling against his back. Many nights Jamie would talk about things he learned in school, explaining it all nice and easy.

If he was home right now, he might be playing checkers. Or maybe Ma would be reading from the Bible. He shook his head. He'd sooner be in his own bed, warm under his quilt. Lying down on a sliver of blanket, he leaned his back into Leighton's broad shoulders and closed his eyes.

"My name's Captain Edward Mathers—commanding officer of Company G."

Billy listened to the words of his new commander and glanced at the members of his company. Most of the soldiers

34

were older. Charlie said a couple were lawyers; some had even been to college. But mostly, Charlie told him, the others were like them—just plain farmers.

"Reveille will sound at five," Captain Mathers continued. "The regiment will form ranks by company. You will be given a description of the day's duties. For the next week and a half, your days will be filled with company, battalion, and regimental drills, target practice, policing camp, and digging sinks." He added the last with a smirk on his face.

Billy nudged Leighton. "What's he mean, diggin' sinks?"

"Gonna be pissin' in a hole in the ground," Leighton replied.

By the end of his first week at Camp King, the only relief Billy had found was when he finally received his own wool blanket. He cringed each time the drill sergeants screamed at his slowness or leaned into his face, hurling torrents of mean words. Increasingly frustrated, Billy walked away from drill one afternoon. Harry ran after him, telling him the sergeants' hurtful words were just army talk. At roll call the next morning the sergeant major shouted Billy's name and ordered him to step forward. A few others were called, including Leighton. Terrified, Billy inched forward, timidly, brushing his shoulder against Leighton.

"Is he sore at us?"

Leighton's face flushed. "Looks like you and me gonna be doin' extra drills 'til we get things right." He shook his head in disgust. "Sergeant major's put us fellas in a new squad. Already give us a name."

"What name?"

"Billy Boy, you and me is in the Awkward Squad."

"Then we ain't in trouble?"

"Naw, just slow is all."

Billy Boy

Billy liked having Leighton at his side. When the teasing got bad, Leighton would slap him on the back and tell Billy to laugh. Said laughter was like a shield of armor. If you laugh, Leighton said, the hurtful words can't go all the way to your heart. Billy tried to imagine the shield whenever the drill sergeants or other privates teased him, but mostly the taunts still managed to pierce his heart. He reckoned his shield was plum full of holes.

Near the end of the training, Billy's excitement was renewed when he at last slipped into his uniform. He received baggy light blue woolen trousers and two coats: a dark blue single-breasted frock coat, and, for daily wear, a four-button sack coat. The sack coat was shorter and fit him best; he sweated too much in the frock coat. As a private he was told he would receive only two pairs of gray flannel underdrawers, two gray flannel shirts, and two pairs of woolen stockings. His footwear was a pair of black leather brogans called bootees. Unlike most of the others, he liked the dark blue woolen forage cap with the 17TH REGIMENT in brass and his company letter "G" ornamenting the crown.

"Looks like you can put another soldier in there with you, Billy Boy," laughed Leighton as he buttoned his frock coat. Suddenly three brass buttons popped from Leighton's coat, disappearing into the tall grass.

"The uniforms only come in four sizes. Ain't one of them fits us good," said Harry as he tried to hold his woolen trousers up with a piece of rope around his waist.

"Josh walks like a large-fin duck in them oversized boots," said Jeb, watching him waddle across the ground.

"Here, little fella, stuff these in your bootees." Charlie laughed and tossed Josh a pair of woolen socks.

36

Billy stared at the pile of tow-cloth trousers and cotton shirts in a heap by the tent. He spotted the buttons from Leighton's uniform in the grass, dropped to his knees, and scooped them in his hand.

"I can sew these buttons on for you, Leighton. I like to sew buttons." Billy jumped up from the grass, his eyes darting back and forth between his friends.

"Billy Boy, I'm thinkin' you and me is gonna get along real fine." Leighton grinned and threw off his coat.

"Get up, all you lazy toadies! Roll them blankets! Get up, Billy." Harry tapped him on the shoulder. "It's August eighteenth! We're mustering into service today."

Billy moaned, rubbed his eyes, and rolled off his blanket. He pushed back the flap and squinted at the brilliant sunrise. He had heard that Major Gardiner, the mustering officer, was going to make all the companies stand ranks until the full dress inspection was over. And already it was hot and muggy. Billy needed to hurry, what with his friends mostly dressed and already checking their packs. He hoped Harry would put things right in his knapsack. Colonel Roberts held Sunday-morning inspections, and Harry always made sure things were in place for Billy. Slipping into his trousers, he glanced around the tent. Harry was gone.

The sun was high by the time Major Gardiner walked across the grass to Company G and greeted Captain Mathers. He paced in front of the first row, his face stern, his dark eyes flashing. Suddenly the major stopped, faced the privates, and loudly ordered them to empty their knapsacks. Harry stole a glance at Billy's pack and hissed under his breath as the articles spilled onto the ground. Major Gardiner stepped in front of Billy, staring at him from head to toe. He took a step backward and with the toe of his boot spread the articles across the ground. For a moment he hesitated, and then all of a sudden he kicked the knapsack aside. Leaning into Billy's face, his voice was deep and guttural.

"Where's your regulation knife, Private?"

Billy winced, blinked his eyes. He tried to swallow, but his throat was too dry. He slid his hand down the side of his coat, felt the solid lump in the pocket, reached in, and pulled out the knife.

Behind him, a soldier moaned fitfully about the heat and fainted to the ground, noisily scattering the tin utensils in the air.

Major Gardiner shook his head in disgust at both Billy and the collapsed soldier and lashed out at Captain Mathers before he turned and marched away.

At last it was over. In spite of everything, Billy felt proud when Adjutant General Hodson presented the regimental colors and he marched in the formal dress parade, passing in review before his senior officers.

The night sky swirled orange as Billy stared at the rows of campfires throughout Camp King. It felt good to be with his friends.

"Rum's been flowing all through this camp tonight," said Charlie.

"Don't nobody feel much like goin' to bed," said Leighton. "Our last night on good ol' Maine soil for a long time." He turned his head to the raucous privates at a nearby fire.

Jeb shook his head. "I ain't never seen folks so liquored up."

"Looks like you're gonna get your chance to see a drunkard up close," answered Harry. "Ol' Lars Soule is staggering this way."

Reeking of tobacco and rum, a burly, disheveled Lars leaned over and passed his bottle to Jeb. "Hey, Berwick boy? How 'bout a little drink?"

Billy watched as Jeb reluctantly accepted the bottle and took a short swig. He quickly handed it back. The private grunted in approval and looked around. Billy lowered his head.

"Hey," Lars yelled, stifling a large belch. "Ain't you one of them dumb cusses in the Awkward Squad?" Billy shuddered as Lars shuffled toward him.

"Here—take a drink." He belched again and laughed.

Billy turned his head away from the bottle. "Pa says drinkin's a curse."

"Well, your pa ain't here now, is he?" Lars leaned his face into Billy's.

"Ain't wantin' to."

"What a whimpering little toad." Lars turned and hollered to his buddies at the next campfire. "Hey fellas, we got us a real sissy boy here. Says his pa don't want him to drink." Hooting and laughter erupted.

Billy hung his head, ran his fingers through his hair, then tore at a fingernail.

"Looks like we got us a Sunday soldier. You know what a Sunday soldier is, boy?"

"Reckon I don't."

"Well, see here . . . A Sunday soldier is a name we give you dumb little cusses—"

"Shut your mouth, Lars." Leighton's face was raw with anger.

"Oh, look, it's another fool from the Awkward Squad."

Billy heard Harry leap to his feet, saw the heels of Harry's boots charge at the drunken private. "If you're looking for a fight, you can start with me. Seems to me we should be getting along, Lars, but if it's a fight you want, I'll take you down right now."

Harry yanked off his sack coat, tossing it to the ground in an angry flourish. Lars raised the bottle and rushed toward Harry, rum spilling over his head and shoulders as he swung it around in midair. Harry ducked his head and lunged forward, grabbing the private's arm and twisting it hard against his back. The bottle fell onto one of the rocks that circled the campfire and shattered, the strong scent of rum fouling the air. In seconds Lars was on his knees, wincing in pain as Harry held his grip, preventing the private from striking back, his free arm dangling limply at his side. Out of the darkness, Lars's drunken friends shouted and lurched for Harry. Leighton jumped to his feet. Charlie picked up a piece of broken glass. Unsteady on their feet, the privates retreated, staggering back to their fire.

Harry waited a few moments and then released his hold, pushing Lars to the ground with his foot. "Go on now, back to your friends."

Wincing in pain, Lars pulled his arm into his chest. He struggled to his feet. "You fellas ain't heard the last of this!" He turned and spit on the ground. "Especially the Sunday soldier," he shouted from the shadows.

Billy's head fell to his chest. He got up, moved slowly from the campfire, and disappeared into the tent. He lay still as his friends slowly entered the tent, rolled out their blankets, and settled onto the ground.

"You okay, Billy Boy?" Harry tapped him on the shoulder. Billy rolled onto his back but said nothing.

"I know you ain't asleep."

"Wonderin' is all."

" 'Bout what?"

"Wonderin' mostly—just who the enemy is." He wiped his eyes with the back of his hand.

"Aw, them fellas are a bunch of bullies for sure, but they'll be all right after a time. It's just the liquor talking."

"Wish I was like you, Harry."

"Billy Boy, I like you just the way you are." Harry leaned close and whispered, "Besides, want to know a secret?"

"Reckon."

"Always wished I was as tall as you."

"You mean that, Harry?"

"You betcha. If I was taller . . . Well, thing is, I had to learn to fight my way through things, what with me being so short." Harry paused and took a deep breath. "All the blustering I do? It's just so folks will take notice."

Billy stared in astonishment.

"Anyway, don't you worry none. We're in this army together. I'm right by your side, just like I told you. Go on now and get some sleep."

Harry slipped across the tent floor and disappeared beneath his blanket. Propped on his elbows, for several moments Billy stared at his long legs stretched out across the blanket. Wiggled his socked toes. Maybe things were going to be all right after all. Settling back down, he waited for sleep, for dawn, and for the troop train that would carry him far from home.

Chapter 5

E lijah was in a run for his life, and only his callused bare feet could save him. He ran hard over the rocky field with only the dim light of a quarter moon as his guide. Ol' Joe said five miles west was the railroad, the steel rails north his path to freedom. Fear swelled in Elijah's throat. At the edge of the field he ran into the forest, growing more anxious with every step that took him deeper into the darkness and his own uncertainty. His foot caught on a protruding root and he stumbled, collapsing on his hands and knees. He took long, deep breaths, gulping down air.

Dawn was approaching. He knew he had little time to rest—only a fleeting moment to summon his will. He listened for his pursuers. The muffled hooting of a great horned owl was the only sound in the stillness of the night.

With his short frame and wide, strapping shoulders, Elijah was growing up just like his pappy; that's what the other slaves said. And, at the age of just sixteen, he was the strongest slave in the county. That's why he was sold to Mastuh Fowler for fifteen hundred dollars.

Elijah shook his head. That's when things changed. The new mastuh owned a large tobacco plantation near Danville, Virginia, far away from his pappy on the Ramsey farm. Tears welled in Elijah's eyes as he remembered hugging Pappy goodbye. Mastuh Fowler had yanked out his whip, cracked it in the air, and struck him hard across his back. "You're my property now, nigger," he had shouted. Wrenched from his pappy, Elijah had crawled into the back of the wagon, filled with loathing for

42

his new mastuh. But Pappy ran up to him, and before Mastuh Fowler could push him away, he had whispered in his ear. "If he keep hurtin' you, my boy, then you run. Run like the wind."

Three months later, Ol' Joe, he told Elijah the same thing.

Elijah startled.

He waited. Listened to the darkness. There it was again! The distant, hoarse-ringing bay of bloodhounds.

He prayed his pappy's strength still ran through his veins. He needed it now to stay alive.

He shot a glance in either direction and then ran to higher ground, low branches whipping his cheeks until they bled. A small open space at the top of the hill offered a view of the surrounding forest. Elijah studied the nearby ridge and the rocky ledges on the other side. The faint line of morning rose pink and yellow along the eastern horizon, reminding him of Ol' Joe's warning—*Run by night, sleep by day*. He needed to find a place to hide soon, safe from the bloodhounds. He ran deeper into the woods toward the nearby ridge, hoping its narrow ravine would offer shelter and a place to hide.

His strength waned; bile rose in his throat as he ran across the forest floor, and he tried to ignore the sharp shooting pains from his feet, the calluses now raw and bleeding. He summoned God as he ran, mindlessly pleading for mercy if Mastuh and his bloodhounds found him alive. He reached the ridge and gasped with relief at the ravine below. He fled down the steep embankment.

The bays of the bloodhounds echoed off the rocky ledges. Their fierce howls startled him, and he lost his footing. Half tumbling, half running, his body weightless, he tucked his shoulders and rolled, landing in a mass of ferns. He crawled on his hands and knees, cool stagnant water oozing between his fingers and toes. Bullfrogs croaked and clamored out of his way.

Elijah struggled back to his feet and scanned the bog. A shallow stream ran through the middle of it. Barely a few feet wide, the water cut an easy path through the dense woods. The water was only up to his ankles as he stepped into the middle of the creek, grateful for the sandy bottom that soothed his stinging feet. He made his way downstream, not caring about his direction, his only thought to elude the slave catchers. He had heard stories of escaped slaves overtaken and torn to pieces by the bloodhounds. Only when it was safe would he think about the Blue Ridge Mountains and the rail lines north.

He moved quietly down the stream until the sun poked a fiery head over the treetops. He stepped anxiously onto the muddy bank and scanned the dense thicket around him.

The sound of fast-moving water caught his attention. Not far ahead, the stream emptied into a wider river, big enough that the bloodhounds would lose his scent. Too frightened to cross the deep water, Elijah hugged the banks, walking ankle-deep, grasping at branches hanging low over the water. Before long he spotted an uprooted oak half submerged, its wide trunk and gnarled roots sprawled across a sandy beach. Sunlight blinded him. It was time to hide. Dropping to his hands and knees, Elijah crawled beneath the tangle of tree roots and burrowed in the damp sand.

He wondered how far away he was from the Fowler plantation, surely the biggest farm he had ever seen. Ol' Joe said Mastuh owned nearly a hundred slaves. His old mastuh used to work in the fields beside the slaves, but not Mastuh Fowler. His three sons rode their horses up and down between the tobacco rows, watching, taunting the slaves, and snitching to Buckra, the overseer. Suddenly Buckra's beady dark eyes flashed in front of Elijah's face. He winced, trying to muffle the low moan rising in his throat.

Right off, things had been bad with Buckra. Ol' Joe said the overseer feared Elijah's strength, unusual for someone so young, and worried that Elijah might cause trouble. That's why Buckra tried to break him like a wild horse. Elijah shook his head to scatter the horrifying images that raced through his mind. He couldn't let the slave catchers find him. If the bloodhounds didn't tear him apart, Buckra would.

Ol' Joe had saved Elijah's life last night. It was only a few hours ago now. Elijah was asleep when a hand fell over his mouth.

"Hush now, boy, and listen up," Ol' Joe whispered to him. "You be in trouble. Mastuh and Buckra be in the curin' barn tonight. Mastuh say he sell you at the auction block. Now Buckra all worried Mastuh Fowler see what he done to you. Ain't no white folk pay money fo' you now. So Buckra, he gon' come after you tonight. He evil, boy. He do sumthin' bad so Mastuh don't see what he done."

Elijah asked the old man what to do.

"You gotta run, boy."

"Where to?" he had asked.

"Run to them Blue Ridge Mountains in the west, 'til you come to the railroad goin' north. That be the way of the Drinkin' Gourd. Git yo'self to Maryland, place called Sandy Spring. Quaker folks there help you git to Canada. Then you be a free man. Hide in the day and run by night. Go on now."

Elijah ran.

Huddled now in the upturned trunk, he prayed the bloodhounds had lost his scent. He needed to sleep, to escape from his thoughts. He stretched his legs, rolled onto his back, and settled down in the sand. In an instant, pain shot up and down his spine like bolts of lightning.

He screamed.

Granules of sand had penetrated the flesh of his lacerated back. Wincing, he rolled onto his belly and buried his head in his arms. Pain overwhelmed him, and in seconds, everything went black.

Elijah wakened several hours later, the burning in his back lessened to a dull throb. Hunger gnawed at him. Crawling out from his hiding place, he inched across the sand, cupped his hands, and drank from the river. Fearful the slave catchers would search up and down the river, he no longer felt safe at its edge. He needed to run west, to the Blue Ridge Mountains, and find that railroad going north. He turned from the river, raised his face, and studied the landscape where the sun dipped behind the distant hills. He hurried up the grassy bank and ran; ran like the wind.

Chapter 6

In the gray and humid September dawn, Billy gazed out across the Potomac River. The bivouac at Fort Dupont, high on the Anacostia ridge, offered quite a view. All of Washington lay below. As he buttoned his flannel shirt, he heard his friends talking about some soldiers who had disappeared from the fort during the night.

"Deserters," Leighton grumbled under his breath. He took a huge gulp of air, sucked in his stomach, and squeezed into his light blue trousers.

Balancing on one leg, Josh hopped across the grass and slipped his socked foot into his boot. "Them two privates ain't got no clothes 'cept these uniforms. Army's gonna catch them for sure."

"Naw, they'll steal some other clothes. Head for the woods." Leaning over to tighten his boots, Leighton cursed loudly when a button popped from his trousers. "Ought to be getting skinny with the rations they feed us," he added.

"Why they goin' in the woods?" Billy asked.

"Hidin' out, so the army don't catch 'em," said Leighton.

"But ain't they just cuttin' out for home?"

"Billy Boy, I told you. You can't go home just 'cause you don't like the army. Remember, three years unless sooner discharged?" Leighton picked the button up off the ground and tucked it in his pocket. "Come on, let's get to the cookhouse before the grub's all gone."

Grabbing his knapsack and jacket, Billy hurried down the trail, following Leighton down the trampled path. "Josh says them fellas gonna get caught," he said.

"Yeah, well, if they do, the army's gonna shoot them."

"Shoot them?"

"Articles of War, Billy Boy."

"Them articles shoot fellas who run off?"

"Sure enough. It's wrong what they done."

As they walked through the wooded hillside, Billy patted his coat pocket, reached inside, and wrapped his fingers around a hunk of wood, pleased that he had remembered to bring it along. After drills, in the evenings while his friends played cards, he drifted throughout the encampment, lonely and frustrated that he couldn't share in a game of dice or a hand of poker. The fellas tried to teach him, but Billy just couldn't remember the rules. So Billy spent most of his evenings just feeling homesick. Sometimes he would stare at the Potomac and imagine it was the Little River, pretending that he and Pa and Jamie were fishing along its banks. One evening he stopped to watch Ethan, an older private, whittle a corncob pipe. For several nights Billy watched in quiet fascination as Ethan skillfully carved the bowl of the pipe out of a corncob. Finally, the gray-haired private encouraged him to try it, showing him how to do the same thing with the right piece of wood, peeling its bark and shaping it into another life.

Billy ran his forefinger along his carving. He had finished it the night before and was anxious to show it to his friends. He glanced up as Leighton rushed off the beaten trail and ducked into the peach orchard. "Sergeant says we ain't to steal from the farmers," he shouted, even though Leighton was already out of sight.

Billy waited for several minutes, glancing nervously in either direction. One branch snapped, then another. Breathing heavily, Leighton at last emerged from the orchard, arms filled with plump, ripened peaches. "Last of the season," he said with a grin. "Let's go get our breakfast."

Holding his tray of food and a mug of steaming coffee, Billy sat on the ground beside Harry, Charlie, Josh, and Jeb. Leighton plopped down behind him and carefully lifted the peaches from inside his buttoned jacket. In spite of the muggy air, Billy sipped his coffee, welcoming the bitter taste. He reached into his knapsack and pulled out his whittling. Feeling shy, he fingered the carving, his gaze lowered to the ground.

"You ain't no card player, but you sure can whittle!" Charlie reached for the carving, turning it over and over in his hands.

"Say, that's a mighty fine piece," said Harry as he snatched it from Charlie's hands. "I didn't know you could whittle."

"Been watching Ethan."

"Whittled you a regulation soldier, all right," said Charlie.

"Well, not quite." Harry pointed to the soldier's frock coat. "You need two more buttons here."

"No matter," Billy said with assurance. "Leighton ain't got all his buttons." A soft thud landed on his neck—liquid, mushy, and warm, trickling down his back.

"Been meaning to give you one of these overripe peaches, Billy Boy." Leighton said, leaning over to ruffle Billy's hair. Taking the good-natured joshing in stride, Billy laughed, and using the back of his hand, wiped the juice from his neck.

"Been here more'n a month and seems like garrison duty's only good for drills, poker, whittling, and stealing peaches," said Harry.

"Yeah, well, I ain't complaining," said Charlie. "Not sixty miles west of here sits Lee's army. Think about the Twentieth Maine that got the call to strike tents and march four days ago. I reckon they're just about on top of those Confederate boys by now."

Chewing on a lump of tobacco, he stretched his legs and leaned his back against an elm. "We may be bored and all, but this ridge ain't such a bad place."

A distant rumble of artillery jolted their early morning calm. Booms thundered down the river. Billy flinched.

Harry leaped to his feet. "That's cannonading—from the west! Battle's going on for sure."

A bugle sounded, and the boys hastily responded to the call.

"A battle is under way this morning, men, at Sharpsburg, Maryland, near Antietam Creek," said Sergeant Noyes. "General Robert E. Lee has led his Army of Northern Virginia into Union territory for the first time. We have eighty-seven thousand troops there under Major General McClellan's command—enough to drive the Confederates back into Virginia.

"It's time," Noyes continued, pacing back and forth, his hands behind his back, "for Company G to be trained in the engines of war. I've sent for an artillery instructor from Livingston's battery to teach you how to use the big guns—howitzers and mortars. You'll be practicing on them today, so move your lazy hides to the clearing behind the ridge!"

Flashing a wide grin, Harry glanced at Billy as they approached the target field. "We ain't likely to be bored today," he said. "Look at those twelve-pound howitzers! Must be what's firing at Antietam."

"Ain't likin' them big guns. Only like my musket is all," said Billy.

They hurried past the tethered horses and moved closer to the howitzers, mingling with the other privates as they circled the large guns. Finally Sergeant Noyes called the company to attention and introduced the artillery instructor, a tall, thin man with thick yellow hair and a jutting chin.

"The Dutchman," whispered Harry. "Heard one of the privates say he was a miserable ol' skunk."

The Dutchman ran his hand over the howitzer and stared intently at the anxious men. He cleared his throat, hesitating before he spoke.

"Firing a smoothbore cannon is a team effort. It requires as much precision as your drills. Experienced gunners should be able to load and fire a fieldpiece every thirty seconds." His eyes were cold. "If you can't, well," he paused, lowering his voice, "you can be sure the Rebs will see you in Hell.

"The corporal is the gunner—the one who does the aiming." The Dutchman leaned over and picked up the long sponge and rammer. "On the command 'Load,' crewman number one sponges the bore—like this," he said as he rammed it into the cannon. "You men, two and three," he said, pointing his finger at Billy and the soldier next to him, "for the next two rounds, you will be the load crewmen. Two passes to three, three to four. Four," he continued as he picked another private for the team, "you will receive the round from three—four places it in the muzzle and ignites the charge . . ."

The Dutchman helped the load crewmen issue the first round. The smoothbore cannon fired, and the projectile belched from the muzzle and shot across the field, exploding in a grove of pine and snapping branches, scattering them in a haze of white smoke.

Billy clapped his hands over his ears. Horses whinnied, pumped their hooves backward over the ground, straining their reins against the posts. Over his shoulder, Billy glanced at the frightened animals.

The Dutchman stepped back and shouted to the load crewman to begin the next round. Billy turned around, nervous, uncertain what to do. He froze. One of the privates shoved him into the gun carriage.

"Pick up the projectile, you blasted fool," the private whispered. "Hurry! Pass it off."

Billy placed his hands on the projectile and hesitated. Sweat trickled beneath his shirt and ran down the back of his legs.

"Private! Are you daft?" The Dutchman stepped forward, eyes flared with anger. "I said a round goes off every thirty seconds, not thirty minutes."

"Ain't sure is all." Billy swallowed hard.

"Oh, you *ain't sure?* You pick up the projectile and hand it off! Lunkhead," he muttered, loud enough for the others to hear.

Billy tried to ignore the muffled laughter as he lifted the projectile from the gun carriage and handed it off. Moments later the cannon fired. Billy felt the earth shake beneath his feet.

Suddenly one of the horses reared, snapping the leather reins from the post, and bolted across the stony field, the limber and ammunition caisson still hitched to its back. Soldiers scattered in all directions as the ammunition crate bounced loose from the caisson and tumbled onto the ground, tossing shells into the air.

"Watch out for the caisson!"

"Look out! It's gonna hit that boulder!"

"Shoot the blasted horse!"

"She's wild!"

The frantic horse ran straight at Billy. Darting to the side, his gaze steadfast on the horse, Billy recognized her white-eyed fear.

"Don't shoot her!" he screamed. "She's just scared is all."

The sorrel mare angled past the boulder, but the caisson smashed against the rocky outcrop and overturned, throwing her to the ground. Pinned, with the limber pushed against her side, the spooked horse thrashed her legs wildly in the air.

Outraged, the instructor pushed through the crowd of soldiers.

"Corporal, shoot the damn horse. She's useless to us."

The corporal raised his musket and aimed at the mare's head.

"No! Don't shoot," cried Billy as he ran in front of the corporal. "She ain't hurt. Scared is all."

"Out of the way, farmer," shouted the Dutchman.

Ignoring the officer, Billy inched toward the horse, crooning softly. Nostrils flaring, the mare panted wildly, ears flattened against her head. As Billy crouched down next to her on his knees, the horse made a high-pitched squeal. Still, Billy moved slowly to her, stroking her between the eyes, careful to dodge her thrashing legs. He caressed the mare's long damp neck, applying pressure until her head stopped whipping back and forth.

Around him, the men grew quiet. Billy glanced nervously at the corporal. The corporal frowned in response, grunted, and slipped his finger from the trigger, his gun still aimed at the horse.

Slowly, Billy reached for the reins, his crooning growing softer. He signaled to Harry. Nodding, Harry moved in slowly, unhitched the horse from the gun carriage, and backed away. Then Billy raised himself off the ground and, standing stock-still, gave a firm tug on the reins. The mare seemed to calm completely, settling her legs slowly to the ground.

Billy looked up as the Dutchman placed a hand on the corporal's arm and lowered the musket. Billy smoothed the horse's neck and spoke to her firmly, tugging on the reins and prodding the horse to her feet. He stood square to her, then turned sideways and took several steps forward, aware that the horse shadowed his footsteps across the field. When he reached the line of posts, he walked to the one farthest from the big guns and tied the reins securely with a double knot.

"What's your name, farmer?" The Dutchman was suddenly behind him.

Billy turned and quickly lowered his gaze to the ground. "You sore at me, sir?"

"What's your name?"

"Private Laird."

"You work with horses much, Private Laird?"

"Sometimes. Like when Mr. Hall—"

"Horses spook easily around heavy artillery. Nice work just then."

"Ain't no need of shooting her. Scared is all."

The officer stared at him, contempt written plainly on his face. His jaw tightened. "We'll be firing all morning. You'll remain here for the rest of the drill and mind the horses. It's about the only thing you're good for," he said as he turned abruptly and strode off.

Billy walked along the posts, checking the ties on each of the horses. Earth spattered on the ridge beyond as the large guns erupted in thunderous roars. He moved among the horses, stroking their heads and necks, relieved that he was no longer part of the loading crew.

As evening gathered over the ridge, Billy stared out across the Potomac, turning up his collar and buttoning his jacket. The last rays dropped behind the western hills. It was strangely quiet, as if something was missing. The distant cannonading had ceased. He wondered if the battle was over or if the cannons would fire again at dawn. As darkness settled around him, he leaned his head back and studied the sky. He hadn't remembered to look for the North Star since coming south. Excited, he searched first for the now-familiar place in the sky to locate the Big Dipper. Panic rose in his throat. *Why ain't she there?* Confused, he spun around, trying to remember her place among the myriad stars. He must have missed it somehow. He raised his eyes above the Potomac River. *Nothing.* Frantic, he ran to higher ground, spun in circles as he stared at the sky. Then he lowered his gaze. *I see it!* The Big Dipper was well below the treetops, much lower in the sky than he remembered. And then he spotted the North Star—almost in front of him. In the darkness, Billy called out a silent hello to his pa.

Chapter 7

The next morning, October 7, the 17th Regiment moved out. President Lincoln had given orders to General McClellan to cross the Potomac and find the enemy. The company wasn't headed too far, too fast, though. The sergeant ordered the men to march to the Capitol grounds, stack arms, and wait there for further orders.

Throughout the morning the sun blazed tirelessly.

"I'm tired of sitting," said Harry. "Been here all morning. Besides, there ain't an officer in sight. See that round building, Billy?" Harry pointed a finger down the long walkway.

"Yeah."

"That's the Rotunda. It's been used as a hospital since the Battle of Antietam three weeks back. Wounded lying just about everywhere around Washington. Let's take a walk."

Billy was awestruck by the massive stone buildings around him. Magnificent shade trees lined the walkways that stretched across swaths of bright green grass. As he and Harry drew closer to the Rotunda, they saw several soldiers wandering around aimlessly, bandages covering their faces and bodies. A woman approached them, walking beside a soldier who moved unsteadily on his wooden crutch.

"He's only got one leg," Billy said loudly.

The soldier stopped and stared at him, a deep frown across his face. "Reckon you boys ain't seen any fightin' yet." He spat on the ground. "What's your regiment?"

"Seventeenth Maine, Company G, sir," Harry said.

Pushing his crude crutch hard into the grass, the soldier hobbled closer, his frown melting into a smile. "Seventh Maine," he said, before he stumbled, falling facedown onto the ground.

"Hurry, boys, help me lift him," said the woman.

Billy and Harry raced to the soldier's side, each cupping a hand under one of his armpits, and easing him carefully onto a bench a few feet away. The woman thanked them as she checked the man's dressing. His leg had been amputated high above the knee. Trickles of blood seeped through the gauze. The woman sighed and brushed dirt and dust from the front of the man's shirt.

Billy turned his attention to the dark-haired woman. She had deep shadows under her eyes, although the rest of her face was ghostly pale. Her gray dress was stained and wrinkled. She caught his long glance.

"I'm Isabella Fogg. I'm from Maine, too—Calais."

"You come down here to help the soldiers?"

"My son's in the Sixth Maine Regiment," she answered. "He came to Washington last year, and I volunteered for the Maine Soldier's Relief Agency to be near him. Now I help tend to the sick and wounded from Maine."

The soldier glanced at Billy and Harry. "What fort you boys at?"

"Dupont," said Harry. "Garrison duty on the Potomac. Been here over a month now, but we're finally moving out. You were at Antietam?"

"Yep. My first engagement." He glanced down at his stump, and sighed deeply. "Took a minié ball right through her. Still, I reckon I'm one of the lucky ones." He paused, nodded his head toward the Rotunda. "At least I'll be going home."

Isabella frowned and gently scolded the soldier. "Hush with that talk, Reuben. These boys got a long road ahead."

57

"Are there many wounded in the Rotunda, ma'am?" asked Harry.

"More dying than wounded," answered Reuben instead.

Billy turned to stare at the Rotunda, curious about what lay inside its granite walls.

"It's a terrible sight in there, boys," said Isabella.

Reuben shook his lowered head. "Make no mistake, there's a devil out there for sure. And it's hell you'll find on that battle-field."

Isabella smoothed his matted hair.

"There's no mercy. I'm a God-fearin' man, but I was merci-less out there, too—all of us—nothing but damned savages on that field. And the blood everywhere; oh Lord, so much blood."

Turning her back to Billy and Harry, Isabella placed her arm around Reuben and held his head gently against her as he wept inconsolably. She glanced back at the boys. "You best be going now—Godspeed, my Maine boys."

Without a word, Billy sped off toward the Rotunda, climb-ing the wide stairs two at a time, stopping only when he'd reached the top. Harry's footsteps clattered behind him. Inside, they stood in silence, staring at the bright paintings that cov-ered the high white walls in the Grand Hallway. The air was putrid.

"Smells like a rotting deer carcass in here," said Harry.

Slowly they walked into the round hall. Billy grabbed Harry's arm, sucking in his breath at the horrific scene on the marble floor. Men lay crushed against one another, their bat-tered bodies filling the room, their moans echoing off the walls.

"Ain't even got pillows," Billy whispered. "Just lyin' there in their bloody uniforms."

Billy watched in stunned silence as women in soiled dresses tended to the wounded and dying; everywhere he looked he saw mangled bodies, torn flesh, and sorrowful faces. Behind him, someone moaned and begged for water. He turned and stared shyly at the soldier. A fair-haired woman, carrying a pan of water, dressings tucked under her arm, nudged Billy's shoulder. She was clearly in a hurry.

"Please give that man some water," she said. "Use your canteen."

Billy dropped to his knees. Deep blue eyes stared at him through charred skin; pus oozed across the soldier's nose and face. The hair on half of his scalp was singed. Pulling his canteen off his shoulder, Billy placed his hand gently under the man's shoulder and raised his head, careful not to touch the blood-soaked bandage around his neck. He held the canteen to the man's mouth, letting only a trickle of water touch the blackened lips. The soldier drank, raised his eyelids, blinked, and closed his eyes. Billy cradled his head and shoulders for several moments. Then he loosened the buttons on the soldier's jacket. With his face so damaged, it was hard to tell how old the soldier was.

"What you thinkin' happened to him?" Billy asked as he glanced up and saw Harry standing behind him.

"Gunpowder; blast from a projectile, most like. Burned him good. Poor fella."

Easing the man's head gently onto his rolled coat, Billy took a deep breath and sat down on the floor. He looked around at the other wounded, unsure of what to do, when a soldier raised his arm and motioned to him. Billy went to him.

"I'm Billy," he said, leaning over and smiling at the soldier who looked near his own age. Sweat trickled down the young man's brow. Instinctively, Billy leaned over and pushed the damp, matted hair away from the soldier's forehead.

"Davey. One Hundred and Eighteenth Pennsylvania. Am I gonna die?"

Billy turned his head, hoping Harry was behind him. He would know what to say. But Harry was already down another row. Billy turned nervously back to the young soldier, wondering how to answer his question.

"Am I?" Davey asked again. Billy lifted the man's jacket and stared at the blood-soaked dressing wrapped tightly around his waist. He worried that the man would die.

"Reverend Snow says God calls us home."

"Well, God's about ready to call me, I reckon. You know any prayers?"

"Some."

"Say one for me—will you?"

Billy ran his fingers through his hair. He took a deep breath. "I-I-I don't rightly know—"

Davey coughed. "Anything, please."

"Ma reads me one from the Bible. About the Lord being our shepherd." He ran the lines through his mind and then spoke. "I shall not want. And he lies me down in green pastures—leads me beside waters . . ."

Weakly, Davey joined in. "Though I walk through the shadow of death, I shall fear no evil . . ."

"Thou is with you or—or—guess I ain't rememberin' much else. Right sorry."

"You done just fine. Thanks."

"Reverend Snow says the Lord hears our prayers no matter what." Billy wished he had something to give the soldier. He patted his hand against his pockets. Empty. Suddenly he remembered his knapsack, yanked it off his shoulder, and looked inside. There it was.

"I whittled this here." Lifting it from the knapsack he placed the carved piece under Davey's trembling hand. "I'm wantin' you to have this, Davey."

The young soldier fingered the carving, raised it slowly in front of his face. "Thanks. It's real nice." He winced in pain. "And thanks for the prayer."

"No matter." Billy sat beside Davey until the young soldier closed his eyes. Finally he stood, hesitating briefly; hoping Davey was only asleep, he moved on. He found other wounded men, eager to talk, and for a long while he busied himself up and down the rows, meeting a farmer from New York who had lost an arm, a carpenter from Brunswick, Maine, and a blacksmith from Pennsylvania, a burly man with thick shoulders who had taken a bayonet in his side. Billy started to tell the blacksmith about the horse that had spooked from the howitzers when he felt a light tap on his shoulder.

"Time to move out," Harry said quietly.

Reluctantly Billy nodded good-bye, got to his feet, and followed Harry across the floor. He wished he could stay longer. It surprised him how much he liked talking to the soldiers. It didn't seem to matter that he couldn't remember a whole prayer or have much smart to say to them. Just that he was there.

"You done good in there," said Harry as they stepped out into the sunshine. You soothed them soldiers down like you done with the mare. You done real good."

Chapter 8

The 17th Regiment marched into the grassy lowland. "We're in Virginia now—enemy soil," Leighton said as Billy stepped beside him. "We just might be shootin' Rebs before this day is out."

"Not unless they're bivouacking with us," said Harry, suddenly appearing in front of them. "Sergeant says we're camping here for the night."

"In this bog?" Leighton moaned.

"We ain't marched but a mile outta Washington," said Charlie.

Billy dropped his heavy pack and looked around. It was a dismal area teeming with mosquitoes.

"We're gonna be fightin' all right," Leighton said as he flapped his blanket at the air.

Like the others, Billy slept fitfully in the heat, buried beneath his blanket as mosquitoes swarmed and buzzed throughout the night. At roll call the next morning the sergeant said they were marching eighteen miles to Ball's Crossroads, the 3rd Brigade's encampment.

By late morning the heat was unbearable. Struggling under the heavy weight of his pack, sweat ran down Billy's back, his legs, and into his boots, soaking the ill-fitting leather that rubbed against his heels and ankles. He watched curiously as other soldiers tossed blankets and overcoats into the ditches alongside the road to lighten their packs in the oppressive heat. Dust rose up on the trampled road, and he sneezed yellow dust and spit brown spittle from his mouth.

By the end of the day, Billy's feet were chafed and swollen, and his legs ached from the arduous march. He groaned in dismay when the corporal suddenly appeared, telling him to report to Sergeant Noyes for picket duty.

"You gonna be all right?" Harry asked. "You ain't been on night sentry before."

Billy shrugged his shoulders and reached for his sack coat, haversack, canteen, and rifle.

"Make sure you stay awake. You know the sergeant's a real bugger."

Sergeant Noyes issued Billy twenty rounds of ammunition and repeated the picket instructions as he escorted him to the guard post, an open knoll overlooking the crossroads. "You'll be relieved in four hours, Private Laird. Any questions?" he asked.

"No, Sergeant."

"Stay alert. We're on Reb soil now."

The moon was almost full, casting a faint light over the hilltop. Billy listened carefully, trying to separate familiar night noises from anything unusual. Fighting exhaustion from the long march, he stifled a yawn. He blinked several times; his head felt heavy. Soon, his chin fell to his chest. Suddenly he jerked his head upright. Harry's warning echoed in his ears. He needed something to help him stay awake. He ran his hand over his mouth, trying to remember all of the sergeant's instructions.

Walk the perimeter! Check everything!

Grabbing his rifle, Billy walked along the crest and down the slope to the crossroads, wincing as his boots rubbed his blistered feet raw. He walked a short distance down one of the lanes, stopped, and listened for faint stirrings in the surrounding woods. Hearing nothing, he turned and headed down the other road before working his way back up the hillside.

Weariness tore at him, and he gazed across the hilltop. A stand of birch glistened white in the moonlight.

He was curious about birch, wondering if the pale-colored wood carved easily, if it would be soft, like pine. He hurried across the clearing. Leaning his musket against one of the trunks, he broke off a small limb, sat down on the ground, and pulling his knife from his haversack, began peeling the thin white bark, careful not to nick or gouge the naked wood. He decided he'd whittle Daisy, his nineteen-year-old mare, born when Billy was but two months old. Maybe he could send the carving home, surprise his folks. He imagined them opening the package and seeing Daisy all carved from wood. No longer sleepy, Billy ran his hands along the smooth birch and cut into the wood, grateful for the moonlight over his shoulder.

"Private Laird!" Sergeant Noyes loomed out of the darkness.

Billy jumped up from the ground, clutching the half-carved wood and his knife. "Sergeant—"

"What the hell are you doing?"

"Whittlin' is all."

"Where's your musket?"

Billy scanned the ground around him. The musket still lay against the trunk of a birch, well out of reach. Sergeant Noyes pushed his face close, his jaw jutting out from his neck. "What kind of whittlin' do you think the Rebs will do to a Yankee soldier?"

Billy took a deep breath and lowered his head.

"They'll whittle a bayonet right through your heart! And with our picket killed, well, Rebs might as well walk into the bivouac and slaughter us all! What the hell do you think picket duty is for, Private?"

"Things was quiet," Billy said meekly.

Sergeant Noyes shook his head. "Private, when we reach our next encampment you'll be confined to your tent. I intend to have you court-martialed for violating the rules of picket. Now get back to your post until I return. And it ain't under this damn tree!"

"Yes, sir." The sergeant's words terrified Billy. He knew from Harry that a court-martial meant you had done something the army didn't like.

"And get rid of that blasted hunk of wood."

Billy dropped his knife into his haversack and stared for several moments at the carving clutched in his hand. He let it slide between his fingers, watching it land in the tall grass before he kicked it wildly into the trees. Picking up his musket, he flung it over his shoulder and walked quickly across the clearing to the top of the knoll.

He looked for the North Star, but a thick bank of clouds had moved across the moon and stars. Billy was alone and scared. A crash of thunder rolled across the sky; in minutes a drenching rain pelted him. His fear and the soaking cold kept him awake, his hands clutched tightly around his musket until his picket was over.

Rolled in a soggy blanket, Billy was nudged awake in the still-dark morning.

"What's happening, Sergeant?" asked Harry as he rolled over in his blanket and saw the sergeant standing over Billy. "What do you want with Billy—Private Laird?"

"He should be court-martialed for his miserable picket."

"Court-martialed? Why?"

The sergeant grumbled, ignoring Harry's questions. "Laird, this must be your lucky day," he said sourly. "It seems there are other orders for you."

"Orders?" Billy stumbled to his feet.

"You're being dispatched to Livingston's battery at Edward's Ferry on the Potomac. In Maryland, to be precise."

"The one with them big guns, Sergeant?"

"Why Livingston's battery, Sergeant?" Harry rushed between them. Leighton and Josh bolted from their beds.

"Artillery's frightening the horses. The Dutchman's been after the captain to transfer Laird. Thinks Laird can mind the horses."

"When's he supposed to go, Sergeant?" asked Harry.

"He's to report to Sergeant Riley on October seventeenth." Taking a step closer to Billy, the sergeant said, "You'll be Riley's problem soon enough, Laird. You'll sooner wish you were court-martialed than face that hot-headed Irishman."

"I c-c-can't—I can't leave my friends!" Billy stumbled backward, nearly toppling Harry. Leighton let out a low whistle, his eyes wild with anger.

"Sergeant—" Leighton and Harry said in unison, but the sergeant brushed them aside with a wave of his hand.

Billy felt the wind knocked out of him. "I-I-I can't go—you ain't understandin', Sergeant. Things is hard for me—fellas poke fun and—and when I ain't knowin' what to do, Harry—and Leighton—they watch out for me. I can't . . ."

Sergeant Noyes walked away.

For the next several days, Billy hardly left Harry's side. Harry pleaded once again with his superior officer to keep Billy in Company G, but the court-martial for Billy's failed picket duty still posed a threat, and Harry had no better option than to comfort his friend.

"Don't you worry none," Harry said on Billy's last evening before his detachment. "Most likely Company G's going to be right close to artillery once we start to fighting."

Leighton smacked Billy lightly on the back of his head. "If Livingston's battery ain't got no Awkward Squad, then they'll have to send you back here, Billy Boy."

Throughout the long night, none of the assurances his friends offered brought Billy any comfort. In a few short hours, he would be truly alone for the first time in his life, and it terrified him. With dawn skulking over the eastern hills, Billy at last curled into the folds of his blanket. At first light, Corporal Leavitt would escort him to Livingston's battery.

Chapter 9

Early in the evening Elijah followed railroad tracks through withered cornfields. Weak with hunger, he crawled on his hands and knees through the dry and crusty soil, hoping to find some forgotten ears of corn among the brown stalks. He had eaten little since running away from Fowler's plantation; mostly he'd gathered berries or found remnants of crops cast off and left to rot in sun-bleached fields. Occasional orchards offered fallen fruit when he dared to walk among the scanty trees. Hugging the foothills of the western mountains, Elijah had followed the rail lines for several days. The ringing bays of the bloodhounds were long behind him, but he was careful just the same.

In the sheen of starlight he spotted rooftops and the lofty spire of a church. He studied the landscape. West of the railroad town was dense forest that offered Elijah cover as he maneuvered around the town in an arc-shaped path. As in other towns along the railroad, he was hopeful of picking up the tracks at the northern end of town. He stepped away from the rail embankment and headed for the forest, staying low, moving stealthily through the thicket.

Slowly he angled his way past the town, turning sharply east out of the forest after spotting the last light in a farmhouse window. There they were. Moonlight glinted off the rails, like a long straight line running beneath the North Star. He stopped suddenly. *Laughter*. He dropped down on his hands and knees. Clouds moved across the moon, darkness closed in around him. He saw the faint glow of cigarettes a short distance in front of him.

Slave catchers? He flattened his body on the ground, fearful the heavy beating of his heart would echo in the night. He could hear voices. There had been a battle nearby—in the fields. Bull Run. Manassas. Yanks, he heard them laugh, "crushed, pushed north to Washington." *White folk soldiers would give Elijah to the slave catchers!*

How close was he to Sandy Spring? He raised his head. In the distance he could see hundreds of campfires and the haunting outlines of tents, endless rows of tents. He had nearly walked right into the soldiers' camp. There was nowhere else to go except to double back. He remembered crossing another rail line a while ago, but it was heading west, not toward the Drinking Gourd. Crouched low, he tiptoed backward, back to the forest, where he stopped and listened. A southerly breeze rustled the grass, carrying the voices away from him. He knew the soldiers were close, only now he couldn't hear them. Every few feet he stopped and listened for the voices, breathing more easily when he reached the forest edge. He picked up his pace and ran until he found the rails running west. He stepped over the tracks onto the wooden ties, not daring to look back.

It terrified Elijah to follow the rails west, but he had no other choice. The tracks would keep him from getting lost, and as soon as he could find a path north, he would leave the rails and follow the star. Desperately lonely for Pappy and Ol' Joe, his strength diminishing, he walked the rail ties through the long night.

Dawn was breaking. He would have to find a place to hide soon. Which way to go? Should he hide close to the tracks or turn into the forest, following the star? The North Star was quickly fading in the early morning light. It would be hard to follow it under the thick cover of trees. And he might get lost, even die in the forest. Unsure of what to do, he continued along the tracks, talking out loud to the Lord, pleading once more to show him the way. The rail lines sloped gently downward through the wooded ravine, and on lower ground he saw a gray stone bridge a short distance ahead. His heart pumped with excitement. *Creek flowing the way of the star!* That gave him a path through the woods!

But Ol' Joe's words haunted him, reminding him to follow the railroad north, not a creek. Tired and hungry, he sat down on the cool steel, not knowing whether he should follow the creek or the westerly rail.

The sun spilled over his bare shoulders, the welcome warmth also providing a burst of awareness that he was out of time. He slid down the bank, the voices in his head talking, urging him on. *Lord showed me the creek, he sayin' go that way. Follow the Lord's path, not the railroad.*

As he turned his back to the familiar tracks and Ol' Joe's warnings, Elijah hoped his friend would forgive him.

He slept most of the day. The sky was overcast, threatening rain. Hunger gnawed at him, and he scavenged the forest floor for berries. Finding nothing, he stayed close to the creek, the water his only nourishment. He slept again, and when he awoke he felt weak and light-headed. When it grew dark, the rain fell, bouncing noisily off the leaves and splattering cold droplets down his back.

Elijah stumbled over root stumps, and branches scratched him as he made his way along the bank of the creek. Dizziness blurred his vision, and he finally lay down on a patch of moss, deciding to sleep until dawn, praying he would feel stronger in the morning.

He opened his eyes to the chatter of birds above his head. Sunlight filtered through the trees. He sat up, rubbed the sleep from his eyes, and leaned over the stony bank for a drink of cool water. He stood up, relieved his dizziness was gone, although his legs were still weak. He walked along the creek for what seemed like hours, scouting the landscape for an orchard or a cornfield. Each step grew heavier; exhaustion filled every extremity of his body.

Dizziness again. He pressed the palms of his hands against his temples. The forest spun in circles, blurring flashes of green and black; his legs buckled, and he felt himself falling. He reached for a low branch, but it snapped and sent him crashing, facedown on the ground.

He awoke just after sunset. Using his arms for leverage, he tried to get on his feet, but he was too weak and he crashed back down. He wondered if the bloodhounds would find him like this. He crawled back closer to the bank and lay under some low-hanging branches. He thought about his pappy, sitting outside their log hut on a summer's eve smoking his corn-cob pipe, telling stories as crickets chirped in the warm fields. He thought about Sundays, when the preacher came. Under the cool shade of the willow oak, Elijah would sit with the other slaves and listen to his comforting words, grateful for such rare and peaceful moments. Sometimes in the evenings, the slaves sang songs around a fire. His favorite was the song where everyone clapped their hands and stomped their feet in measured beats. It was the only time he could remember when everyone smiled.

Billy Boy

Hold your light, brother Robert
Hold your light on Canaan's shore
What makes ol' Satan for follow me so?
Satan ain't got nuthin' for to do with me
Hold your light, hold your light
Hold your light on Canaan's shore

He tried to say the words out loud, or hum the melodic beat, but he was too weak to move his lips. So he played it over and over in his mind.

Elijah hold the light.

The spiritual gave him hope, and in a half-whisper, he uttered a small prayer. "Lord say he help the little folk. Lord, you take care of Elijah now."

Chapter 10

Billy was despondent. As he dogged the corporal's steady footsteps across the Virginia countryside, he could hardly believe he was on his way to a new company. He was afraid of what would happen to him without Harry and Leighton. He would sooner face a court-martial than be in Livingston's battery. He hated those smoothbore cannons, needing all them fellas to load the projectiles and fire her. Awash in despair, he walked in silence throughout the long morning, watching the sun climb higher in the cloudless sky.

By the time they reached the crest of a steep hill, Billy's heart was racing and his head throbbed. A cool wind brushed across his face, refreshing him. Beside him, the corporal squinted in the sunlight, scanning the wide river below them.

"See that small creek that spills into the Potomac?" said the corporal as he pointed his finger toward the distant hills. Glumly, Billy glanced his way, shrugged his shoulders, and said nothing.

"That's Goose Creek. And across the river from her—see that small clearing on the other side? That's Edward's Ferry, Livingston's bivouac." He glanced expectantly at Billy.

"We swimmin' across?" Billy asked, suddenly a little curious.

"Just about," laughed the corporal. "We'll walk farther up this side of the river and cross at White's Ford. It's shallow there; water won't be much above our waists."

Fingering his cap, Billy took a deep breath and swallowed hard. "Corporal," he asked timidly, "you thinkin' the sergeant's gonna let me go back to my company and my friends?"

The corporal placed his hands on his hips and blew the air from his cheeks. His answer was sharp and biting. "You ask Sergeant Riley that question, Private, and you'll be real sorry you did."

Billy sighed. He turned his gaze away from the corporal to stare vacantly across the river, only half aware of the hand suddenly resting on his shoulder.

"Look, you'll make new friends soon enough. It don't matter much what company you end up in." The corporal started a hurried stride down the hill. "Things will work out." Billy followed, kicking aimlessly at the tall grass.

Crossing the river had been uneventful, and by the time Billy and the corporal reached the carriage path to Edward's Ferry, their uniforms were almost dry. The shady path at last opened onto a clearing. They went directly to the sergeant's tent and, finding it empty, headed across the field toward the long row of caissons at its edge. Over the corporal's shoulder Billy spotted the sergeant, a stocky, broad-shouldered man with a tangled mass of curly reddish-gray hair spilling from his cap.

"What the bejesus?" shouted the sergeant as he dropped a tow hook on the caisson. He reached into the opened crate and pulled out a handful of surgical knives and crude saws, turning an angry face to the corporal. "Do these look like shells to you, Corporal Leavitt?" Tossing the instruments back into the box, the sergeant spit a wad of tobacco and wrenched the tow hook under another lid.

The corporal tried to keep a stern face. "Guess you'll be doing surgery on the Rebs, Sergeant."

"No doubt the docs have my ammo." Sergeant Riley peered into the crate. He slammed the lid shut.

Turning his attention away from the caisson, the sergeant walked over to Billy, standing just inches from his face. His eyes bore down on him; the veins on his thick neck bulged red. Billy shied backward, shifting his weight back and forth and staring at the ground.

"Sergeant," said Corporal Leavitt. "Private Laird, Company G—"

"You as good with horses as the Dutchman claims, lad?" the sergeant interrupted, leaning over and pushing a finger into Billy's chest. "I've no use for a plodding farmhand, mind you."

"Yes, sir—sir, I was wonderin' if I-I-I could go back—" He raised his face, twitched as the sergeant's eyes, black as a ferret's, narrowed.

"What is it, Private?" His breath was hot, and smelled faintly of stale coffee.

"I-I-I, well, Harry, my f-f-friends—"

"Ah, Sergeant Riley." Corporal Leavitt pushed in front of Billy. "Private Laird needs to feed the horses—so, ah, I'll take him over to the corral now. We've not much time left before the last drill."

Sergeant Riley turned back to the wagon. "Suit yourself. I'll know soon enough if he's up to the task." He reached for his tow hook. "And find my ammunition, Corporal."

Corporal Leavitt gave Billy a push and hurried him across the clearing. At the edge of the field he stopped abruptly, turned to Billy, both hands on his hips. "You simple fool. You almost got yourself in a lot of trouble. You're in the army! You do what you're told, and you don't ask for special favors."

Pointing a finger toward a cluster of trees, he shouted, "Get yourself over to the other side of camp. Untie and corral the horses."

"Ain't fair," Billy whispered under his breath as he stared at his boots. He felt the corporal's hand on his back, shoving him forward. He stumbled and, turning, glanced at a face full of anger. "Get moving. And don't expect me to help you out again."

Billy walked in silence, kicking up clods of dirt with the toe of his boot. He winced as he strode past a line of smoothbore cannons. Camp looked much like Company G—rows of tents, clusters of soldiers playing games of chance, rolling tobacco, writing letters, and polishing bayonets. But it didn't feel the same; it was unsettling without his friends. Billy headed for the stand of trees, choosing a path that ran behind the tents. A small group of soldiers was sitting around an unlit fire, smoking, and they glanced up as he walked past. From the corner of his eye he saw someone dart quickly from the group, and he hurried his pace.

A hand fell firmly on his shoulder and spun him around. He stared into the swarthy, strangely familiar face, recognition tying his stomach in knots. *Lars Soule.* The bully from Camp King.

"So it's you—the Sunday soldier," bellowed Lars as he squeezed his fingers around the sleeve of Billy's jacket. "Look-a-here, fellas. Remember the dumb li'l cuss from the Awkward Squad?"

Billy's heart raced with fear as others closed in around him. Even though instinct told him to wrestle free and run, before he could move away, Lars grabbed his shoulders and twisted him around, pushing his face in front of the other privates.

"This ain't no Awkward Squad here, you dumb little toady." He shoved Billy at the others. Billy tried to block out the taunts, the laughter. But Lars grabbed him again by his shoulders, and leaning in close, spit tobacco in his face.

"Listen up, Sunday soldier—we got us a war to fight down here. And me and my boys don't need any simpleton getting us killed." Lars pushed Billy to the ground. "We'll have some fun at drill tomorrow morning. You'll soon see this company's got no place for the likes of you."

As Lars and his friends turned away, Billy rolled onto his feet and ran blindly toward the grove of trees, past the tethered horses, losing all sense of following the corporal's stern orders. He kept on running, the echo of laughter exploding behind him.

A gusty wind off the river swirled around him as he reached the hilltop above Edward's Ferry. For several moments he paced back and forth along the bluff, repeating that hated word—*simpleton . . . simpleton . . .* He gazed out at the wide Potomac, at the lush Virginia meadows on the other side. He sighed heavily at the view, the scattered stands of ash reminding him of autumn and home. He spotted Goose Creek emptying into the wider river, the woods flanking its banks, and for a moment he wished himself in the middle of the forest, away from the taunts, and far from Lars Soule.

As Billy walked along the edge of the bluff, a jackrabbit spooked in front of him and disappeared into the thicket. Finally, as a shield from the sharp wind, he sat down under an oak tree and leaned his head against its trunk. He opened his haversack and glanced at the three-day ration of hardtack, salt pork, and bully beef issued before he left, but nerves had curbed his appetite. Setting his pack on the grass, he tried to figure out what to do.

Too frightened to return to camp, he watched the sun drop behind the hills, listening to the wind carry imagined howls of laughter. As darkness settled, he grew anxious about Corporal Leavitt. Was he looking for him? Would it mean another court-martial? His pulse quickened. *I ain't never goin' back there. I ain't.* He ran his fingers frantically through his hair. Maybe he'd cut out like them others done. Then he remembered Leighton saying it was wrong to desert.

Suddenly the image of Lars's face flashed in front of him. He shuddered at the thought of morning and what might happen to him at drill. *But Leighton says the army will shoot you if you run away.*

Tears welled in his eyes. Misery overwhelmed him, and he slumped to the ground, his body wracked with sobs.

Long moments passed. Finally he sat up, and clasping his arms around his knees, he raised his face to a full moon and a sky full of stars. From the high hilltop he spotted the Big Dipper and traced his finger to the North Star. Pa said home would always be right under that star.

"Pa!" he cried out loud to the darkness. "Pa! I'm wantin' to come home."

In spite of Leighton's warnings, his decision was made. He was not going back to Edward's Ferry. He remembered Leighton telling him that the privates who deserted would need to hide out in the woods. There were woods on the other side of the river, along Goose Creek. He could hide there for a time.

He was going home.

Chapter 11

Billy flung his canteen and haversack over his shoulder and went to grab his rifle. He hesitated a moment before deciding to leave the gun, tossing it angrily into the thicket and turning away. It was a long hike back up the river to the crossing point, and more difficult at night. He glanced at the bright moonlit fields below.

The Lord's made me a lantern, seems like.

Quietly he made his way down the opposite side of the hill, careful not to stumble and alert the soldiers on picket duty. He thought about Harry and Leighton and the others, wondered if his friends would understand and forgive him. Loneliness ate at him.

He walked for most of the night, following the river until he spotted the wide bend where he had waded across the day before, at White's Ford. Although the moon was fading in the predawn light, he recognized the steep banks across the river. The current was moving faster than it had been the day before. He wished he could swim across, but he needed to keep his haversack dry. Taking off his sack coat and wrapping the haversack and canteen in its folds, he raised it above his head and stepped into the dark, cold water.

The shale of sand and gravel on the river bottom was slippery, reminding him of wintry days sliding across the ice on Frog Pond. He slipped more than once and fought to keep his balance as the fast-moving water tossed him off the crushed bedrock. The river rose to his chest, and the heavy weight of his clothes pulled him downstream, pushing him with the current.

Billy Boy

Too late, he realized, to take off his boots and dig his toes into the gravelly bottom. The force of the river pressed against him, and he twisted and strained his body sideways toward the opposite side. Gradually the water dropped below his waist and he regained control of his footing, moving freely toward the shore.

Catching his breath, Billy stared at the steep, smooth banks and readied himself for the slippery climb. He plunged his arms into the sleeves of his coat, repositioned his haversack and canteen, and dug his fingers into the bank. He searched for a handhold as his boots slid against the slippery clay, teasing him back to the river's edge. Above his head, he saw a thick root jutting out. He grabbed hold of it and pulled himself upward. Straining, his fingers clawing dirt and gripping at every root, he inched his way to the top. He swung his arm over the edge and in one great heave rolled his body sideways up and over onto the grassy crest. His strength drained, he swallowed mouthfuls of air as his heart hammered in his chest.

Wet clothes stuck against his skin, sending cold shivers up and down his body. Cupping his hands, he blew warm breath over his fingers, red and sore from the gritty climb. He lay down on dew-laden grass, listening for a rustle in the brush, a sudden movement in the trees. Hearing only the night insects' rhythmic trill, he closed his eyes and pretended he was home, warm and dry under his quilt, his little brother snuggled beside him.

Billy awoke to the sun on his face. Fearful of being spotted, he forced himself to his feet and looked across the fields. He could move quickly through the grassy landscape, but he'd have to stay low. He darted across the field and spotted a lone apple tree at its edge, its limbs overburdened with unpicked fruit. He grabbed a handful of apples, stuffed them into his pockets, and hurried off.

By the time he reached Goose Creek, thickening clouds blocked out the late-morning sunlight. The woods seemed darker, more frightening in the graying sky. Glancing across the river at Edward's Ferry, he darted into the cover of the trees, hugging the bank of the creek as he moved into the forest. He would sooner be in the meadows, and sooner feel the wind rustling through the tall grass than the dampness of the gloomy forest. He was scared and alone. The wet leather of his boots chafed his feet, and he stumbled over tree roots hidden under decaying leaves. He cried out once, spooking the birds high in the treetops. He sniffed and brushed the sleeve of his jacket across his runny nose.

He wanted to turn back, hide closer to the Potomac River, but fear drove him deeper into the woods. He stopped several times and splashed water from the creek over his face. Once he sat down on a boulder, looked around, and tried to rest. But the stillness unnerved him, and he slid off the smooth rock and moved farther upstream. At last the afternoon sun burned through the clouds, filtering welcome light down through the trees, briefly lifting his dispirited soul. He spotted another small clearing beside the creek just beyond the branches hanging low over the bank. He was desperately hungry, now anxious to sit in the warming sunlight and eat one of the apples.

He pushed the needled limbs away from his face. Suddenly he yelled as he fell into the pine tree, branches snapping against his weight. He stared in shock at what he saw there on the forest floor.

A colored boy lay sprawled across the ground where he'd been sleeping. The snap of tree limbs had startled him awake, and in an instant, fear flashed across his dark face. He rolled over on his side and staggered to his feet.

Before Billy could speak, the boy backed away, each step inching him closer to the creek. His bare feet sank in the shallow water and he jerked backward. Water swirled around his knees, pushing him off his feet. In a rush to regain his balance, he lost his footing and flipped on his back. Screams pierced the air before he disappeared under the muddied water.

Billy scanned the river, waiting for the boy to surface and swim to shore. Seconds passed. He began to panic and ran along the river's edge, glancing in every direction. There was no sign of him.

Finally the boy broke through the water, his face turned upstream, his eyes filled with terror as water rushed into his nose and mouth. The current buried him, and then spit him up, hurling him like a log as he moved swiftly downstream. Boulders peppered the riverbed like jagged fence posts.

He can't swim! He's gonna hit them rocks! Billy realized.

Tossing his canteen and haversack to the ground, Billy yanked off his jacket and boots, his heart racing. His blistered feet burst open on the stony ground. Cold water stung the open flesh. He thrust his body downstream, kicked his legs furiously, and used his arms to guide him to the half-submerged boulders. Brown water rushed around the bedrock. He couldn't see beneath the surface. He dove under, spreading his fingers like tentacles in search of the body. In the murky darkness, he felt him, flattened against a boulder, pinned by the current. Billy yanked and pulled, but his emptying lungs cried out for air. Propelling his legs to the surface, he breathed deeply and then dove again. Using his back to break the force of the water, he wrestled the body away from the rock and pushed it to the surface. With one arm, he grabbed the lifeless form around the chest, his free arm paddling water, groping for leverage. The creek splashed over him and he rolled on his back, his face downstream. Kicking his feet, one arm in a frenzied backstroke, he angled toward the bank.

Once in shallower water, Billy planted both feet in the sand. Slipping his hands under the colored boy's armpits, Billy dragged him to the grassy clearing. Sinking to his knees, his chest heaving, Billy studied the boy's inert body. Brown water slowly drained from his mouth. Billy rolled the boy onto his side, and in seconds bile and water erupted from his throat.

Billy watched the boy's chest move up and down in faint, shallow breaths. Moments passed before his eyes flickered open and met Billy's. "Slave catcher . . ."

"I ain't no slave catcher! I'm a soldier; least, I was . . ."

"White folk . . . slave catcher . . ." The boy's voice faded as he collapsed on the grass.

Elijah's first sensation when he awoke was warmth. Wood smoke tickled his nose. Eyes pinched closed, Elijah listened, his body motionless. Over the crackling flames, he heard water slapping against the rocks. And then he remembered. The creek. He fell in the creek. *Slave catcher!* He rolled his hand across his chest, his fingers touching heavy cloth. *What's this?* Something stirred beside him. He didn't want to look. His eyelids fluttered with indecision.

"You done sleepin'?" the voice asked.

White folk. Slave catcher. *He takin' me back.* He opened his eyes to the tall and fearful white man looming over him. He would have to fight. He tried to raise his head off the ground, but his weakened body resisted, pulling him down.

"Slave catcher?" Elijah moaned.

"Told you already, I ain't no slave catcher. Why? You a slave?"

"Why you pull me from the creek?"

"I seen you can't swim is all. Thing is, first time at Frog Pond, Josh—"

"You takin' me back?" Elijah cried out.

"I ain't doin' nuthin'."

Confused, Elijah watched the man lean over and pick up a handful of branches stacked neatly in a pile, tossing them onto a small fire burning in the center of the clearing.

Elijah was suddenly conscious of his fingers fiddling a button—the jacket that was keeping him warm, alive, for the slave catchers. For the reward. "This your jacket?"

"Yeah. You was shakin' bad. Why ain't you gotta shirt?"

Baffled, Elijah shook his head. "White folk don't care if a nigguh got no shirt."

"You lose it?"

"No, suh."

"Then why ain't you got one?"

Elijah sighed and rolled over on his side, holding the jacket close around him. His forehead exploded in pain, the woods whirled in rapid circles around him. "Why you keep askin'?"

"Wonderin' is all. You hungry?"

"Yes, suh."

"You got a haversack?"

"What's a haversack?"

"Ain't you got one?"

"No, suh."

"Where you keepin' your food?"

"Ain't got no food."

"How come?"

The white man stood up and walked away from the fire, leaned over, and reached for a leather pouch. Elijah stiffened, ignoring the question. He needed a weapon. Afraid to raise his head, he used his fingers to search the ground around him. He touched a rock the size of his fist, and wrapping his hand around it, dragged the rock close to his side.

The man pulled a knife from his pouch and looked his way. Elijah gripped his fingers tightly around the rock.

"Got some salt pork here." Holding his pouch, he dropped to the ground, sat cross-legged, and placed the salt pork on his knee. He dug his knife into the greasy meat. "Why you ain't got any food?"

Salt pork. How long had it been? A picture flashed through Elijah's mind—sitting on the steps of the log hut with Pappy, eating chunks of warmed salt pork and moist corn cakes. Pappy telling stories as they ate under the stars, the long day in the fields finally at an end. Hungry, he tried to sit up. Dizziness washed over him. He lowered his head slowly onto the flattened grass.

"No matter. Stay there."

"What you gonna do?"

"Gonna feed you is all. Harry said I did a good job helping out them fellas in the hospital."

He inched his way over.

Still, Elijah locked his gaze on the pale blue eyes studying him as a piece of salt pork dangled from the knife. He had no strength to resist; he felt sure he was going to die at the hands of the stranger. But the man carefully picked the salt pork off the blade and slipped it into his mouth. Bewildered, Elijah closed his lips around the meat, his starvation overwhelming his will to fight. He eagerly accepted more. The white man sat beside him, feeding him chunks of the salt pork; then he cut up an apple and fed him a few slices. Elijah swallowed hard, fighting the longing to close his eyes in sleep. Consciousness slipped slowly from him; his eyelids drooped, blinked open, and finally shut.

"Why white folk save Elijah?" he whispered as he drifted into darkness.

He wakened to find night settling, flames from a small fire crackling and sparking the air. The white man was still there, sitting nearby, his long legs huddled against his chest, arms wrapped around his knees. There was no hint of meanness in his face, eyes blue as a perfect summer sky. Elijah coughed. The man startled, jumped to his feet, grabbed a canteen, and kneeled beside him. Elijah didn't move as a hand cradled his neck and raised his head. Slowly, water spilled onto his tongue. "Go on now and sleep 'til mornin'," Elijah heard him say as he closed his eyes.

The rustling of leaves wakened Elijah. Opening his eyes, he turned his head as a gray squirrel darted into the thicket, his teeth clamped on the small haversack. In an instant Elijah was on his feet, crashing through the dense brush, suddenly aware that his legs were no longer trembling and the dizziness was gone. Relieved, he grinned as the squirrel abandoned the pouch and scurried up the pine. Leaning over, Elijah grabbed the haversack and pushed his way through the tangle of brush back to the clearing. He stepped over to where the man lay sleeping and studied him, and then he scanned the ground for a rifle, perhaps hidden under the brush. Other than the canteen and knapsack resting by his side, there was nothing else, not even a blanket. The man's dark clothes were crusted with dirt and mud. For a moment Elijah thought about running, but instinct told him to stay, to see what would unfold. Without a weapon, the thin white man posed little threat. He tossed the pouch down to the ground. The man stirred, blinked his eyes at Elijah, and rolled over on his side, back to sleep.

Elijah gathered a handful of branches, feeding them onto the smoldering fire. Slowly the coals rekindled into life. He breathed deeply in the crisp morning air, feeling hopeful for the first time in days.

Lord, give Elijah one mo' chance. But why, Lord, you send Elijah white folk? Leaning over, he picked up the rock he had hidden earlier by his side and tossed it into the middle of the creek.

This time the man groaned awake and looked his way, staring at him for several moments before breaking into a smile. Elijah offered a shy smile in return.

"You feelin' better?"

"Yes, suh, sho' am."

"Reckon you're still hungry."

"Yes, suh."

"We got us two apples and some beef is all."

Sitting up, he reached for his haversack and took out an apple, tossed it to him, and taking out his knife, pulled out the meat and cut it in half.

Elijah ate the apple first, licking the juice from his fingers, staring intently at the stranger who kept sharing his food.

Elijah waited and then spoke. "You be thinkin' 'bout takin' me back?"

"Back where?"

"Mastuh Fowler."

"Don't know no Master Fowler. You just run off?"

"Yes, suh."

"Name's Billy."

"Billy, suh."

"Ain't you got a name?"

"Elijah."

"Elijah," Billy repeated. "Reverend Snow read that name afore—in the Bible." He tossed the apple core into the fire. "Thing is, I run off, same as you. Cut out from the army."

Shock jolted Elijah to his feet. "Army, suh? They lookin' for you?" he asked, blowing air out of his cheeks. "Oh, no, suh."

"You sore at me? I mean, 'cause I deserted and all?"

Elijah stared at Billy in disbelief, then glanced at his clothes, badly soiled but the jacket distinctly blue. "What army you in?"

"Army of the Potomac, Seventeenth Maine Regiment. Leighton says the army'll likely shoot me."

"And where is this Leighton?"

"He's my friend." Billy let out a deep sigh. "Leighton and Harry and, and—all of them back there, 'cept me. You got a friend, Elijah?"

Nodding his head, Elijah gazed into the woods, a vacant stare across his face. "Ol' Joe, he my friend. Elijah never gon' see Ol' Joe again."

"Then you ain't got a friend?"

"No mo', suh."

"You wantin' to be my friend?"

Elijah's eyebrows arched. He turned away and looked out across the creek. "White folk don't be makin' friends with no slave," he said a few moments later.

"Why not?"

"That just the way it be."

"Reckon it ain't needin' to be that way."

"When you leave these woods, maybe you tell slave catchers about Elijah. Slave catchers pay you money."

"I ain't tellin' no slave catcher." Billy shouted. "Besides, I'm needin' to stay here. Leighton says if you desert, you got to hide in the woods for a time."

"How far you run from?"

"Other side of the Potomac—crossed it and came into these here woods."

"Why you run away no how?"

"Wantin' to go home is all. Ain't we gonna be friends?"

They stared at each other in awkward silence. Finally, Elijah turned away without answering. He paced a few steps, paced back, and turned away again. From the corner of his eye Elijah watched Billy walk to the creek, plop down on the bank, and cup his chin in his hands. Billy sat there, never once turning around for most of the long afternoon as Elijah stayed and tended the fire, staring vacantly, occasionally shaking his head in frustration. Finally, with a push of his hands on his knees, Elijah got up and walked to the bank.

"Billy, suh?" Elijah sat down on the grass beside him.

"Yeah?"

"Elijah never had no white folk be his friend. Why you want this nigguh fo' a friend?"

"Needin' one is all. Like my friend Harry. Thing is, I ain't always sure what to do. Harry figured things out most times."

"Maybe Elijah try."

"Figurin' things out and all?"

"Yes, suh."

"Then you'll be my friend?"

"Only some."

"Why only some?"

Elijah pointed a finger at his dark skin. "Elijah no white folk like this Harry. So Elijah only some."

A hint of a smile crept across his face.

Billy grinned. Tension collapsed into relief, expressed in a fit of giggles, and he folded his arms across his stomach. Embarrassed, he erupted into another burst of explosive laughter.

Elijah couldn't remember a time when he'd ever heard someone laughing out loud like that. The sound was infectious; without warning, he found himself chuckling, too, even though he was in the middle of chewing his share of Billy's beef. In seconds he was mimicking Billy's laughter, heavy chortles exploding from his throat. Tears spilled down his cheeks, and he doubled over and hugged his belly. But then his laughter collapsed into a hacking cough; his eyes bulged as he gasped for air, and he fell onto his hands and knees.

Elijah heard footsteps rushing toward him. Still coughing, he raised his head to the noise, but his watered eyes saw only a blurred figure moving quickly to his side, now looming over him. He saw only a hand arched as if to strike him. His scream echoed across the clearing.

"No, suh! No, don', don', suh!"

"You're chokin'! Gonna slap your back is all."

But Elijah heard only the sharp cracks of the whip that had snapped against his back, one after another, each violent lash tearing open his flesh. He cried out, his body twitching at each imagined lash. He collapsed, falling limply to the ground.

Elijah knew his head lay against the white man's chest, but he lacked the strength to resist. He didn't move as arms enfolded him, rocking him slowly, back and forth, before exhaustion crumpled him.

Chapter 12

"You ever been fishin', Elijah?" Billy sat on the bank, warmed by the late October sun, elbows propped on his knees as he stared at the sluggish creek. The water was considerably lower than it had been the day before when it was swollen from the rain.

"No, suh." Elijah picked up a stone and tossed it into the creek.

"Pa taught me. Thing is, I ain't much good at it." Billy glanced at Elijah. "We ain't got nuthin' to eat. One apple is all," he said, wrinkling his brow. "Wish we had us a fishin' pole."

"Mebbe we just catch 'em with our hands." From his rocky perch Elijah leaned over and peered into the shallow water.

"Too hard, I'm thinkin'." Billy twisted to his side, leaned over, and picked up a branch. "Hey, I could whittle us a spear." Excitedly, he pulled his knife from his trouser pocket and dug into the limb, furiously shaping its broken end into a fine, sharp point.

"Look!" Billy exclaimed, overwhelmed with self-satisfaction as he held up the spear. "Learned me to whittle from Ethan."

Elijah let out a low whistle and grabbed the spear, touching its pointed end with the tip of his finger. "Ooh, suh, that be mighty sharp."

Within minutes Billy had carved another one, jumped to his feet, threw off his socks and boots, and waded into the water, striking his new weapon erratically at the air.

"We're needin' to fish where the water ain't movin' so much," he said, and led the way downstream until he found an eddy wide enough for the two them. He glanced up at a wide-trunked oak, its yellow leaves shadowing the water's edge. "Pa says to always fish in the shade."

Holding the spears above their heads, they positioned themselves at opposite ends of the eddy, each poised to strike the first trout. At each imagined movement, Billy repeatedly jabbed his spear beneath the surface, stirring mud and gravel from the creek bed. "Them fish just skedaddlin'."

Elijah shook his head. "You just scarin' them fishes away. Let Elijah do the fishin'." Billy lifted his spear out of the water, uttered his dismay at the flattened tip, and waded out of the eddy.

"Bad luck is all," he groused as he stepped onto the red bank of mud under the oak, tossing his ruined spear to the ground.

"Billy, suh, you be listenin' and watchin' them woods while Elijah fish."

"You mean like picket duty?"

Elijah shook his head. "Don't know nuthin' about this picket duty. Maybe you just whittle sumthin' for Elijah."

Billy's spirits immediately brightened. He turned and studied the oak tree and snapped off a low branch, its decaying leaves crumbling in his hands. "I'll whittle a fish. Don't worry none, Elijah. I'll watch them woods, too."

Elijah shook his head. Sometime this white boy act just like a child. As Elijah stood quietly in the eddy, his spear arched above his head, Billy stretched his long legs over the bank and began stripping the bark.

Elijah stood unmoving in the shallow water. Suddenly Billy heard a small splash as Elijah's spear shot through the water. Billy looked up as Elijah raised the spear, its tip piercing the gills of a brown trout.

Elijah swung the spear over the bank and shook the fish off the tip. The fish flopped for a few seconds and then lay still on the sand. Billy clapped his hands.

The long afternoon passed before Elijah speared another fish and waded back onto the bank. He started a small fire, careful to use only dry twigs to lessen the smoke. Billy scooped up both fish and set them on the flattened surface of a large rock, wiping his blade against his trousers.

"Pa and Harry always cleaned 'em, but I seen them do it." He sliced off the heads and slit the bellies, using his fingers to pull out the tangle of guts. Then he ran to the bank and on his knees leaned over and rinsed the fish, removing the last of the innards. As he set the fish back onto the outcrop, he hesitated, not sure how to remove the spine and its network of fine bones. He jabbed his knife against the spine, tearing chunks of raw meat before he sighed and dropped the fish onto the flat rock. "Needin' to cook the fish with them bones, I'm thinkin'."

"Elijah do the cookin'," Elijah said as he folded the spliced bellies over a twig and held them over the fire. The oily fish dripped and sizzled over the coals.

Billy plopped to the ground and, resting his chin in his hands, studied Elijah's naked back hunched over the fire. His skin was ragged; seams of red bumpy ridges ran from his neck and disappeared into the band on his trousers. "Elijah," Billy asked quietly, "how come your back's all tore up?"

"Whuppin's, Billy, suh."

"Who done that to you?"

"Mastuh and the overseer."

"Why'd they go and tan you so hard like that?"

"All slaves get whupped," he said, not turning around. "Mastuh Ramsey, though—he Elijah's first mastuh—he treat

93

my pappy and me good most time, but we worked hard. We work in the fields all the time, every day. But sometime on Sundays, Mastuh let the slaves have a preacher come and we sing by the fire." Elijah paused and poked a finger at the soft underbellies of the fish.

"Then who's Master Fowler?" Billy asked.

"Mastuh Ramsey go on and sell me to Mastuh Fowler. He bad. He whup me for no reason. Elijah don't do nuthin'. Then his overseer, Buckra, he whup Elijah with a rawhide strap most days." Elijah winced. "Ol' Joe, he tell me Mastuh gon' sell me at the auction block. That night Elijah run away, like Pappy and Ol' Joe say."

"Ain't right, hurtin' people like that," Billy said, shaking his head. "You ever gonna see your pa again, you thinkin'?"

Elijah lowered his head. "'No, suh, Elijah don' think so."

"Then you got no place to go?"

"Ol' Joe, he tell Elijah, go to Canada and be a free man. He say follow the North Star." Elijah turned a blackened twig away from the fire.

"North Star! My Pa says our farm's right under the North Star. Thing is, I'm followin' her home." Billy jumped to his feet and, walking away from the fire's reflection, searched the sky. "Needin' to find the Big Dipper first," he said, pointing his index finger low in the northern sky. "It's got a big handle on it—like a soup ladle."

"You be lookin' for the same as the Drinkin' Gourd," Elijah said. "Billy, suh, be goin' to Canada?"

"Naw, Berwick. That's in the state of Maine. About near as far, I'm thinkin'.'"

Elijah slid the fish onto a rock. "All cooked." He peeled the hot skin and picked at the flakes of meat. "Fish taste real good.

Ol' Joe, he say go to Sandy Spring, Maryland. Quaker folk there put me on the Underground Railroad to Canada."

"Maryland? I know where that is; it's just across the river."

"Elijah get all the way to Maryland?" His eyes flashed wide. "Just like Ol' Joe say?"

Wiping his greasy fingers against his trousers, Billy smacked his lips as he devoured the last of his fish and settled down on his earthen bed. "We'll leave in the mornin'. Needin' to steal us some food."

"No, suh. Elijah don't steal nuthin'."

"It ain't stealin'. Them fellas in the army do it all the time. Leighton don't get in trouble for it."

Elijah offered no response as he tossed the last of the branches onto the fire and watched the flames spiral higher. Finally he lay down beside Billy. "Buckra whup a little nigguh gal with a hickory stick. Whupped her so bad she nearly die. Just 'cause she go and steal a potato, she so hungry. No, suh, Elijah don't steal nuthin'."

"All right, then. I'll do it. Besides, Leighton says if you desert you got to steal some other clothes. Army will catch me right quick if they see me in these clothes."

Billy thought some more about what lay ahead. He knew Elijah would be scared to cross the Potomac, to step into a river far wider and stronger than Goose Creek.

"Elijah?"

"Yes, suh?"

Somethin' I'm needin' to tell you."

"What that be?"

"That river, the Potomac? Like I already told you, I crossed it before. It's pretty big and all. You ain't gonna be scared, is you?"

Elijah sighed deeply. "Elijah gonna cross this river—this river make Elijah a free man."

Daylight dawned gray and heavy, a fine mist hanging in the air. Anxious to make the crossing before the rain, Billy woke Elijah, telling him they needed to hurry. As they emerged from the forest onto the open fields, Billy pointed to the Maryland countryside on the other side, to the distant army encampment at Edward's Ferry, before rushing into the safety of the tall grass. Wind whipped against a darkening sky as they climbed a sweep of rolling hills and turned away from the river.

"Need to find me some clothes right off," Billy said. Haystacks dotted the harvested fields, and a sharp longing for home went through him when he spotted a farmer gathering forkfuls of hay. He felt a nudge against his ribs.

"Clothes over there," Elijah said, pointing to a farmyard in the other direction. Clothes were hanging to dry from a line strung across the yard.

Billy nodded, and dropping to his hands and knees, followed Elijah through the overgrown field. As they inched closer to the farmyard, Billy poked his head up over the grass, spotting nothing but dairy cows grazing behind a fence near the barn. Heavy with laundry, the clothesline sagged almost to the ground.

"Stay here and keep a-lookin'," Billy whispered. "You see somethin', whistle is all." He crawled slowly through the thicket, stopped, and turned his head to Elijah. "I ain't never stole nuthin' before neither."

"Mebbe, Billy, suh, you can get me a shirt," Elijah said with a wry grin on his face.

Billy nodded, and in seconds disappeared in the dense undergrowth, staying low until he reached the rain barrel at one end of the clothesline. Hearing no whistle from Elijah, he sprang from his hiding place and, running the length of the line, grabbed handfuls of clothes as pins snapped and dropped to the ground. He scanned the farmyard, spotting only an orange-striped cat rolling in the dirt. Clutching the damp clothing, he raced across the open yard and leaped into the cover of the tall grass, dropping onto his hands and knees. Elijah grinned. Without speaking, they moved quickly down the field, finding shelter in a stand of oaks.

"No matter if these don't fit good," Billy said, examining the bundle of clothes in a heap on the ground. He held up flannel shirts, trousers, and a woman's skirt. He tossed the skirt to the ground and handed Elijah a shirt.

"I'm gon' wear this shirt all the time. Ain't nobody see this back again. Ain't nobody."

Billy's clothes hung loosely on his thin frame, and taking the long lace from one of his boots, he tied it around his waist to keep the trousers from sliding off his hips. Except for his short sack coat, which he wanted for its warmth, he shed his army clothing, and stuffing it all under a bush, he covered the discarded clothing with dried leaves and dirt. Sadness rushed through him. It was the last connection to his friends and a reminder he was leaving them behind. He thought long and hard about Harry. Worried if he would ever see him again. He glanced over at Elijah, ever grateful for his new companionship, and his promise to figure things out for him like Harry had done.

They followed the river upstream, watchful for army encampments or soldiers on picket along the Maryland shore. They made their way slowly, shadowing among the trees and studying the landscape before darting across open fields. By late afternoon Billy had found White's Ford, and pointing his finger, explained to Elijah how they would work their way across the river after dark.

"Thinkin' I'll get us some food." Billy said, tugging at Elijah's elbow. "There's a farm way over there."

Elijah nodded. "We both go this time, Billy, suh."

They spotted a nearly vacant garden behind the large red barn. The farmhouse sat farther down the lane, almost out of view. Crawling beside Elijah, Billy watched as his friend dug his fingers into the dark soil and pulled out a handful of forgotten potatoes.

A low growl pierced the air, followed by barking.

Startled, Billy looked at Elijah and saw the terror streak across his dark face. "Let's go."

"Lord, don't let that be bloodhounds." Elijah scooped up the potatoes and darted into the cover of the thicket, Billy close at his heels.

Shouts erupted from the farmyard. "Asa! Get over here!"

Billy turned to look. Halfway across the garden, a yellow retriever stopped, turned its head to his master's voice, and then turned back to Billy, unleashing earsplitting barks.

"Asa? That skunk's gonna get you again! Get back here." His master's voice was firm. Whimpering, the dog retreated.

Billy and Elijah sprinted across the field to the river, sliding at last down the embankment to an overhang at its edge. They each downed a potato.

Elijah raised his face to the three-quarter moon disappearing through the thickening clouds. It had started to rain. "Billy, suh, we need to cross now, and you gon' have to help me," Elijah said. "Take off your shirt and wrap your things in it."

Billy nodded. Tucking the shirt and belongings under one arm, he turned to Elijah as he waded into the shallow water. "Take my hand—if I stop, then don't you move neither."

"Billy, suh, you sure we can cross the river like this?" Elijah whistled under his breath and reached out to grab Billy's hand.

"It ain't so bad." Billy stepped into the dark waters and, planting his boots heavily on the shale-covered bottom, tested his balance before urging Elijah forward. With each step, Billy moved slowly, cautiously, pausing every few feet as Elijah inched his way behind him. As the river deepened, the current made them even more unsteady in their wobbly footholds. The cold water swirling around their chests swelled and slapped their faces as the wind funneled down the river, turning the Potomac into a torrent of white-capped waves.

A crack of thunder echoed against the steep banks. The sky was black.

Elijah's fingernails dug into Billy's clenched hand. The sudden pain startled Billy, and he slipped on the shale, jerking Elijah off his feet.

"Elijah, dig in, dig in!"

Fear and adrenaline drove Elijah's bare feet into the gravelly bottom. Billy tried to do the same, frantically searching for a foothold. For an instant his boot felt secure, and then suddenly he felt himself sinking into the river bottom.

"Don't step no farther, Elijah. Got a boot stuck."

Billy pulled and tugged to free himself, but his boot sank deeper and deeper. Clutching his shirt-wrapped belongings tighter to his chest, the fingers on his other hand locked with Elijah's, Billy heaved his weight forward, wresting Elijah off his feet. Elijah yelled as the current lifted him, hurling him against

Billy's shoulder. The impact spiraled Billy off his feet. He felt his foot sliding from the boot.

"Hang on, Elijah!" Wrapping one arm around Elijah's waist, Billy frantically clawed the water. *I can't lose my boot!* he thought.

At last he felt the tip of the leather and tugged. The boot broke free from the river bottom's hold, and he tucked it under his arm. Slowly, still holding onto Elijah, Billy moved with the current, angling them toward the shore. In seconds, they waded into shallow water, holding each other. Half stumbling, they collapsed on the muddy bank.

Billy picked the soggy clay out of his boot and let out a low laugh.

"Why you be laughin', Billy, suh?"

Billy pointed to the bootlace tied around his trousers. "Boot didn't have no lace is all."

"No more rivers, Billy, suh, no more rivers."

They crawled up the slippery bank and scurried for cover in a grove of firs.

"Ain't knowin' our way in this rain," said Billy as he folded his arms against the cool dampness. "Can't see the stars."

"Billy, suh, we'll just lie down and sleep now. This the only thing to do."

To shield themselves against the muddied ground, they gathered and stacked pine branches and lay down on their crude beds, backs pushed against one another for warmth. In spite of the soaking cold, they quickly fell asleep.

Billy opened his eyes at the first stirring of the approaching dawn, the incessant chattering of sparrows. The rain had stopped. He rolled over onto his back and nudged Elijah awake. They crawled out from under the dripping branches, warming their chilled bodies and dampened clothes in the generous sunlight.

Billy was impatient to get moving, but Elijah would not hear of it. "Billy, suh!" he said. "We wait for dark."

"But the army—"

"We wait here, just 'til dark. Elijah listen good for the army, won't let nobody find us."

"All right then." Nestled under the fir trees, Billy and Elijah ate the last raw potato and drank water from the canteen before settling in for the long wait until evening.

Chapter 13

As soon as the stars appeared, Billy and Elijah headed out. They moved off in the direction of the star.

In the early darkness Billy stumbled, fell onto his knees, and found himself on hardened sand. Suddenly he glanced in either direction. "This here's a road. The North Star went and led us right to a road."

Walking on flat ground was easier, and they moved at a steady pace through the wooded countryside. Just before daylight, they veered off the road into a pine grove, and made beds of leaves and dried pine needles. After just a few hours' sleep, Billy awoke. Impatient at remaining in hiding for the rest of the day, he woke Elijah and prodded him to continue down the road. Reluctantly Elijah agreed, insisting they hug the woods that flanked its edge.

A short while later they heard the clamor of hooves behind them. They ran into the thicket, ducked behind a scrub bush, and watched silently as a pair of horses trotted by pulling a wagon, plump burlap bags piled in the tailboard. The driver wore a broad-brimmed black hat, and talked and gestured animatedly to the woman sitting next to him wearing a large white bonnet. Billy and Elijah waited until the wagon was safely out of view and then scurried down the side of the road listening for sounds, careful to move within the cover of the underbrush. After several miles, the wooded lane opened onto a sweep of yellowish-green fields.

"Them fields all alfalfa," Elijah said as he hurried through the deep green growth to a giant flat boulder crowning the hillside.

He leaned against the rock's smooth, sun-warmed surface to rest his back. Billy climbed to the flattened top and, using his hand to shade his face from the blinding sunlight, gazed out across the rolling landscape. In the far distance, he spotted a white steeple rising above a cluster of dark green spires. "There's a town over in them trees. Sandy Spring, I'm thinkin'."

Elijah climbed to the top of the rock, craned his neck, and looked out across the fields. "Yes, suh," he said as he studied the landscape. He turned and faced Billy. "Elijah stay on this here rock. Billy, suh, you go to town and see if it be Sandy Spring."

"How am I gonna do that?" Billy asked.

"Town be havin' a sign somewhere."

Billy looked down. "Can't read no sign."

Elijah turned a puzzled look at him. "Can't read? But white folk get schoolin'."

Billy's cheeks burned crimson. "Had trouble with learnin'."

"It's all right, Billy, suh." Elijah turned and looked at Billy, flashing a wide grin and nudging his shoulder. "Now you be just like Elijah.

"Now you listen good," Elijah said, staring into Billy's eyes. "You go to a store and ask where Sandy Spring be. You don' say nuthin' about your nigguh friend. And you don' say nuthin' about the army. Then you come right back!"

"All right, then. Still got them coins in my haversack. Maybe I can buy us some bread." Taking the coins from the pouch, Billy stuffed them into his trouser pockets.

Billy walked along the busy main street and studied the colorful storefronts, each a striking contrast against the drab, gray buildings. He spotted a general store at the corner and hurried inside, where he was greeted by whiffs of freshly baked bread. Overcome with sights and smells he had not seen since

Berwick, he stood mesmerized in the center of the aisle, staring at the well-stocked shelves. A fair-haired lady holding a straw basket moved by him and offered a gentle smile. He smiled shyly back and headed toward the counter. Nervous, aware of curious stares, he stepped timidly past a group of men sitting around a potbellied stove and leaned his elbows over the worn countertop. Jars of candy sticks and golden candied ginger captured his attention.

A plump man, nut-brown sideburns framing his ample cheeks, appeared behind the counter. "What can I get for you, young fella?" he asked, peering over his spectacles.

"I'd like me a loaf of bread."

The storekeeper grabbed a round loaf off a shelf behind him and set it on the counter. Taking a step back, he placed his hands on his hips and waited.

His head lowered, Billy pulled the coins from his pocket and arranged them in a neat row beside the bread, too fearful to look up and catch the storekeeper's watchful gaze.

"That's more'n you need."

"Then I'll have me some cheese."

The storekeeper lifted a block of white cheese from the glass case, sliced a wedge, and placed it on a scale. He studied the scale, glanced back at the row of coins, then wrapped the cheese in brown paper and tied it with string.

The fair-haired lady moved up beside Billy, her shoulder brushing lightly against him. In an instant the sweet scent of lavender perfumed the air.

Billy continued to stare at the money, wishing Harry were standing beside him.

"Just take what you need is all," he mumbled finally. He stole a glance at the sweet-smelling lady. He thought she was the prettiest thing he had ever seen, what with her thick flaxen hair, the stray wisps curling around her face.

The burly storekeeper shook his head, placed his palms on the counter, and leaned into Billy's face.

"Have the money you need there, Hiram?" the fair-haired lady asked in annoyance as she set her basket on the counter. The storekeeper counted the coins, dropped a fistful in his apron pocket, and pushed the rest toward Billy.

Billy's eyes widened in surprise, and he darted a quick glance at the jars of candy. He had already spotted the candied ginger, but was too nervous to use his fingers for counting the pennies the way Harry had taught him. Maybe there was enough money for one piece. "Some ginger candy, please."

The storekeeper scooped up the remaining change. "You from around these parts?" he asked, putting several ginger slices into a small paper bag. He turned and hesitated, dangling the bag in the air, waiting for an answer.

"No—no, sir." Billy said. "Is this Sandy Spring?"

"What business you got in Sandy Spring?" The storekeeper asked, arching his eyebrows.

"We was—I mean, um, I was needin' to get there is all."

"We? Who's we?"

Fumbling with the button on his shirt and shifting his weight, Billy made no reply. He looked over at the fair-haired lady again and then lowered his gaze to the floor.

"You and your friend—walking, are you?"

"Yes, sir."

"You'll get there by nightfall. Looking for someone in Sandy Spring?"

After a long hesitation, Billy answered, stumbling on his words. "I ain't supposed to say."

"Got you a pair of bootees, I see, boy," said a voice behind him. Billy spun around. One of the men sitting beside the stove glared at him, and then looked down at Billy's boots. Pockmarks dotted his face. He leaned over and nudged the man next to him, pointing a finger at Billy's boots. "Ain't them army boots you wearing, boy?"

"What do you mean, you ain't supposed to say?" The storekeeper had raised his voice. "Why—"

"That's about enough of your questions, Hiram—and yours, Peyton," the fair-haired lady interrupted. "This young man didn't come in here to state his business—or to discuss his boots. Give him his bag of candy and let him be."

Billy turned his face to the fair-haired lady. She spoke to him softly. "Get your goods. I'll help you find your way to Sandy Spring." Then she turned and offered an icy glare to the storekeeper.

Hiram tossed the bag to Billy.

"Well, Cyrus, I've a feeling you'll be doing some scouting down the turnpike later," said Peyton.

The fair-haired lady bristled and nudged Billy toward the door. She took his arm and escorted him down the shaded street and around a corner. Finally she stopped and faced him.

"That's the Norbeck Road over there," she said, pointing her finger. "Follow it to the Washington-Brookville Turnpike. When you reach the crossroads at Olney, take the road to the right. It goes straight into Sandy Spring." Her lovely face widened into a smile. "It's only a few miles from here."

Billy looked down at the ground and shuffled his feet. "Them's a lot of things to remember."

"Are you sure you'll find it, then?"

"Reckon." He felt awkward in her presence. "What's this town?"

"This is Rockville. And what's your name?"

"Billy."

"But you're not alone, Billy?" she asked.

Avoiding her eyes, he shook his head from side to side.

"Do you have friends in Sandy Spring?"

"No, ma'am."

"Then why are you going there?"

"Quakers got a railroad."

She gasped, turned her head, and glanced nervously in either direction.

"Where did you hear such talk?"

"Elijah says I can't say."

"Elijah?"

"You know Elijah?"

"No, no, I don't know any Elijah. But I am beginning to understand," she whispered. "I have a friend in Sandy Spring who can help him."

Billy let out an excited cry.

"Hush, hush!" she said, looking around again. "Those men in the store, Peyton and Cyrus—the ones by the stove—they're mean-spirited. They don't take kindly to strangers—or runaway slaves. Peyton fought for the South, was wounded at Bull Run."

He saw the worried lines across the woman's brow. She pushed wisps of hair away from her face. "Sandy Spring is a Quaker town, and folks here know some of the Quakers are helping runaways. I'm afraid that's why Peyton and Cyrus were wondering about your business in Sandy Spring. Tell me, why did he ask about your boots?"

"Ain't sure."

"Well, when you get to Sandy Spring, go to the Friends Meeting House. It's a two-story brick house, down the lane from J. P. Stabler and Co. It's a store much like the one we were just in. My friend is Johanna Samson; she's tall with red hair. Most likely she'll be there." She looked tenderly at him. "Will you be all right?"

"Yes, ma'am. If I can remember all you told me." He shuffled his boots, not wanting to turn away from her. "You got a name?" he asked awkwardly.

"Sarah." She looked at him with the worried eyes of a mother and then repeated the directions for him. "You must go now, Billy. And, please, for goodness' sake, be careful. Your friend must stay out of sight at all times—it's very dangerous for him. Knock on that Meeting House door even if it's in the middle of the night. If no one is there, Johanna lives just down the lane, in the brown house. Wait for her until morning. Not all of the Quakers help runaways, but she will help your friend."

"Yes, ma'am—Sarah." Billy wanted to ask Sarah to go with him. He twisted the paper bag.

"Now, you must hurry. Your friend will be worried about you," Sarah said as she brushed her hand against his cheek. "Godspeed, Billy. And may you both be safe in this uncertain world we live in."

He turned and walked slowly down the street, shoulders slumped, arms filled with bread and cheese and the bag of ginger candy. Before he reached the corner he turned around and spotted Sarah in the middle of the street. He waved a hand wildly in the air, and felt his heart beat rapidly when she waved back.

Chapter 14

It was nearing dusk when Billy darted off the road into the brush and crossed the alfalfa fields to the rocky outcrop. He called out to Elijah.

As Elijah emerged from the thicket, his eyes widened at the loaf tucked under Billy's arm.

"Oh, Billy, suh!" he said, smiling, as he stretched his stiff body. "You done real fine."

They sat down on the flat boulder and ate hungrily, watching the sun drop in the pink and yellow sky.

"Got me some ginger candy," Billy said as he reached into the bag and handed him a piece. "You like ginger candy?"

"Never had none." Elijah looked curiously at the honey-colored sweet and rolled it in his fingers. He winced at the first bite and spit it from his mouth, his lips puckered. "Billy, suh, this be nasty-tastin'."

"My brother Jamie don't like it much neither."

"You find where Sandy Spring be?"

Billy told him about the storekeeper who asked so many questions and about Sarah. "She smelled real pretty, Elijah. Just like lavender."

Elijah stirred nervously. "Billy, suh, why this purty-smellin' missus take you outta the store?"

"She told that storekeeper not to be askin' about my business is all."

Elijah stiffened. "They be anybody else in the store?"

Billy scratched his head, trying to remember. "There was some fellas sittin' around the stove. Asked me about my boots."

"Why they askin' about yo' boots?"

"Ain't sure."

"You get them boots in the army, Billy, suh?"

"Yeah. Except we call 'em bootees." Billy's eyes blinked wide. "Thing is, that fella called them bootees, too."

Elijah shook his head. "Oh, there's gonna be trouble. White folk in the store know you was in the army."

He stood up, placed his hands on his hips, and stared out across the green fields. "That road in town only one take us to Sandy Spring?"

"Reckon. Sarah says it's only a few miles. I'm rememberin' how to get there mostly. Turnpike she calls it. Runs out the other side of town. Then we're needin' to find her friend at the Meeting House."

"What this friend's name be?"

"Johanna Samson." Billy dug into the paper bag, pulling out his last piece of ginger candy. "She's a Quaker."

"That what Ol' Joe say!"

Billy and Elijah settled against the boulder and waited for the darkness. The cold evening air penetrated their flannel shirts as they huddled together, passing the hours watching for the stars.

Billy blew warm air over his fingers. He looked up just as a shooting star darted across the heavens and disappeared into the darkness. "You see that shootin' star?"

"Yes, suh."

"Pa says it means them stars just plum wore out. Fall right out of the sky."

"Where they go?"

"Ain't sure. Land on the ground, I reckon." Billy's eyes pierced the sky. "What makes them stars come out, you thinkin'?"

"Oh, they already up there. Stars is like candles, come out in the dark only."

Billy shook his head. "Naw, candles is got to be lit."

"Come nighttime, Lord light them stars all by hisself."

"He lights all of them?"

"Yes, suh."

"Why does he do that?"

"Lord light them stars so little folk find their way in the dark. Preacher say Lord take care of the little folk." Elijah stood and stretched his arms and legs. "Stars all lit up now. We go, Billy, suh."

They moved across the alfalfa, emerged from the thicket, and hurried down the empty road.

As they neared Rockville, Elijah took the lead, searching for the turnpike Billy said was on the other side of town. He cut a wide path around the perimeter, watchful for vigilant dogs, creeping through open areas between the scattered homes on the outlying streets. Elijah breathed a sigh of relief when he spotted a road on the eastern side angling toward the hills. He stretched his tight back and listened, and hearing nothing, motioned Billy out of the thicket.

As they moved easily down the road, Elijah felt his heart beat with excitement. He thought of Ol' Joe and wished he could tell him he had found his way to Sandy Spring. Soon he would be on the Underground Railroad, and before long, he would be a free man.

Out of the stillness, hooves beat a tattoo on the turnpike.

Elijah froze in place, reached out and tugged on Billy's shirt, signaling him to be quiet. He stared into the darkness.

Riders were approaching—with lanterns!

Elijah pushed Billy off the road, into the gully. The hooves grew louder. The riders were closing in. Elijah leaped down the embankment, sliding, tumbling, loose dirt flying in his face. Voices shot through the dark.

"The gully, Cyrus! I see him! Wait! I think there's two of them!"

"A nigger's with him all right!"

Elijah raced over the stony ground. He heard Billy trip, stumble. Elijah grabbed Billy by the arm, pulling him back to his feet. Pine needles lashed their faces. The underbrush tore at Elijah's feet and he stopped once, gritting his teeth as he pulled a pinecone from the ball of his foot.

Hooves echoed over the stones.

Elijah prayed they would lose their pursuers in the forest, but the trees thinned; moonlight spilled across a clearing.

There was no place to hide.

"There's a light across the field—a farmhouse!" Billy shouted.

"No, suh, not the house!"

"Got no choice. They're catchin' us."

Then Elijah saw the dark silhouette of a fence only a few feet away. "Jump the fence. Follow me."

They leaped over the rails, Billy tailing Elijah, running straight for the cows, disappearing in the middle of the herd.

The riders emerged from the trees, the light from their lanterns bouncing in the darkness. In an instant there were shouts, a shuddering thump of hooves, horses whinnying to a hurried stop.

"Cyrus, follow the fence line! Look for the gate."

The startled herd lowed, their harness bells clanking noisily. "Let's head for the barn," Elijah whispered to Billy, urging him to crouch down and move with the cows, staying close to their underbellies.

"Come out or we'll shoot!" a harsh voice sounded in the darkness.

Slowly, quietly, Billy and Elijah inched their way to the barn as the frightened cows moved across the pasture.

Elijah crawled under the fence and slithered along the barn's clapboards, in search of an opening. The doors were latched. He dropped to the ground, signaled for Billy to follow, and dashed around to the back. An opening, at ground level. A buggy rested in the center of the earthen floor. Quickly, Elijah scanned the stone foundation and the wooden sills that supported the main barn above them. There were no stairs, not even a ladder to the upper level. No place to hide.

He moved under the sills, groping and pushing on the planks in the cobwebbed darkness. Mastuh Ramsey's barn had a trapdoor in the middle of the floor for sweeping the dirtied straw onto the ground below. He pushed at the floorboards above him; sweat trickling down his face. Nothing. The planks were solid, tight.

He shot an anxious glance at Billy, crouched beside the buckboard, muttering to himself. Then it hit him. The center of the floor. Elijah raced to the buckboard, climbed onto the springy platform, and standing on its seat, pushed hard against the planks directly over his head.

The trapdoor creaked open.

He looked down at Billy, nodded, and then raised the trapdoor just wide enough to glance around the interior of the main floor. The doors were still closed. Elijah pulled himself up through the opening, leaned over, and extended his hand to

Billy. Billy braced his foot on the sill and let Elijah lift him through the hole. Quietly, Elijah set the trapdoor back in place.

They stood motionless, listening as the horses' hooves clattered to a stop in front of the barn. In the distance a door slammed. Footsteps raced across the farmyard. Someone shouted, "What's goin' on here? Who are you?"

"Ezra! Put your rifle down—it's Peyton and Cyrus. We chased a slave and a white boy—a deserter, we're guessing—chased them into the pasture, but they headed for your barn!"

Elijah heard the men dismount.

"Barn door's shut tight. Must be hiding on the lower level where I keep the buggy."

Footsteps scrambled toward the back of the barn.

Billy looked up at the lofts above his head. "Maybe we can hide in the hay," he whispered.

"They find us there." Elijah bit his lip as he listened to their pursuers race through the level below them. His eyes darted about the barn, searching frantically for a hiding place.

Hogsheads! On a small, high platform attached to the wall between the two lofts were four large wooden casks. Ladders leaned up to both sides of the platform. Elijah tugged at Billy to tiptoe across the floor and then nudged him up the ladder to the main loft, climbing each rung quietly behind him. *Lord, let them hogsheads be empty!*

When they reached the loft, he pulled Billy close, whispering, "We gonna hide in them hogsheads up on the platform." Billy nodded. Slowly, they climbed a short ladder and stepped onto the narrow platform.

Trying not to make a sound, Elijah opened the lids. The casks were empty. He helped Billy lift his legs over the rim and burrow down inside. "Don't move and don't you come out 'til

114

Elijah get you. Elijah gonna put the lid on now."

The voices outside grew louder. Rustling by the barn door. Elijah stepped into the cask beside Billy, struggled to squeeze his broad shoulders past the upper ring. The wood pressed tight against him; he was stuck.

The barn door rattled open.

Elijah took a deep breath, sucked in his stomach, hunched his shoulders, and pushed down hard. Splinters of wood jabbed his flesh like needles; his blood was like oil against the roughly hewn slats, sliding him at last deeper into the barrel. He was in, just as the light from the lanterns spilled through the room—except the lid lay on the platform floor.

"Reckon they kept on runnin'. Don't see how they would have gotten in here."

"Like as not, we'll take us a look around. Plenty of hay up there to hide in. Keep your rifle cocked, Peyton, while I check out the lofts."

Beads of sweat trickled down Elijah's cheeks, mingling with his blood, stinging him. He listened as one of the men climbed the ladder. Suddenly there was the frightening sound of a pitchfork swishing through the hay.

"Gonna have to push some of the hay onto the floor, Ezra."

"Go ahead, Cyrus, I ain't sleepin' tonight—not with some runaway about."

For several agonizing minutes Elijah listened to the repetitious sound of the prongs sinking fiercely into the hay. He swallowed, fear racing through him. He worried about Billy in the next barrel. *Lord, don't let them look in that barrel.* Startled mice scurried across the loft.

"This loft's clean. Lemme check the hay on the other side. What's the best way to get over there, Ezra?"

"You can use that platform up there with the hogsheads as a bridge," Ezra answered. Elijah sucked in his breath. "Or, you can use the rope. There's a pulley straight across the beam."

Elijah's silent prayers were answered when he heard a rope swaying across the barn, the thud of boots landing on the opposite loft. He listened for several more minutes, as the fork again pierced the hay.

"Looks like they got away. Must've run off into the woods somehow. They ain't up here."

The pitchfork clanged against the wall. Footsteps climbed down the ladder.

A horse whinnied. "The horses! By the God! They're stealin' our horses. Hurry!"

In spite of the rush of retreating footsteps, Elijah waited. Instinct told him someone was still there.

Moments passed.

Someone chuckled below.

"Looks like you gone and scared yerself some horses out there, Chesapeake! Out there nuzzlin' their legs, I reckon. Old cat like you still scaring the bedevil out of the horses. I'm headed inside . . . There's no runaways around here."

The barn door slid shut along its tracks, and Elijah heard the latch click. After a few more minutes, he climbed out of the hogshead and, stepping quietly, raised the lid on the other barrel. Elijah placed his hand on Billy's head and touched his matted, sweaty hair.

"We all right. We safe, Billy, suh." He reached under Billy's arm and helped him out.

"We rest here a bit. Then we go."

Billy followed Elijah down the ladder, stepping lightly across the hayloft and then settling down. Rolling onto his side, Billy leaned his back into Elijah's shoulders as they burrowed under the straw. Both were still trembling. A half-hour later, Billy was asleep.

Elijah lay quietly, listening for stirrings in the night, waiting for his heart to quiet.

I never think white folk ever gon' sleep beside Elijah. This all hard to figger out. I didn't pray for no white folk. And Billy, suh, he my friend now. Yes, suh, he act just like a chile and then he go and save Elijah's life. What all this mean, Lord?

His question unanswered, Elijah closed his eyes, willing himself to waken long before the dawn.

Chapter 15

A cold wind riffled through his hair as Billy beat his fist
against the door of the Friends Meeting House. Leaves
swirled in the darkness as precious moments passed. Suddenly,
the door opened. Billy raised his head, staring timidly into
green, deep-set eyes. The woman's height startled him; her
fiery red hair was pulled away from her face and tucked tightly
under a small lace cap. The wind rushed into the hallway, flattening her pale blue dress against her legs.

"Are you Johanna Samson?" Billy asked meekly, his body
shivering.

"I'm Johanna. Thee looks very cold." She stepped to the side
of the entryway, holding a lantern. "Come in."

Billy hesitated, took a deep breath, and stepped inside. He
was greeted with a rush of warm air and the sweet scent of
spruce burning in the woodstove. A low slat wall on either side
of the stove divided the room into equal sides. The room was
stark, the clapboard walls without plaster. Even the beams lacked
pegs for holding lanterns or hanging coats. Billy thought Johanna
Samson must be very poor to live in such a cheerless house.

"Would thee like to sit down?" she asked as she closed the
door behind her and motioned him to one side of the room.
He stepped across the floorboards and sat down on a long
bench, casting a shy glance at the tall woman.

"What brings thee to my door at this late hour?" she asked.

"Miss Sarah said you could help my friend, Elijah," Billy said,
swallowing hard.

"Sarah?"

"Yes, ma'am. The lady from the other town—Rockville. She's right pretty and all."

Eyebrows arched on Johanna's face. "Of course, Sarah Mayfield. Indeed, Sarah is a lovely person. Tell me, how may I help Elijah?"

"Elijah, well, he says Ol' Joe told him about the railroad in Sandy Spring gonna take him to Canada."

"I see." Johanna paced across the floor, stopped, and came back. "And where is thy friend now?"

"In them woods over yonder." Billy's fingers tingled, and he rubbed his hands back and forth across his trousers. Miss Johanna seemed nervous all of a sudden. He worried as she turned and walked to the window, pressing her face to the glass and peering into the darkness.

"Has thee told anyone else about me?"

"Just Elijah."

"And what is thy name?"

"Billy Laird."

"Thee is not from around here. Where is thee from?" Her voice sounded harsh of a sudden, and Billy shuddered.

"Maine," he said. "You sore at me, Miss Johanna?"

"Maine?" Johanna shook her head and moved across the floor, sitting down on the bench beside him. Her voice was softer this time. "Forgive me. I am sorry if thee felt offended by my tone. Thee is an abolitionist?"

Crossing his arms, Billy stared at the floor, biting on his lip for lack of anything to say. "I'm not understandin'," he said shyly.

"Tell me, then, how thee came to help Elijah."

"Miss Johanna, I'm just wantin' to go home is all."

"To Maine? Now it is I who does not understand."

"Thing is, I mustered in the Seventeenth Maine Regiment—"

119

"Thee is a soldier of war?" Johanna asked.

"I run off."

He saw her wide, erect shoulders slump; she turned away from him and sat silently, her eyes pinched shut. Long moments passed, and Billy worried that the strange woman was sore at him for running away.

He stirred awkwardly, got to his feet, and took a step toward the door.

"Is thee denying war?"

Billy hesitated and turned to her.

"Ma'am?"

"Does thee not wish to fight another?"

"I ain't afeared to fight."

"It is not fear that I speak about. Does thee understand I am a Quaker?"

"No, ma'am."

"Please, come and sit down. Let me explain. Quakers oppose all wars. We believe it is wrong to fight—to kill another child of God or to take violent action against anyone. I believe it is honorable that thee chose to walk away from war."

"Captain sent me away—to another company—away from my friends, who always . . . well, they help me, and . . . " Billy squirmed nervously and finally sat down on the bench, struggling with his words. "Besides, reckon I ain't wantin' to hurt no one— but Pa says folks that kill are doin' the Lord's work and all."

"God is in each of us, Billy. If thee does not want to hurt anyone, then the spirit of Christ as thee hears it is the truth that shall guide thee."

"You a preacher lady? You don't seem old enough . . . Reverend Snow back home, he must be—"

"No, Billy, I'm not a preacher. And I shall be thirty-four next month. Now, tell me more about this Elijah."

"When I cut out from Livingston's battery I run into the woods by Goose Creek. Leighton says you got to hide in the woods for a time—so the army don't catch you. Thing is, I found Elijah lyin' by the creek."

"Was he hurt?"

"Hungry is all. I went and fed him what I brung."

"And thee became friends?"

Billy shook his head. "He thought I was a slave catcher." He looked at her. "I ain't."

"If I help Elijah, how does thee plan to get home?"

"Don't rightly know."

Johanna stood and walked again to the window. "It is late and Elijah must be cold. Bring him to the horse shed across the lane in the woodlot," she said pointing her finger against the pane. "Be very careful that he is not seen. Stay close to the trees. I will return with food and blankets for thee both."

The horse shed was lit by candles, and picking up one of the candlesticks, Elijah scanned the small space. It was swept clean of all clutter. Except for a sprinkling of hay over a plank floor, the stalls were empty. Elijah spotted only a single harness on a row of wall pegs, and holding the feeble light above his head, he could find no saddle or bags of feed. He was relieved. The shed was little used. A hinge creaked and Elijah moved the candle toward the sound. Holding the door open with her shoulder, Johanna entered the barn carrying a tray of food; blankets were tucked under her arm.

Elijah stared at the tall woman who called his name. *This missus sho' don't look like Missus Fowler in her fancy silk dress.*

"Thee must be Elijah." Johanna set the tray down on an overturned crate and let the blankets fall from her arm. "I am Johanna," she said as she glanced at Elijah's bare feet. "Would thee like a soapstone from the woodstove to warm thy feet?"

"They all right, missus."

"I brought bread and soup."

Billy yelped with excitement and ran across the barn floor. He reached for a bowl and spoon, grabbed a slice of dark bread, and plopped down on the floor. Elijah stared at the thick slices covered in smooth yellow butter. He hesitated, raised his head, and looked questioningly at Johanna.

"Thee must eat."

Elijah picked up a piece of bread, touched the creamy butter, and licked it from his finger. "This real good, missus." He reached for the bowl of soup.

Johanna glanced around the small room. "There is a loft above. Spread your blankets on the hay. Finish eating. I will come by early in the morning. Thee must not leave this shed. There is no meeting for worship until the third day, so thee will not have to worry about people milling about. Not all Quakers—or Friends, as we call ourselves—help runaways find their way to Canada, so thee must always remain in hiding. Tomorrow we will discuss what needs to be done." She stood and turned toward the door. "Good night."

"Good night, Miss Johanna," said Billy.

Elijah set his bowl of soup on the floor and hurried across the room, sliding a plank board into the hooks that flanked the barn door as soon as Johanna disappeared from view.

"She's a nice lady—'cept I ain't understandin' her much," Billy said as he sponged the last of the broth with his bread and placed the empty bowl on the tray.

"Yes, suh, she all right." Elijah walked slowly across the floor, picked up the blankets, and tossed one to Billy. "Go on up the ladder now, Billy, suh." Blowing out the candle, he fumbled in the instant darkness, climbed the rungs, and settled on the straw beside Billy.

"Miss Johanna sure talks like a preacher," Billy said.

A cold rain beat against the shingled roof. Sheltered in the hay, Billy and Elijah listened to the patter of raindrops, pulled the blankets over their heads, and drifted into peaceable sleep.

Chapter 16

E lijah and Billy watched from the window as Johanna stood in the small graveyard outside the horse shed. She had barely moved in the past half-hour. "What she doin' out there like that? She all right?" Elijah wondered aloud. "You go on out there, Billy, suh, and see if she be needin' sumthin'.'"

Johanna turned her head as Billy closed the shed door and walked over to her. "This is the grave of Philip Thomas who died when he was only twenty, way back in 1754," Johanna said. "He was the first member of our Quaker settlement to be buried in the graveyard."

"You all right, Miss Johanna? I come out 'cause you been standin' here a long time."

A smile passed over Johanna's face. "Thee boys need not be concerned. I was holding in the light—praying silently."

"Ain't you got a church for that?"

Johanna nodded. "Friends hold meetings for worship here, in this brick house. But our worship is different from what thee is accustomed to. Men and women sit on separate sides of the room and wait in silence upon the Lord."

"Then why you out here all by yourself?"

"To seek God's will by this first grave. In many ways thee reminds me of Philip Thomas; I feel a kinship to him with thee. There is a long history of the Thomas family in this area. Some were disowned as members in our religious society for their participation in the Revolution. It was a family divided on our ancient testimony of peace with all men. So I came here to pray. I have been struggling with how I might help thee and yet not violate this testimony."

"Testimony?"

"The Testimony of Peace speaks to our belief that we are against violence of any kind. Friends oppose all wars and participation in military action. It is a belief that guides us in our everyday actions. And I have been waiting here to see this matter as God would see it rather than as human beings would see it."

"You askin' God about me?"

"I do not ask God; I listen. My truth springs from the leadings of my heart. While I was standing here, beside this grave, awareness filled my soul."

Billy glanced at her, trying to read the calmness he saw in Johanna's face as she raised it to the morning sun.

"God helped me achieve a sense of clearness," Johanna said. "It is as if God said to me, 'Thee must ease the suffering of this young man who is but a victim of this war.' Thee turned away from darkness and into the light, Billy, and I know now what needs to be done."

"You ain't sore then?"

"I am at peace with my decision."

Billy sighed, but the comfort of Johanna's arm around his shoulder felt reassuring.

"Run and tell Elijah to stay in the loft while we walk into town. Thee will be leaving soon, and I will not send Elijah away without a pair of boots. These October days are turning cold."

Billy and Johanna walked down the hillside into a small ravine. Stopping beside a clear spring bubbling across a hollow of fine white sand, Johanna told Billy the spring was a small tributary of the Anacostia River. Its crystalline water, she said, gave the name Sandy Spring to the early Quaker settlement.

"When we get to Stabler's General Store, thee must speak very little to the proprietor. Mr. Bentley is a kind and decent man and once helped an escaped slave, but Elijah is running with thee, a soldier of war, and that is a different matter. I will let Mr. Bentley think that I am buying boots for thee."

"Yes, ma'am."

For the rest of the way Billy and Johanna angled their way in silence up the ravine and onto the gravelly lane that led to the town.

"It is early yet, so I am hoping there will be no one else about at this hour," Johanna said as they entered the main street. "In spite of the war, we see few strangers here."

As Billy followed Johanna up the steps into Stabler's, he thought of the general store in Rockville and of pretty blonde Sarah standing in the aisle. But inside Stabler's he saw only a tall, dark-haired storekeeper who turned and nodded at him as he fanned the flames in a potbellied stove and slammed shut its cast iron door.

"Good morning, Richard," Johanna called as she walked briskly across the floor.

"And a fair morning to thee, Johanna," Richard Bentley said with a smile. His bushy eyebrows raised in curiosity as he glanced over her shoulder. "Thee has a friend this morning?"

"This is Billy, a friend of Anna Dickinson's, from Philadelphia," she said. "And most in need of a new pair of boots."

"A pleasure to meet thee, young man," Mr. Bentley said, casting a glance at Billy's boots. Again his eyebrows raised and a slight frown crossed his face. "Hmmm . . . well . . . ," he muttered as he turned back to the stove. "I must make the coffee, and then we shall see about new boots. Would thee both like some coffee since thee is about so early?"

"No, I—" Johanna startled at the sound of heavy footsteps behind her. Billy spun around and saw a short, heavyset man with a thick, graying beard walk into the store.

"Has thee perked the coffee yet, Richard?" asked the bearded man. "A frightfully cold morning. It seems winter may be close upon us. A pleasant morning to thee, Johanna."

"Ah, Edward . . . thee shares a cup of coffee with Richard before thee handles the mail?" she asked, smiling.

"Aye, it's coffee and news we share each morning," said the postmaster. "The telegraph keeps me well informed, and Richard and I discuss the events of this dreadful war."

"Thee may grind the beans for me, Edward," said Richard.

Glancing curiously at Billy, Edward removed his wool cap, stuffed it into his pocket, and walked over to the stove. Reaching for a square tin container on the shelf, he opened the lid and measured several spoonfuls of beans into the grinder. "Word is that General McClellan may soon find himself out in the cold. It's rumored that President Lincoln will remove him from command of the Army of the Potomac."

Billy's eyes widened with curiosity.

Edward carried the ground beans to Richard, who tossed them into the coffeepot and placed it on top of the stove.

"It is as we suspected, then, my friend," said Richard. "How could Lincoln not grow impatient with McClellan's ineptness in pursuing General Lee's army?" With a wry grin, he glanced at Johanna and Billy. "Imagine two old Quakers so knowledgeable about the strategies of war."

"In all but the fighting we are," said Edward.

Billy swallowed hard, glanced quickly at Johanna, and turned to the postmaster. "Army's got a new general?"

Edward's eyes narrowed and he hesitated before he spoke. "Aye, lad," he said slowly as he held his gaze on Billy. "General Ambrose Burnside. I hear that he has not distinguished himself in battle, but it appears the president has no other promising candidate." He leaned over the stove and warmed his hands. "This new general speaks of a rapid march south to Richmond."

"A rapid march?" asked Billy.

"Indeed, the Union troops are moving out as we speak," answered Edward. "And Burnside claims his grand divisions will take Fredericksburg by Thanksgiving."

"All the troops moving out to—?"

Billy bit his tongue and glanced at Johanna.

"Thee certainly brings the news to Sandy Spring, Edward," Johanna interrupted as she reached for the empty mugs on a small pine-board table.

"Oh, and that's not all. Peyton Foster, that ol' scoundrel from Rockville, came into the post office yesterday."

Taking a mug from Johanna's hand, Edward poured the coffee. "Would thee like a hot cup, Johanna? And thy friend?" Johanna nodded her head, and he handed a steaming mug to Billy.

"Tell me about Peyton," said Johanna.

Edward sipped loudly. "Oh, yes. Peyton says two fugitives are on the run together—a deserter from the army and a runaway slave. Claims they were headed here. Can thee imagine a more unusual pair!"

Startled, Billy turned quickly to Johanna, spilling some of his coffee across the floor. "S-s-sorry, Mr. Bentley," Billy stammered. The storekeeper's eyes lingered on Billy for several moments.

"It's no bother, lad," Richard Bentley spoke in a near whisper. "Thee does not need to worry about a thing."

Johanna paced nervously across the floor.

"Why would the fugitives come to Sandy Spring?" Johanna asked, moving between Billy and the postmaster, her tall frame blocking Edward's view.

"Thee knows there is talk that some Friends here help runaway slaves. But I fear these abolitionist groups are becoming more and more militant, and I do not believe that we should become entangled in this growing violence. There are more peaceful means to press for the abolition of slavery that Friends can pursue. And doubtless a Friend would not help a soldier of war."

Johanna opened her mouth to speak, but Richard interrupted. "I long for the day, Edward, that thee will come with telegraph in hand declaring that this terrible war is ended," he said.

"We must pray it will be so," Johanna said quietly.

"Well, I know thee is expecting a telegraph, Johanna, so I will leave and tend to my business. Good day to you all," Edward said, smiling politely. He put down his coffee mug and left the store.

Richard Bentley stood silently for several moments, took a long deep breath, and stared at the array of boots stretched across the long table. "What size boot does thee need, lad?"

"I-I-I——"

"Thee needs a size ten," Johanna said quickly. "And I fear we have lost much time already. He will not need to try them on."

In spite of Johanna's urgency, Richard stood before the table for several moments. Finally, he reached for two pairs of brown leather boots and handed them to Billy. Turning to Johanna he said, "If I may assume correctly about this matter, then I under-stand two pairs of boots are needed."

Johanna stared in stunned silence.

"Billy must no longer wear the ones he has on now, Johanna. The lad's boots are army issue."

Richard reached into a bin and tossed Billy two pairs of socks.

"Richard . . ." Johanna started.

Richard gently placed a finger on her lips. "Thee is a most resolute woman. Thee need only to ask for my assistance and yet thee chooses to turn away."

Billy glanced back and forth at Johanna and Mr. Bentley, confused by their stern expressions. "You sore at Miss Johanna?" he asked.

"No, lad," Mr. Bentley said, his face breaking into a smile. "Johanna is a most willful woman, and I am merely humbled in her presence."

"Thee is a good man, Richard. What do I owe for the boots?"

"Thee owes me nothing."

"Thank you for them boots, Mr. Bentley," Billy said shyly.

The storekeeper bowed his head and clasped his hands behind his back. "And a safe journey, I pray."

Billy poked his head out over the loft at the sound of the door creaking along its rusty track. Yellow light flickered in the sudden draft, casting wavy shadows against the wall as Johanna entered the shed, the lantern raised above her head.

"Miss Johanna!" Billy called out in sudden relief.

"They all gone now?" asked Elijah, creeping on his hands and knees beside Billy and peering down at her.

"Yes, our meeting for worship is over. Only a few Friends gathered this evening, and Isaiah Brooke, the only one on horseback tonight, tethered his horse to the hitching post out front. It was fortunate that no one required use of the shed. And, I have sweets for thee both."

Johanna hung the lantern on a spike protruding from the rafter and reached into the pocket on her apron. "Elizabeth Applewhite made sugar tarts."

Excitedly, Billy leaned back and pulled the ladder across the hay, and with Elijah's help lowered it over the loft until it landed with a heavy thud on the floor.

"I have much to discuss," said Johanna as Billy swung his legs onto the ladder and, skipping the last few rungs, leaped onto the floor. Picking up an empty crate, Johanna turned it over, clutched the folds of her dress, and sat down.

"This be about the Underground Railroad, missus?" asked Elijah as he scrambled down the ladder behind Billy. Billy handed him a tart, all the while licking the sugar off his own.

"Yesterday when we talked, I explained that the Underground Railroad is only a name given to the escape routes to Canada. And homes that offer food and shelter along the way are called stations."

Johanna reached into her apron pocket and pulled out a folded piece of paper. "I received this telegraph tonight before our meeting for worship. I've been waiting for a reply from my friend Anna Dickinson, a Quaker at one of the stations in Philadelphia. She is willing to help thee," Johanna said, moving back to the overturned crate. "Anna and I have done this before; we send hidden messages in our telegraphs. I have great trust in her."

Johanna fidgeted, stood up, paced a few steps and back again, and sat down on the crate. "This evening, after I read the telegraph, I asked Mr. Bentley for the use of his wagon on the Sixth Day, so that I may take thee both to Ellicotts Mills."

Johanna looked directly at Elijah. "Thee will be hidden in the tailboard, under blankets."

"Where we goin', Miss Johanna?" asked Billy.

"Anna will meet us at the Emory Methodist Church in Ellicotts Mills. From there thee both will take the train with Anna to Baltimore."

"This white folks' train station?" Elijah jumped to his feet. "No, Missus Johanna. Slave catchers be there."

"But there is a way to fool the slave catchers, Elijah," she said. "Hear me out, please."

Johanna turned and faced Billy. "Anna is about thy same age. Anna and thee will travel as husband and wife; Elijah will pass as thy slave. There are still many white people, slave owners in Maryland, who bring their slaves with them on the trains—it will not be an uncommon sight. The slave catchers will not stop thee. They linger at stations looking for runaways who have no papers or try to steal rides by hiding under the cars. They will not bother slave owners or question them about thy slaves."

"Elijah ain't got no papers!"

"Husband and wife?" said Billy, panicked.

Johanna took a deep breath. "Anna will get papers from the provost marshal or the station master if it becomes necessary. This way, thee both will be able to ride the train to Philadelphia instead of walking, at great risk, over a hundred miles."

"Elijah don't know, Missus, don't know . . . This Philadelphia be in Canada? Elijah be free there?"

"No, Canada is still a long distance from Philadelphia, but there are many people there who can help thee. Anna has friends at the Anti-Slavery Society. Thee is a free man in spirit only now, but soon, thee will be a free man under the law."

"Anna's friends help Billy, suh, also?"

Billy filled with despair when he saw Johanna shake her head.

"The people I speak of at the Society help only runaway slaves. But that is why I have asked Anna to help. She is far more able to find a way to get thee home, Billy. Anna will see that thee rides the train north."

"But if I'm a husband and all—"

"No, Billy, I forgot to answer thy question. Anna and thee will not really be married, but papers will say that thee are husband and wife—slave owners—and that Elijah is thy slave. It is the only way for Elijah to ride the train."

Billy jumped to his feet and paced rapidly across the floor, dropping his tart in the excitement. "I ain't never talked much to a lady before. Ain't knowin' how to be married."

"It is only for a short while—to fool the slave catchers until thee arrives in Philadelphia. Then Anna will take thee both to a safe place where thee will wait until it is time for Elijah to leave for the next station." Johanna folded her hands on her lap.

Billy continued to pace, kicking at the scattered wisps of straw on the floor.

"Is all right, Billy, suh," said Elijah as he walked over to him and placed a hand on his shoulder. "Missus Johanna, she tryin' to help us now."

"I ain't knowin' how to be married."

"Billy, suh, we just gonna pretend. We got to fool other people on the train. Like you fool the white folk in the store."

"You mean where I got them ginger candies?"

"Yes, Billy, suh. Now you fool the people on the train only. They go and think you be married, but you ain't, no, suh."

"And you'll be with me?"

"Yes, suh."

"All right, then." Billy sat back down beside Johanna and scanned the floor for the rest of his half-eaten tart.

Johanna smoothed the folds of her skirt and continued. "There will be two trains. Thee will board a train in Ellicotts Mills—it is a short ride into Baltimore. Anna will know what to do. When thee arrives in Philadelphia, Anna will take thee to the people who will help thee get to Canada."

"They white folk?" asked Elijah.

"They are freemen, colored people. They call themselves the Vigilance Committee. They have offered aid and comfort to escaped slaves for many years."

"They nigguh folk like me?" Elijah asked with excitement.

"Thee must not call thyself by such a name, Elijah. It is used by evil people who do not see thee as equal in the eyes of God. They are colored men who have earned or bought their freedom."

"Then Elijah go to Philadelphia, missus. See his people. This a good plan."

Johanna stood and lifted the lantern off the spike. "There is still much to work out, but it is late. I will see thee both in the morning."

Chapter 17

The old farm wagon bumped noisily along the dusty turn-pike. On the buckboard beside Johanna, Billy was glum. Elijah lay motionless in the tailboard, layers of blankets piled over him. Johanna had given Billy strict orders not to talk to Elijah at all, not even when there was no one around.

"This is Ashton, but we most often refer to it as Porter's Corner," Johanna said.

Billy nodded but said nothing as he glanced at the approaching crossroads. It was a small settlement with only a general store, a blacksmith, and a wheelwright's shop. They rode in silence through the open countryside, an endless landscape of apple orchards and brown hillocks speckled with decaying cornstalks.

Billy was thinking about Harry and Leighton and his other friends. He was glad he had Elijah for a new friend, but he sorely missed his pals from home. That telegraph man at the store said all the troops were on the move south. Some big fighting was in store, for sure. Billy was worried his friends would get hurt by one of those big guns. He wished he had had the chance to say good-bye to them before he cut out, and he hoped they weren't too sore at him for what he had done, but they probably were. Not wanting to think about that, Billy slipped his haversack off his shoulder and pulled out his knife and a small block of wood he had found in Johanna's shed. He studied the wood, turning it over and over in his hands, and began to whittle. Flakes of soft pine fell steadily onto his lap.

Johanna shot a puzzled glance in his direction. "What is thee doing?"

"Whittlin' is all," Billy answered, brushing the chips off his trousers. He couldn't tell her he was carving the Meeting House. Elijah wanted it to be a surprise when they said their good-byes at the station.

"Ethan taught me mostly."

"And who is this Ethan?"

"Private, same as me." Lowering his head, he finished shaping the Meeting House's chimney and then stared at his progress. Except for smoothing the tiny notches marking the windows, it was almost finished. Yesterday he had nearly taken a fit trying to get the windows just right. Seemed like every time he went to carve one, he got confused, there being so many and all. Finally Elijah had grabbed the knife, and from the loft, peered through the cracks. He nicked the wood, marking a place for each window so Billy would know where to put them.

The rhythmic gait of the bays slowed, and the heavier clopping of hooves echoed noisily in his ears. The wagon rattled and bumped across a stone bridge that was arched over a shallow river.

"What's this river, Miss Johanna?"

"It's the Patuxent River. When we crossed the bridge we left Montgomery County and entered Howard County."

"We almost there, you thinkin'?" He stretched the stiffness from his neck and shoulders and then looked down again at his whittling. Pleased with the result, he blew away the loose pine chips, rubbed the wood against his shirt, and tucked it into his haversack.

"Ellicotts Mills is about fifteen miles from Sandy Spring. We have another hour at least. We must pass through Highland and Clarksville first, and then we will be there."

Looking out across the fields, Billy twisted sideways in his seat when he spotted a small boy beating a stick against the rails of a wooden gate as he herded cows to a higher pasture. Near Jamie's size, he thought. Doing chores. Suddenly gripped with longing, he stared at the dark-haired child, watching intently as the boy poked the cows playfully with his stick, hopping from one foot to another in his own imaginary game. Billy yanked off his hat and started to wave at the child when the clatter of an approaching wagon spooked him.

Clouds of dust filled the air as the fast-moving wagon narrowed the gap. Billy turned and looked at Johanna and saw that she was trembling, the knuckles of her long hands white against the leather reins.

"Those two men in the wagon are in a frightful hurry," Johanna said nervously, with another glance over her shoulder. Her gaze dropped to the blankets covering Elijah. There was no movement beneath the dark wool.

In seconds the wagon was alongside them. Clucking his teeth, the driver pulled back on the reins and his sorrel mare fell into a slow trot.

Billy pulled the brim of his hat down over his forehead and stole a glance at the driver, who was smiling. His passenger, a man with ruddy hair, was looking intently at Johanna. Billy tried to remember the faces of the men who had chased him into the barn, but he couldn't recall them. He pressed his back against the seat, shielding himself behind Johanna's shoulders.

"Lovely morning!" the driver shouted.

"Indeed." Johanna nodded in response, never turning her face in the men's direction.

"Where might you folks be from?"

Billy relaxed. The voice seemed friendly enough.

"Not far from Porter's Corner," Johanna replied.

"Going to market in Ellicotts Mills?"

The ruddy-haired passenger leaned over in his seat, scanning the nearly empty tailboard until his eyes rested on the pile of blankets. "But then you're not bringing anything to sell I see," he added. "Or mebbe you are selling blankets?"

"We are meeting a friend at the station," Johanna answered. "We left early this morning, and the blankets kept us warm."

"Well, mebbe I'll see you at the market. I surely wouldn't miss a red-headed beauty like you," the man said.

"If thee has a mind to do the Lord's work, I would hope you would join us," Johanna replied tersely.

The man's face flushed red; the driver chuckled and pumped the reins and called out to the horse. The mare broke into a fast trot and the wagon lurched forward, spewing dirt and dust in the air. Cages stacked in the tailboard of the passing wagon toppled to the floor, causing the laying hens inside to flutter and squawk, their feathers spilling through the wooden slats.

The wagon wound its way through Highland and Clarksville and climbed the last long hill to Ellicotts Mills. A cool salty breeze swept over the crest as Billy gazed at the wooded vale. He pointed to a white steeple rising above the treetops.

"That's the Emory Methodist Church thee sees," Johanna said. "And that smoke rising above the hills comes from the trains at the bottom of the Patapsco River ravine." Johanna rested the reins on her lap and turned to face Billy. "My journey with thee and Elijah is nearly over. Thee must trust in Anna."

Billy lowered his head and said nothing. Just thinking about Anna and pretending she was his wife made the hair on his skin rise. Johanna called out to the horses and the wagon plodded down the steep grade into the woods.

The white steeple loomed large in front of him. They were close to the church, and Anna. Billy looked at his hands, which felt warm and clammy. He rubbed the flat of his palms back and forth over his thighs. His breath came fast.

"Thee must relax. Breathe deeply," Johanna said in a soothing tone.

"I ain't likin' this marryin' is all," Billy mumbled.

Oak trees lined the lane, their leaves a blend of green and gold against the pale blue sky, and the long shadows of late autumn cast a deepened blue across the hardening ground. The horses shook their long necks and came to a stop in front of the church. Then Billy saw her, a slender woman in a dark red dress standing at the top of the steps. He lowered his eyes and turned away.

"It is so good to see thee, Johanna!" Anna called as she ran down the church steps.

"And I am so pleased to see thee again as well."

Johanna tapped him on the arm. "Billy, will thee kindly tie the horses?" Lifting the hem of her dress, Johanna climbed down as Billy hoisted the reins over the wagon and leaped to the ground, eager to disappear in the shelter of the horses.

"Thy dress is bright, Anna! And thee was wise to think of wearing such a fine plumed hat as this."

"I cannot dress as a Quaker and be seen with a slave. Is he——?"

"Under the blankets. Is anyone about?"

"The pastor is at another parish and graciously allowed us to go inside. We will be safe here for a short while."

"Elijah? Thee may come out now."

Billy tied the reins to the rail and patted the bays' damp necks. He scrambled back into the tailboard, yanked the blankets off Elijah, and tossed them onto the ground. He grinned as

Elijah stirred and raised himself onto the buckboard, all the while squinting in the bright sunlight and rubbing his eyes.

"You all right?" Billy asked.

"Elijah fine, Billy, suh."

"Thee both must hurry inside the church. We will talk there," said Anna as she collected the blankets and dropped them into the tailboard. Elijah stood and looked about, breathing deeply of the fresh air.

"Hurry!" Anna said.

Elijah stared in wonderment. Sunlight streaked through stained-glass windows, filtering red, yellow, and purple hues onto rows of polished pews. He stepped slowly and stopped, mesmerized by a painting on the whitewashed wall—the gentle face of a man with long brown hair, a ring of brushed gold adorning his head.

"That's Jesus," Billy said quietly as he walked up beside him.

"Yes, suh."

Elijah walked slowly down the aisle following the beams of light, running his fingers lightly along the tops of the smooth benches. He glanced at the front of the chapel, at an altar topped with shiny candlesticks and a cloth of red velvet. The figure of Jesus bound to a large wooden cross hung on the wall behind the altar.

Elijah turned to look at Billy. "Never been in a place like this before."

"Why ain't you been in a church?"

"They for white folk."

"Ain't you got a place to hear about God?"

"Yes, suh, under the willow oak," Elijah said.

"You go to church under a tree?"

"Lord hear us just the same." He pressed his back into the pew and sat silently for several moments.

"You see Miss Anna? She purty, you thinkin'?"

Before Elijah could respond, the church door opened and the rustle of skirts interrupted the stillness. Billy sucked in his breath, turned and watched as Anna moved down the center aisle. Black ringlets dangled from under her hat. Her skin was smooth and very pale and her eyes were the color of cinnamon drops. Goose bumps rose on his skin.

"Hello, Billy," Anna said as she unpinned her hat and smoothed a few tendrils of hair away from her face. "And thee is Elijah?"

"Yes, Missus Anna."

Billy tried to return her greeting, but the words stuck in his throat. His mouth was dry. Embarrassed, he lowered his head and ran his fingers through his hair.

"Elijah," Johanna said, "Anna has a trunk outside on the steps. Would thee and Billy bring it inside? Billy, you go out first to make sure there is no one about."

Bringing the small trunk inside, they placed it at Anna's feet. Raising the skirt of her dress, Anna knelt on the floor, lifted the lid, and removed a bundle of clothing. "I did not know if thee had the proper clothes to travel on the train," she said, glancing up at Elijah. "Here is a pair of pantaloons and a shirt. The shirt is one that household slaves most often wear. And here is a hat." Handing the clothes to Elijah, she then turned to Billy. "Thee could use a clean shirt. Thy sack coat is worn by civilians, so it should not draw attention to thee." Offering a faint smile, she handed Billy a shirt.

"Thee will be called Billy Dickinson, which is my last name," Anna continued as she latched the trunk and straightened the folds of her dress. "And Elijah, thee will be called Daniel. Thee is a household slave—from the Dickinson plantation—not far from Sandy Spring. And we are traveling to Philadelphia to visit my mother who is ill."

"Daniel?" Billy looked confused. "Why you callin' him Daniel?"

"To fool the slave hunters, Billy. I suspect Elijah is worth a great deal of money to his master. And his master surely placed a notice in the newspaper offering a reward. There are always slave hunters who prowl the train stations and read the notices, hoping to find runaways. The notice would print his name and his description."

She turned and looked at Elijah. "Should thee hear thy true name, do not respond or turn thy head to anyone."

"Yes, missus."

"Good. Thee both must be watchful at all times, and think only about thy new names, Daniel and Billy Dickinson. A simple mistake may get thee caught. Daniel, thee should not have to speak at any time—and Billy, thee must pay attention to me. Let me answer questions from the train agents or strangers." Anna looked at Billy, her small eyes dark with intensity. "And thee must not ever talk to Daniel as if thee are friends. Can thee remember that?"

"Yes, ma'am," he answered, staring down at the floor.

Johanna spoke up. "The station will likely be very crowded. Mr. Stabler says the Baltimore and Ohio Railroad out of Ellicotts Mills carries thousands of men and supplies to the western front."

"Yes, it is so. That may be a help to us," said Anna. "Now thee both must change thy clothes." She pointed to a darkened corner of the chapel.

"Missus Anna, what if this plan go wrong?" Elijah asked as he followed Billy back to the front of the chapel. "What we go and do then?"

"It is a wise question. Johanna tells me thee knows about the Vigilance Committee in Philadelphia. If things go wrong when we get to Philadelphia, thee must find thy own way to the Anti-Slavery Society office, on Fifth Street. Thee will find Mr. William Still, a colored man, at this place. Remember this name, for he is the one who will help thee."

Johanna leaned forward on the pew. "How will they find this place or Mr. Still without thee?"

Anna thought for a moment before saying, "Our train will stop near the Schuylkill River. But thee must turn away from the river and head straight into the city—it is not far to Fifth Street. Mr. Still's office is on the corner of Fifth and Market. To be safe, thee both should only walk at night and hide during the day. Or . . . " she hesitated and looked at Billy. "Thee could ask a merchant for directions to Hyde Street. That is where I live."

"It worries me so that thee faces much danger—"

"Johanna, the Lord has prepared me well for His work. I do not fear the risks I take each time I help a runaway or speak out against such evils."

The whistle of a train echoed up the hillside. Billy glanced at Anna.

"We must go now," said Anna. "Johanna, thee may drive us close to the station, but it is better if thee says thy good-byes here. Since we have a slave, we should not be seen with a Friend." She wrapped her arms around Johanna's waist. "I will send thee a telegraph when we are in Philadelphia. Do not worry, my dearest friend. I will keep them safe."

Billy reached for his haversack. "Miss Johanna," he said, "I whittled this here for you—finished it on the wagon." He placed the carving in her hand. "Elijah and me was wantin' to thank you is all."

"The Sandy Spring Meeting House," she gasped. "It's lovely, Billy. So this is what kept thee so busy all morning." Johanna kissed him lightly on the cheek. "I shall treasure this always." She turned to Elijah and pulled him close. He hugged her back and closed his eyes.

"Elijah," Johanna whispered. "Thee is a young man still and soon will build a new life. Thee has great courage. And I will be with thee in spirit."

"Same as me," Billy added.

Anna placed her arm through Billy's. "We are married now." With a tug on his arm she led him down the aisle. He stared at the floor. "Thee must not be afraid to look at me, Billy Dickinson! Thee is now my husband."

"Yes, ma'am," he said, the lump returning in his throat.

"Daniel," called Anna. "I will be speaking sharply to thee, but remember—it is not what I feel in my heart. Now put the trunk in the wagon and sit in the back."

Billy glanced at Elijah, wondering if he was as afraid as he was.

Outside, Johanna pulled her shawl close around her shoulders and looked up at the darkening sky. "Look, Billy! Does thee see the flock of geese?" He looked up and nodded.

"Their long journey is almost over."

Johanna reached over and squeezed Billy's hand.

"May God keep thee safe on thy journey home. And may thee and Elijah one day come to walk cheerfully over this world."

Chapter 18

"We need three tickets for Philadelphia," Anna said to the agent.

"Three, you say?" the agent asked, his eyes darting back and forth between Anna and Billy, close at her side.

"Our servant is traveling with us."

"You'll need to change stations in Baltimore. Train to Philly leaves from the President Street station."

"Thank you. Will our servant be able to accompany us in the same car? My husband is not feeling well and may need a strong arm to lean on."

Stroking the thin goatee on his chin, the agent considered her request. "Full price for the nigger."

"What is the fare for all three of us, then?" Anna said as she opened her handbag.

"A dollar thirty-five for the fare to Baltimore, and another nine dollars and seventy-five cents to Philadelphia for the lot of you."

"And our servant, sir?" Anna asked again, a hint of testiness in her voice as she pushed the money into the agent's hand. "Do I understand he may ride in the car with us?"

"Not to worry about your slave, little lady. Ol' Charlie Wurthington is the conductor on the Philadelphia run tonight. Lets niggers ride with their owners. But, a word of caution, if I may: Make sure he don't bother anyone. Lots of folks don't fancy niggers riding in the same car."

"Thank you, sir," Anna said, stuffing the tickets into her handbag.

"Have the slave load your baggage into the car. Train's pulling out soon."

With a nudge to Billy, Anna turned and walked briskly away from the ticket counter and onto the plaza. She glanced behind her. "Stay close to us, Daniel!"

Billy turned around to see Elijah a short distance back, pushing through the crowd with the trunk resting on his shoulder. His face was sweaty with the pain of hoisting the trunk given the injuries on his back, but Anna had kept the load as light as possible. A small hand pinched Billy's arm. He turned back as Anna pulled him close, leaned into his shoulder, and whispered, "Thee must not look about too much. It will only draw attention." A chill ran through him.

The narrow plaza bustled with people. Gentlemen in fine silk suits lifted trunks and cloth satchels up the platform steps and into the filling cars. Ladies in colorful dresses and plumed hats smiled in lively conversations. The noise and busyness excited Billy. Anna hurried him along, searching for empty coaches, tugging on his arm whenever he glanced over his shoulder. Near the end of the plaza a group of people hovered around an aproned woman selling meat pies from a basket. Billy stared longingly.

"Would thee like a meat pie?" Anna asked.

"Yes, ma'am," Billy answered shyly. "And one for—for—"

"Yes, I know." Anna slipped her arm away from his. He watched as she moved gracefully across the plaza and mingled easily in the crowd, smiling and chatting with the pie lady. Suddenly his heart caught in his throat. He recognized the blue cap above the other heads before he saw the uniform.

The man stood among the crowd of pie customers. Billy watched as the woman handed the pies wrapped in white cloth to Anna, who tucked the package under her arm and hurried back to him.

"You see him, Miss Anna, that army officer?"

Anna nodded. "Yes, I saw him. Every train station has a provost marshal on duty, like I told thee about at the church."

"Them pies smell awful good." Billy walked beside Anna. The provost marshal reminded him of his regiment, and he thought about Harry, Leighton, Charlie, Jeb, and Josh, all marching to Richmond. Were they fighting yet? Was Harry looking for him?

Anna tugged on his arm. "We will go in this coach. It is not yet full."

Billy looked over his shoulder. "That marshal's coming this way, Miss Anna."

She pulled him close. "He is only looking about at the passengers. But thee must let me do the talking."

"Good evening," the provost marshal said as he tipped his hat to Anna and glanced at Billy.

"And a pleasant evening to you, sir." Anna's face broke into a wide smile.

"You folks from around here?"

"About a day's ride," Anna said quickly. "We're on our way to Philadelphia to visit my mother."

The provost marshal gave Billy a long appraising stare before he turned and looked over Billy's shoulder. "That your slave?"

"Yes, sir."

"Own a big farm, young man?" he asked.

"Reckon."

"Where?"

"Uh, Porter's Corner."

"Hardly a day's ride," he said, looking perplexed.

"If you will excuse us, sir, we do need to hurry and find seats together—I'm sure you understand," Anna said.

The provost marshal shrugged his shoulders. "I'll not delay you. A pleasant journey."

"Hurry along with the trunk, Daniel!" Anna called, rushing Billy up the platform steps and into the car.

Elijah's new shirt was soaked with sweat, and felt sticky and cold against his back. Shifting the weight of the trunk across his shoulders, he stole a glance at the white man in the blue uniform. He had to pass in front of him to get to the train. Nerves raw, he lowered his head and started by. Almost there. *Put the trunk on the train. Up these steps now.* He placed his foot on the metal step. *One more . . . almost there.*

Smoke billowed and steam hissed down the platform. A shrill whistle pierced Elijah's ears, startling him. He fell against the car, knocking the trunk from his shoulder. The trunk thumped noisily onto the plaza, bounced, and landed on its side at the provost marshal's feet.

Elijah's eyes swept the platform. White folk all turned to look at him. His temples throbbed. Confusion pulsed through his head. *Elijah be whupped now. Yes, suh! Be whupped good.* He spun around and turned away from the trunk, the voices in his head screaming to run. He pushed himself away from the car.

Suddenly Billy was beside him, grabbing his arm, pulling him up the platform steps, and into the car. Elijah stumbled on the steps, got back on his feet, and in seconds was inside. Then Miss Anna was in front of him, taking his arm, guiding him onto a hard bench. He moved into the seat, turned, and looked for Billy. He was nowhere to be seen.

Elijah jumped to his feet. "Billy, suh!"

"Sit back down, Daniel!" Anna hissed. Elijah glanced out the window across the aisle. Where was Billy?

The train lurched forward.

We goin'! Elijah don't go without Billy, suh! He leaped again from his seat. Anna moved quickly in front of him, blocking the aisle and his view of the plaza. The train screeched over the rails. Elijah's heart beat rapidly against his chest. Then Elijah saw him.

Sweat dripped down Billy's brow as he landed inside, the trunk banging against the seats jerking him sideways. Gasping for breath, he stumbled down the aisle and lowered the trunk onto the floor beside Elijah. Relief washed across Elijah's face.

Anna pushed Billy into the empty seat across the aisle and settled in beside him.

"Thee did well, Billy," Anna whispered. She leaned over and peered out the window. Billy looked out onto the plaza. The provost marshal was walking beside the car. Anna had spotted him, too.

"Can't this train move any faster?" Anna whispered through gritted teeth.

As Billy watched, a wiry man pushed through the crowd on the platform, grabbed the provost marshal by his sleeve, and pointed his finger wildly at their window. His face, scarred with pockmarks, was familiar. It was one of them fellas from Rockville who chased them into the barn!

The train whistled its exit. Billy pressed his face against the window, steam and smoke partially clouding his view. His heavy breathing fogged the inside pane. Using his shirtsleeve, Billy frantically rubbed the glass and peered through the opening. He saw the provost marshal reach into his breast pocket and yank out a piece of paper, reading it out loud. The man from Rockville nodded his head.

"Dear God!" Anna whispered under her breath. "Who is that man with him?" Anna turned to Billy. "What can this be?"

"Daniel a good boy, missus," Elijah cried out. "Daniel don't want no whuppin'."

Billy and Anna spun around in their seats. Stern-faced passengers stared coldly at them. Anna shuddered and leaned across the aisle. "Hush, Daniel, I am not angry," she whispered. Turning her back to the passengers, she handed Elijah the cloth-wrapped pie. "Eat this warm pie and try to rest."

Then, smoothing the folds of her skirt and adjusting her hat, she nodded at the glaring faces. "Thee must try not to look worried, Billy," she said as she leaned her back into the seat. "That man with the provost marshal—perhaps it had nothing to do with us."

In a trembling voice Billy told Anna about the pock-faced man. She listened, cinnamon eyes never wavering from his. When he finished, Anna placed her gloved hand on Billy's arm. Her voice was calm. "Baltimore is a large city, and the train stations are most always very busy. If need be, we can lose ourselves easily in the crowd. Do not be afraid," she said. "I wish to sit quietly now and wait upon the Lord."

She handed Billy a meat pie and then bowed her head.

It was easy to believe her, Billy thought. The whole time he was talking, Anna never once looked scared. Maybe things were going to be all right. He glanced across the aisle. Elijah was picking at the morsels of his pie. Billy eagerly reached for his own.

Chapter 19

"We're coming into Baltimore—Camden Station. But we do not get off here," Anna said. "We'll be changing railroads for Philadelphia. Our car will be pulled by horses along the rail lines to the other station on President Street," she explained.

Billy looked confused. "Horses?"

Anna smiled. "I know it sounds strange, but the steam engine is too noisy to operate within the city—it scares other animals. And the embers from the locomotive can set off fires, so the car is pulled by horses." She leaned over in the seat and gazed out the car window.

"There are no civilian guards waiting to meet this train," she said with relief in her voice. "I hope we will move quickly to the other station. The railroads are under military control now, and with so many unscheduled stops for troops and supplies, there's no way of knowing if a train will leave at its posted schedule."

Billy pressed his face against the glass, cupping his hands around his eyes. Under the gaslights' yellow glow, rows of Union soldiers sat on the platform floor, their backs slumped against the station wall. Knapsacks and muskets lay at their feet. A heavyset soldier with curly brown hair passed in front of the other men. Then he stopped and, opening his knapsack, pulled out a piece of hardtack. For a fleeting moment the soldier reminded Billy of Leighton. A sharp pain stabbed Billy's heart.

"I see the station's provost marshal—he's hurrying down the platform," Anna said. "Wait; he is walking to the locomotive on the other rail."

Billy shifted his gaze, following the direction of her finger as she tapped on the window. The provost marshal stopped beside the engine car on the opposite track, shaking his head, his hands resting on his hips. On the top of the car, men hunched over the brake wheel. Billy watched as the provost marshal cupped his hands and shouted. Seconds later, a workman looked over the roof of the car, climbed down the ladder, and walked toward him, wiping a blackened hand across his brow.

"That must be the engineer," said Anna.

"Provost marshal's sore at him, I'm thinkin'," Billy said quietly. The engineer shook his head back and forth, his hands moving wildly as he shouted back at the officer. The provost marshal pointed to the soldiers packed along the plaza. Then he pulled something out of his jacket—a pocket watch—and in a mocking gesture held it in front of the engineer's face.

The car jerked forward.

Billy fell backward onto the seat. Anna laughed.

"Why you laughin', Miss Anna?" he asked, a hurtful look on his face.

"I'm happy, Billy! We're on our way to the other station, and we didn't have to deal with that provost marshal. It seems he is much too busy trying to get the troops out of his station."

Billy watched the lights of the city grow dim as horses ploddingly pulled the train to the next station. The car was not nearly as crowded as it had been, and behind him a young couple seemed unconcerned about the slave sitting across the aisle. Shortly after arriving at the station, and after a few more passengers came on board, the car was hooked back up to an engine, and the train moved off. Anna opened her handbag and pulled out a small green book.

"You gonna read, Miss Anna?" Billy asked.

"Would thee like to look at this book?"

"No, thank you, ma'am." Embarrassed, he turned his face back to the window.

"It's the prose works of John Greenleaf Whittier, a Quaker abolitionist from Boston." Anna touched Billy's hand. "Would thee like me to read to thee?"

He nodded shyly and watched as she turned to a page marked with a ribbon.

"I was reading a poem called 'Yankee Girl.' It is about a young girl and a southern master. Here is the last verse:

"Full low at thy bidding thy negroes may kneel,
With the iron of bondage on spirit and heel;
Yet know that the Yankee girl sooner would be
In fetters with them, than in freedom with thee!"

Billy was silent. How could he tell Miss Anna that he didn't understand the poem? After a long pause, he said, "Them words is real nice."

"It is also what I feel in my heart."

"You thinkin' things is all right now, Miss Anna?"

"Evil lurks in every corner, Billy. Even though we have been safe thus far, I will remain ever vigilant when we arrive in Philadelphia. It is a lesson Mr. Whittier speaks about in his book, *The Little Pilgrim*, when as a young boy he hooks a fish only to lose his prize in the middle of the stream. His uncle warns the young Whittier to 'never brag of catching a fish until he is on dry ground.' "

"Elijah caught us some fish in Goose Creek when we was hidin' and all. Speared 'em good. Then tossed them fishes right on the dry ground—"

"Remember, Billy, no talk about Elijah." She turned back to her little book.

Billy waited for Anna to read out loud again, but she remained silent. He leaned his head against the glass and looked back across the aisle. Elijah was sitting silently, looking out the window, trying not to call any attention to himself. Billy thought about whittling and then remembered he had no wood. Leaning back against the window, he closed his eyes.

When he awoke, endless rows of gaslights were flashing past his window. He tugged gently on Anna's arm. "Miss Anna," he whispered, reluctant to disturb her sleep. "Miss Anna," he whispered again. "Train's coming into Philadelphia, I'm thinkin'." He tugged a little harder.

Anna opened her eyes, sat up straighter, and looked out.

She turned and glanced at Elijah, all the while hastily refastening her hair into a bun. She whispered to him, "When we arrive at the station I will hire a carriage so we can go directly to the Anti-Slavery Society office. I know the hour is late, but Mr. Still is expecting us. Thee will stay with Mr. Still. Billy and I will go to my mother's home for the night."

"Ain't I gonna see Elijah no more?"

"It's Daniel, Billy," Anna reminded him. Billy winced.

"We will return tomorrow afternoon. I suspect the Vigilance Committee will want to interview Elijah as soon as possible."

The brakes screeched as the train slowed its approach into the station. Anna stood, straightening her dress. "This is the

Southern and Western Station—on the corner of Broad and
Prime streets. It's old, far from the taverns and hotels."

The train lurched forward and came to a jolting stop. The
car bustled as passengers stretched their limbs and gathered
their baggage, moving hurriedly into the now-crowded center
aisle. A station attendant opened the car door and set the platform steps in place. A dry, cold wind off the river drifted
across the rail yard, finding its way into the stuffy car. Anna
moved quickly to the front, poked her head out the door, and
scanned the gaslit plaza. Cautiously she stepped out.

"The provost marshal for this station is standing outside on
the plaza," she whispered to Billy as he moved in behind her.
"He seems to be studying the people leaving the cars." Anna
stepped back, pressing her body against the nearest bench,
allowing the crush of passengers to pass in front of her. When
the car was nearly empty, Anna moved to the steps, motioning
Billy and Elijah to follow.

The crowd thinned as people rushed to trolley cars and
horse-drawn carriages waiting on the street. Billy spotted the
provost marshal pacing the plaza, intently watching the last handful of passengers milling near the train. Grateful for the
gaslights' dim glow, Billy hurried beside Anna. Behind him, Elijah
burrowed his face against the trunk carried on his shoulders.

A voice shouted. "Hold on just a minute, over there!"

Billy stopped suddenly, his heart thudding against his chest.
From the corner of his eye, he saw the provost marshal staring
in his direction. "Miss Anna . . ."

"We must not act in haste," she whispered. She turned and
nodded her head at the provost marshal, tucking her arm
around Billy in a casual gesture, and kept walking.

"Miss Anna," Billy said, barely able to choke out the words, "he's coming our way."

"I said hold on!" the provost marshal shouted. Suddenly, he was rushing toward them. "Langford! Burns! It's them all right—they match the description the provost marshal in Endicott Mills telegraphed to us. Over here!"

"Dear God! They are looking for thee, Billy!" Anna's face paled in the yellow light. "Thee must run! Run to the river and hide there!"

"Miss Anna!"

Anna yanked her arm away from the crook of Billy's elbow and gave him a shove. "Go! There is no time! Remember what I told thee. Elijah, run!"

The trunk toppled from Elijah's shoulders.

"What the bejesus!" The provost marshal stopped suddenly, spun around, and shouted over his shoulder. "Langford! Burns! They're on the run!"

Startled travelers scurried out of their way as Billy and Elijah sprinted down the length of the platform. Billy leaped over a trunk, nearly stumbled, caught his balance, and ran out onto the gravel beside the tracks. Elijah ran past him and, turning away from the rails, disappeared between the cars.

"Billy, suh! Come!" He caught up with Elijah and they scrambled onto the far rails and ran into the starless night just as two guards wielding guns ran out of the station.

"The river, Elijah!" Billy screamed. "Miss Anna said run to the river!"

Behind them, shots fired in the darkness.

Billy followed as Elijah leaped over the tracks and crashed into dense thicket. He heard the guards scrambling noisily over the couplings, then the crush of their boots smashing through the bushes. Stealing a glance over his shoulder, Billy lost his footing and fell, his knee landing on a rock. Pain shot through him, and he rolled over onto his back, his hand clutching his knee. "Elijah!"

They could hear the rasp of heavy breathing as Elijah reached down and pulled Billy to his feet, urging him forward. The pain when Billy's foot touched the ground was excruciating, and he cried out. "Can't bend my knee!"

The shouts and stomping boots were getting closer.

"Billy, suh, get down on your belly and don't make no sound," Elijah whispered as he crouched down on his knees. Suddenly all went quiet. They could still hear the guards breathing, only inches away. Silently, Elijah's fingers fanned the ground. He clawed a stone from the soil, pulled back his arm, and heaved it toward the tracks.

Glass shattered.

Boots scraped in front of Elijah.

"They're back at the train! Broke a window!"

Dirt sprayed Elijah's face as the guard retreated.

"You step light as a feather now, Billy, suh," Elijah whispered as he pulled Billy to his feet. He wrapped Billy's arm around his shoulder and moved into the cover of the trees. Pine needles cushioned their steps as they darted around the trunks, hiding, listening for returning footsteps in the pitch black. Every few seconds Elijah stopped to listen.

In a short distance they emerged onto a wide stretch of tangled brush and cattails. Their boots sank in the soft earth. Elijah pushed ahead of Billy, staying low, motioning for him to follow as they worked their way cautiously through the thicket, ever listening.

The underbrush opened to a muddied riverbank rife with litter. Squealing rats scattered through the rotting garbage, trash, and broken glass. The air was foul. Billy placed a hand over his nose.

"Billy, suh, we stay here for a time." Elijah helped Billy settle onto the ground, pushing away the litter, tossing handfuls of sand over the stinking debris around them. It was eerily quiet as Billy and Elijah sat and stared at the Schuylkill River. A lone steamer, a side-wheeler, floated by, the ship's lanterns fluttering in the cold wind. In the near distance, a steam locomotive whistled.

"Elijah ain't never gon' ride no train again, no suh," he said in a half-whisper. He leaned back on his elbows. "Billy, suh, you take good care of Elijah on the train."

"Weren't nuthin'," Billy said, rubbing the swelling on his knee.

"You done good, Billy, suh." Elijah slapped him lightly on the back. He stood and kicked the sand with his boots, finally bending over and picking up a long, thick stick. Breaking the stick's jagged ends, he handed it to Billy. "Stick help you walk. We move on now."

As they walked beside the river, the gaslights from the nearby row houses cast a dim reflection on its dark surface. A few steps in front of Billy, Elijah came upon an overturned boat, its planks rotting and covered with muck and debris.

"Mebbe we could hide under here," Billy said.

Elijah kicked the rotted wood. A pack of large rats scurried from underneath the bow and scattered across the mud. "Billy, suh, we find us another place to hide," said Elijah.

"But Miss Anna said to hide near the river."

Elijah shook his head. "Billy, suh, we on our own now. We needin' to get to Fifth Street and find Mr. Still."

"How we gonna find Fifth Street?" Billy asked, alarm in his voice.

"Elijah don't know yet."

"Then we should hide here. Maybe Miss Anna will come."

"We can't hide here, Billy, suh," Elijah said. "Missus or no, it real bad here. Elijah go and figger things out like he promise."

"You mean like Harry?"

"Yes, suh. Just like Harry."

They moved on, away from the water's edge, past heaps of rubbish. Slowly they pushed through the woods, emerging finally onto a narrow, cobbled street lined with row houses. Chimneys spewed ash and smoke. Keeping to the shadows, Billy dug his walking stick into the cobbled cracks and limped along behind Elijah. They cautiously crossed a half-dozen inter-sections, at last finding a tiny alley, free of the debris that lined the small back streets. They scrambled down the narrow pas-sageway, passing under an arch with open iron gates.

The alley opened into a church courtyard. Elijah glanced around. High walls enclosed it, hiding it from the street. The church was dark. He touched Billy's shoulder and pointed to the wooden stairs near the church's back door. "Billy, suh, under those stairs—this be a good place to hide."

Billy nodded. His knee still throbbed with pain and he was eager to get off his feet. The ground under the stairs was dry and offered some protection from the chilling air. They huddled next to each other. "By thunder, it's cold, Elijah."

"It be all right, Billy, suh. In the morning, we find Fifth Street where the other nigguhs be."

"Miss Johanna said it ain't right, you callin' yourself that."

"Then colored folks."

"You thinkin' Miss Anna might be there?" Billy asked hopefully.

"Missus Anna be lookin' for us, Billy, suh. Don't you worry none."

"We gonna see us the North Star again, you thinkin'?"

"Billy, suh, you go on and sleep now."

When Billy awoke it was still dark, but he knew dawn was not far away. He moved his leg, relieved that the pain in his knee had lessened to a faint, dull ache. He stayed quiet, not yet ready to awaken Elijah.

If he tried real hard, he could almost see the rooster stirring in the barn at home, waking with the sun. For sure Pa and Jamie would be milking the cows and sending them off to pasture. And Ma in the kitchen, most like. He imagined a plate of buttermilk pancakes dripping with chunks of creamy butter and thick maple syrup.

Elijah turned and moaned in his sleep. What would happen to them today? What if he never saw Elijah again? Maybe Elijah would come to the farm instead of Canada—maybe even stay. Then Jamie would have another brother. And Jamie could teach Elijah checkers. Thing is, Billy thought, Elijah would whip Jamie good. But, he reminded himself, Elijah would need the black checkers to win. And the black ones were always Jamie's.

He might never see Elijah again. He might never see Harry again.

He remembered the night in Camp King when Harry told him he wished he was as tall as Billy. Harry was the first real friend he had ever had. For a long time, he had wondered why Harry wanted to be his friend. Then Ma told Billy that Harry had had a little sister named Nora, who fell off her horse when she was five, and hit her head hard. After that, Nora never talked again, and was no longer able to do most things by herself. It was Harry who took care of her, did nearly everything for his little sister. Three years later Nora took a fever and died. Ma said Harry learned to have a bigger heart for special folks. Said Harry wanted to be Billy's friend because he was special in his own way, too.

Leighton and Josh had never poked fun at Billy like the others, but they weren't his friends—not 'til Harry came along. Then with the Awkward Squad and all, he and Leighton took a liking to one another. It seemed to Billy that Leighton's heart went and got bigger, just like Harry's. He was glad that he and Leighton had become friends. Besides, the sergeant major had always kept Harry busy with extra chores. The other privates said Harry was finding favor with the sergeant. He guessed Harry was turning out to be a right smart soldier.

As for Billy—he just couldn't wait to get home.

Chapter 20

L ying on his back, looking up at the plank-board steps above him, Billy rubbed his hands against the cold. Elijah stirred, poked his head out from under the stairs, and peered into the courtyard. The day was dull and gray, the air thick with mist.

"Billy, suh," Elijah said after a while. "Elijah been thinkin'. You needin' to ask where Fifth Street be."

Billy grimaced. "I got to find me another storekeeper? Like before? What if he asks me questions?"

"You don't tell white folk nuthin'."

"Maybe the provost marshal's gonna be lookin' for me."

"You wear Elijah's overcoat. That way you don't look the same. Come outside here." Crawling out from under the stairs, Elijah pulled off his jacket and handed it to Billy.

"What if somethin' bad happens?" Billy asked as he hurriedly unfastened his buttons and slipped into Elijah's jacket. "Jacket's awful big."

"Billy, suh," Elijah said, "ain't nuthin' gon' happen. Just go on and do like Elijah say." He reached for Billy's sack coat and scrunched his nose when he couldn't push his arms through the narrow sleeves. Frustrated, he wrapped the wool coat around his shoulders and crossed his arms to hold in warmth.

"Why ain't you wearin' my coat?"

"Billy, suh, this coat too small for Elijah, so you hurry back before Elijah freeze hisself."

"I'm goin'," Billy said dismally. "Ain't got no money for bread, neither."

Billy brushed dirt and bits of scattered pine needles from his trousers and stretched his stiffened body. Still tender, his knee buckled when he started to walk, so shifting the weight on his leg, he limped under the arch through the alley that led to the main sidewalk. The mist was lifting. The promise of sunlight brightened his spirits as much as the sights and sounds of the awakening city.

He watched a pair of sprightly mares pulling a streetcar filled with early morning shoppers along the smooth rails. Billy headed down the sidewalk, strolling beneath colorful awnings, gazing in shop windows. He paused in front of a haberdashery with its handsome display of fine men's clothing, ambled past a printing office and a barbershop, and offered a passing glance at a storefront window filled with yards of winter woolens, plaids in brilliant reds and greens, mufflers soft with rabbit fur. He broke into a wide smile as he came upon a sweet shop and for several moments stared through the window, watching the candy maker stretch and fold ribbons of saltwater taffy over a marble slab. He pressed his face against the storefront window. On the far shelf were jars of licorice strings, horehound and lemon drops, and candied ginger.

He tapped on the glass.

The candy maker looked up as he stretched the red-and-white-striped taffy across the slab, frowned, and shook his head. Billy shrugged and turned away from the candy shop. He continued down the slate sidewalk.

A short distance ahead, two women in long capes hurried from a bake shop and stepped into the street, their straw baskets bulging with rounded loaves of bread. Behind them the elderly storekeeper, a broom tucked under his arm, stopped and tossed a handful of breadcrumbs onto the sidewalk. His woolly side-whiskers bobbed up and down his ruddy cheeks as he chatted to the gathering sparrows.

"Mornin', mister," Billy said, startling the sparrows as he approached the kindly looking man. Billy stepped quickly aside as the sparrows flapped from the ground like spraying water, disappearing into the eaves.

"Good day, lad." The storekeeper gave him an appraising look from head to toe. His easy smile clouded, and he took a step backward. "I suppose you'll be looking for work?"

"No, sir." Billy saw the look of concern on the old man's face and ran his dirtied fingers awkwardly through his matted hair. "Lookin' for Fifth Street is all."

The old man wrinkled his brow. "Fifth Street, you say?"

"Yes, sir."

"Well, lad, you're nearly there now. This is Third Street." He raised his arm and pointed. "Down this way, just a couple of blocks, and you'll be there."

"Thank you, sir."

The old man nodded his head and began sweeping the walk in front of his door as Billy hurried away.

"Young man! Fifth Street's the other way!"

"Yes, sir," Billy said, waving his arm. He kept on walking. A burst of pain shot through his knee; he slowed his pace and, favoring his leg again, limped slowly down the sidewalk. He stopped suddenly in front of a storefront window that had been shuttered earlier. He let out a low gasp, awestruck by the handsomely carved three-masted schooner, its miniature sails fully extended as if it was running with the wind. He studied the schooner's intricate detail, wishing he could remember everything about it so he could whittle one for Jamie. Reluctantly he moved on, his mind flooding with ballasts and riggings, tall masts, and full sails, all the way back to the narrow alleyway that led to the shelter of the church, and Elijah.

Elijah's lips curled into a smile. "Billy, suh, you been gone a long time. You didn't get in no trouble?" he asked as Billy crawled underneath the staircase.

"Naw." Billy slipped off the jacket, handed it to Elijah, and lay down on the hard ground.

"You find where Fifth Street be?"

"Yeah. We're right close."

"Real good, Billy, suh." Elijah blew warm air onto his hands and pushed them into the pockets of his jacket. "Now, we just stay under these stairs 'til it be dark."

As the moon rolled over the spires of the courtyard church, the pair left their hiding place.

"Moon all misty-lookin', Billy, suh."

"It's them yellow rings around it. Pa says rings mean it's gonna snow."

"I heard of snow, but I never seen any. How your Pa know that?"

"Seen it lots of times afore." Billy cupped his hands, blowing hot breath over his fingers. "Wish we had us some food. I'm starved."

"We find Fifth Street now. Mr. Still, he take care of us."

They moved quietly down the near-vacant street, Billy motioning the way silently to Elijah.

They walked several blocks, finally turning right on a tree-lined street, past elegant two-story brick colonials and ornate verandahs, clusters of trailing ivy spilling over wrought-iron fences. Oil lamps glowed in the pane windows, and chimney smoke billowed dusty gray.

It was ear-tingling cold. Flakes of snow fell silently from the darkness. Elijah shivered and raised his collar as the snow trickled down his neck. He stopped for a moment under a gaslight, staring in wonderment at the specks of white powder shimmering beneath his feet.

"You thinkin' this might be Fifth Street?" Billy scrunched his nose, and brushed the white wetness away from his face.

"No, suh. Nigguh folk don't live in these fancy houses."

"Ain't supposed to be sayin' that."

"Coloreds."

"We lost, you thinkin'?"

"Just keep walkin', Billy, suh. Elijah find the colored folks."

As the long rows of stately homes faded into a business district, Elijah stared at an endless stretch of storefronts, dark and uninviting, snow falling undisturbed on the cobbled street. Discouraged, he guided Billy around the next corner, only to discover another street of imposing homes. Where were the huts for colored folk?

Elijah led Billy down several blocks, turning at last into a darkened district far away from the fancy houses of the white folks' neighborhood. At the next corner he stopped suddenly.

A hauntingly familiar song wafted through the snowy darkness. *Hold your light, brother Robert, hold your light on Canaan's shore . . .*

Was he dreaming? Elijah grabbed Billy's arm. "Billy, suh, you hear music?"

"Yeah, sounds like a hym—hymninal."

"Elijah know this song! Elijah sing it when he dyin' by the creek."

Elijah ran into the middle of the street. He spun around and ran to the sidewalk on the opposite side, making slushy footprints in the new snow. He followed the strains of music, now stumbling, his eyes blinded by the wetness splashing his face.

Then he saw it. A church. The music was coming from inside the church. He heard the rush of footsteps behind him, and turned an excited face to Billy.

"Billy, suh, the Lord, he go and lead us here," he said pointing to the church doors.

The church vibrated with the mantra of the sweet melody. Rows of colored people swayed to the music, their hands clasped across the pews. Elijah stood in the vestibule and gazed in disbelief. Billy stomped the snow from his boots and brushed the flakes from his coat.

At the pulpit, a gray-haired preacher stared back at them with a startled expression. Then he stepped away from the pulpit and whispered to a man standing in the front row.

Elijah was awash with emotion. Was it finally over? Was he free? He bowed his head, whispered into his folded hands, his body shaking uncontrollably. He was only slightly aware of Billy's arm around his shoulder.

"Elijah," Billy whispered. "Preacher and another fella comin' down the aisle."

Slowly, Elijah raised his head and stared into the faces of the preacher and the man walking beside him, a colored man in a wide-lapel suit and bright white shirt. Never had he seen such finery on a colored man.

The man reached out his hand, asking, "Are you Elijah?"

Elijah flashed a questioning glance at Billy. He looked nervously around the room. The singing had stopped; everyone was staring at him. He turned to the man in front of him.

"Yes, suh."

"Praise the Lord!"

The preacher walked over to Elijah. "You are among friends here." With a slight bow, the preacher clasped Elijah's hands and said softly, "Thank you, Almighty Father, for delivering these young men safely into our hands."

"This be Fifth Street? And you Mistah Still?" Elijah asked, addressing the finely dressed man who stood next to the preacher.

"No, this is Lombard Street. It's between Fifth and Sixth streets, but it seems you found me, anyway." A wide smile flashed across the man's face. "Yes, I am William Still."

"Then you know Miss Anna?" Billy said, scanning the room.

"Indeed. I'll send a carriage for Anna at once. We have been looking for you all day. She is most distressed. I heard what happened at the train station. Fortunately, Anna escaped the provost marshal's attention when he pursued you both."

William Still whispered to the preacher, who nodded and pointed to the vestry.

"You boys must be hungry," Still said. "I am only a guest at this church. It is their night of prayer and praise, but the preacher has invited you to share in the food that has been pre-pared. Come, follow me." He placed an arm on Elijah's shoul-der, nodded his head at Billy, and led them to a small room near the back of the church.

The room was plain, the worn floorboards pocked with hobnails. Billy glanced at the ceiling, puzzled at the long tim-bers scarred black. Long woolen capes and coats hung on iron spikes protruding from the walls, and a ring of rusty horse-shoes framed the door. But the plain room felt warm and invit-ing. Billy smelled coffee, and he glanced at the barrel-shaped woodstove, taking in its warmth and welcome smells. On the long trestle table against the wall, a buffet of smoked ham, boiled chicken, deviled eggs, bread, and pickles lay on the checkered cloth.

William Still fixed them each a heaping plate.

"What's this church?" asked Billy, wiping his mouth on his shirtsleeve.

Still smiled. "It's the Mother Bethel African Methodist Episcopal Church. This room is part of the original building—a blacksmith's shop that Richard Allen, the church's founder, bought in 1787. The church has grown considerably since then, but the members like to preserve the symbols of its early history—such as the horseshoes you see on the wall."

Still cut into another loaf of bread and piled thick dark slices onto Elijah's plate. Then he turned to Billy and sliced more.

"I'm anxious to hear your story, Elijah. And you will have the chance to tell me more about it tomorrow, when you meet with the Vigilance Committee—the one that Anna spoke to you about."

"Why Elijah talkin' to this vigilance?"

"What we do is interview—ask questions of—all the runaway slaves that we help. It's important to keep detailed information about them, because sometimes we are able to find their family members or loved ones they have been separated from for many years. We also like to keep a record of the slave's experiences, how they were treated, and so on."

"You help slave folk find each other?"

"Sometimes, yes. My older brother Peter was separated from our mother as a child. Eventually, he escaped from his slaveholder in Alabama and found his way to the Society's door.

Our mama had not seen him in forty years," Still said with great emotion in his voice.

Billy dropped a piece of bread from his hands. "Maybe you can find Elijah's pa!"

"Elijah ain't gon' see Pappy again, no suh. He far away now."

"It's hard to know, Elijah."

"I'm wantin' Elijah to live with me," Billy said with a questioning glance at Still.

"Why Elijah got to go to Canada, Mistah Still?" Elijah asked.

"Until this war is over, and unless the Union army wins, Canada is the only place where he will be free. The slaveholders or their agents are most always in the cities. Even in Philadelphia there are many slave hunters about the streets. You are young and strong, Elijah, and no doubt worth a great deal of money to your master. He owns you still. That is why the only thing you can do is escape to Canada."

"And you, my friend," Still said, turning his attention to Billy. "Anna tells me you ran away from the army?"

Billy frowned and stirred nervously in his chair. "Didn't want to be there is all."

"So you just walked away?"

"Yes, sir."

"Did you volunteer?"

"Yes, sir, with my friends."

"Were you in any trouble?"

Billy held a slice of bread to his mouth, pulled it away, and set it on his lap. "Sergeant Noyes sent me to artillery—take care of the horses getting all spooked on account of them big guns and all. Took me away from my friends—other fellas poke fun at me . . ."

"Poke fun?"

170

"I ain't smart like most folks." Billy stared at his food in silence.

"Billy, it's all right." Still sipped his coffee. "Please, finish your bread."

Billy sat quietly as members of the church filed into the room. For a long while he watched curiously as stranger after stranger walked over and warmly greeted Elijah. Many of them turned and smiled at him; some nodded, while others arched their eyebrows, their faces stern or quizzical. But Billy grinned when Mr. Still heaped another slice of ham onto his plate. He looked up when he heard a voice cry out across the room.

"Billy!" Anna stood in the threshold. She ran over and gave him a warm embrace. Then she wrapped her arms around Elijah's neck, too.

"I could not sleep with such worry. I am so proud of thee both, as I know Johanna will be. God's truth shines upon us all tonight."

"Missus Anna, you save us at the station," Elijah said.

"It was God's will." She turned and looked at William Still. "This wonderful man has searched the streets for thee since last night."

"And may I add that Anna scoured the riverbanks this morning—against my better judgment," Still said. "Which reminds me how tired we all are. I must leave for home now. Elijah, you will stay with my wife, Letitia, and me tonight. Billy, you will stay with Anna. We will all meet in my office tomorrow afternoon."

"Mistah Still, can Billy, suh, go with Elijah when you ask him the questions?" Elijah asked.

William glanced at Anna. "Yes, of course. Anna and Billy will be our guests."

As Still walked into the vestry to gather his coat, Billy's eyes landed on a line of small wooden boxes attached to the wall, each with a peg hole. Above each box hung a framed portrait of a man, and just below the boxes was a small table that held a glass jar filled with colored marbles.

"Why them boxes up there with them peg holes?" Billy asked when William Still returned to the entryway.

"Well, Billy, do you see these portraits? They are members of the church who are running in an election for church trustee. And many people who belong to this congregation do not know how to read or write, so they are given marbles to cast their votes. They place the marble in the peg hole under the portrait of the person they are voting for."

Billy bit down on his lower lip. "Thing is, I can't read neither—for sure I ain't never voted."

"I believe there is always a way to work things out for those who are less fortunate, if we just take the time to care."

"You a preacher, Mr. Still?"

Still looked amused. "No, son, I'm not. What makes you think that?"

"You know things is all—like how folks feel on the inside."

"Suffering is a great teacher, Billy."

Nodding his head in parting, William Still placed his arm around Elijah and walked outside into the quietly falling snow.

Chapter 21

E lijah sat motionless in the straight-backed chair, head bowed to avoid the curious glances of the committee members as they gathered around a long pine table. Only his fingers stirred as he rubbed the yellowed calluses on the palms of his hands. He stole a glance at Mr. Still. The tall man pulled the heavy cotton drapes across the window, the dark blue folds the only color against the wood-slat walls. Then turning to the hearth, William Still reached into the woodbox, picked up a snow-crusted log, and tossed it into the fire. Flames popped and sizzled.

Finally the room quieted as the guests settled into their chairs and faced the committee.

"Elijah," Still said as he returned to the table and sat down beside him, "before we begin, I want to introduce you to the members of the committee here this evening.

"At the far end of the table is Nathaniel Depee. Beside him, Jacob White, then Charles Wise and Edwin Coates. The other people in this room, including your friend Anna Dickinson, are people who bring runaway slaves to our doorstep. They are our trusted friends—such as Samuel Johnson," he said, nodding his head toward the bearded man beside Anna. "His house in Germantown is a station on the Underground Railroad."

Still paused, opened his leather notebook, and glanced at the end of the table. "Nathaniel."

Nathaniel Depee cleared his throat. "The General Vigilance Committee of the Anti-Slavery Society in the city of Philadelphia is called to order this seventeenth day of November, at seven o'clock in the evening, in the year 1862." Depee turned his head and coughed lightly into his hand. "All discussions henceforth will be recorded by William Still, secretary, and will remain in his custody."

Making apologies, Depee turned and coughed again. "Elijah, we thank the good Lord that you reached our society safely. I understand that you have been running for several weeks. The committee wants to hear from your own lips who held you in bondage, how you were treated, what prompted you to escape, and who that is near and dear to you is left behind. And we want nothing more than to help you gain your rightful freedom." He hesitated and glanced around the room. "If you are ready, Elijah, Mr. Still will begin the questioning."

Still leaned back in his chair, turned to Elijah, and offered a faint smile. "Are you comfortable, Elijah?"

"Yes, suh," he answered, despite the quivering in his voice.

"Good." Still explained that he would be writing notes during the interview and reminded Elijah that any of the members seated at the table might ask questions of him as well. "So, Elijah, please tell the committee, what is your last name?"

"Hill."

Still looked thoughtfully at him. "Then your full name is Elijah Hill?"

"Pappy call me Elijah Robeson Hill—after my mama's granpappy."

"Then I will record your name as Elijah Robeson Hill. And what is your pappy's first name?" Still dipped his pen into an inkwell.

"His name be Solomon."

"Solomon," Still repeated. "Tell us about your mama—what was her full name?"

Elijah drew a deep breath and stirred uncomfortably in his chair. After a moment he spoke. "My mama called Elisha—so she name me Elijah. My mama die when Elijah only two. My pappy raised me."

"Do you know how your mama died, Elijah?" Still asked.

"Pappy say one day she real sick pickin' corn. He say overseer come by and leave her be, right there in the field. Just walk away. Say she gonna die nohow—got the fever. But my pappy stop work and carry my mama to the hut and lay her down. Mama don't die in no cornfield, he say." Elijah lowered his head. "Elijah don't remember his mama."

"I'm sorry about your mama, Elijah." Still glanced at the other members of the committee. "Do you have brothers or sisters?"

"No, suh. My baby sister, Lydia, she die right off."

"You mean in childbirth, Elijah?"

"No, suh. My mama have a baby girl. Pappy say baby all fine. Then my mama sleepin' and when she wake up, she fin' that she rolled over on my baby sister and she dead. Pappy say my mama know what she done—so Lydia don't be a slave. He say mama's heart break nohow."

Still bit his lower lips and took a deep breath. "Yes," he said in a low tone. "We have heard of such things before. How old are you?"

"Sixteen."

"And this Ramsey was your master?"

"Yes, suh. 'Til he sell Elijah." Elijah blinked, squirmed uncomfortably in the chair, and rubbed his temples with the palms of his hands. When he looked up, William Still had a puzzled expression on his face.

"Perhaps we will talk more about Master Ramsey at this time," Still said. "What were your living arrangements there, Elijah?"

"You mean where Elijah sleep?"

"Yes, that is what I mean."

"Pappy and me live in the log hut. It all right. Elijah have a bed. All Mastuh's slaves live in huts near Mastuh's house."

"How were you treated by Master Ramsey?" asked Jacob White as he leaned forward, resting his elbows on the table. His brown face was friendly; his close beard was flecked with gray.

"Mastuh treat slaves pretty good, suh. Most times."

"Most times? Then you were whipped by this master?"

"Yes, suh. When Elijah do wrong."

"Such as?" White asked.

Elijah hesitated for a moment, twisting his hands. "Mastuh, he work right in the field with us most days. One time Elijah broke the hook on the horse plough. Mastuh took a fit so he whupped me in the wheat field."

"What did he whip you with?"

"Hickory stick he gone and broke off."

"Did he do this often?" asked Still.

"No, suh. He pretty good."

"What was his wife like?"

"Missus Ramsey? She real nice missus."

"What work did the master do?"

"Mastuh? He grow wheat and corn for the market."

"Did you want to run away from Master Ramsey?" asked Edwin Coates.

Elijah grew nervous at the question. The white man's face was long and harsh-looking, but his husky voice was kind. He shot a worried glance at William Still.

"There is nothing to fear in your answer, Elijah," Still whispered.

Elijah took a deep breath. "No, suh. Mastuh, he not so bad—only sometimes. Mastuh Ramsey even give slaves shoes, but after a time he didn't have no mo' money."

Coates shook his head. "No shoes," he mumbled under his breath. "And how long were you at the Ramsey farm?"

"Elijah born there."

"And your pappy, is he still there?"

"Yes, suh. Pappy stay 'cause he not strong no mo'."

"Where is this farm?"

"Durham, North Carolina."

It was the white man again. "While you were at Master Ramsey's, Elijah, did you ever have any chance for schooling?"

"Oh no, suh. Elijah only walk Mastuh's chillun to school sometimes."

"Can you write your name?"

"No, suh."

Still tapped his fingers lightly on the table and glanced at the other members, hesitating before he asked the next question. "Elijah, you told us you were sold. To whom were you sold?"

"Mastuh Fowler."

"Do you know why Master Ramsey sold you to Master Fowler?"

"Yes, suh. Mastuh have hard times when the drought come. He say he need mo' money 'cause he got debts. That why Elijah didn't have no shoes." Suddenly he looked down at his feet and smiled. "Missus Johanna go and buy shoes for Elijah."

"How much were you sold for, Elijah?"

"Mastuh say he get fifteen hundred dollars when he sell me. White folk say Elijah stronger then most slaves—strong like his pappy."

Still scrawled his pen busily across the paper. Nathaniel Depee pushed back his chair, walked over to the hearth, and tossed another log onto the fire. Flames spiraled up the brick flume. He pulled a pipe from his suit pocket, tapped it against the stone hearth, and with a small silver pin pushed a wad of tobacco into the bowl.

Still glanced up from his writing, and at his nod, Nathaniel walked back to the table. "Elijah, we want to ask you some questions about Master Fowler now," Still said.

Elijah shook his head back and forth before lowering his chin to his chest, his eyes pinched closed. He saw the ruddy face of Buckra, his whiskey breath laughing with each violent crack of the whip. The image boiled in his memory.

He turned to Still. "Elijah don't want to talk about this no mo'."

Still leaned back and tossed the pen onto the table. "I know it's difficult, Elijah. But it really will help you to talk about him. He wasn't like Master Ramsey, was he?"

"No, Mistah Still."

"Is Fowler the reason you ran away?"

"Yes, suh. Mastuh and Buckra. He the overseer."

"How long were you at Master Fowler's before you escaped?"

"Ol' Joe say Elijah there three months' time."

"Three months? Not such a long time with a new slave-holder," said Charles Wise.

Confused by the white man's comment, Elijah fidgeted in his seat, turned, and looked at Billy and Anna. Anna twisted a lace handkerchief in her lap. Billy chewed on his thumbnail.

After an awkward silence, William Still leaned over and spoke in a hushed tone to Nathaniel Depee. Elijah watched as the committee members whispered among each other, finally nodding their heads at William Still.

"Elijah, I know this is difficult for you. So only I will ask the questions right now. Will you try?"

"Yes, Mistah Still."

"Good."

"Where does this Master Fowler live?"

"Danville, Virginia."

"And what crops does he raise?"

"He got this big tobacco farm. Lots of slaves . . . mor'n Mastuh Ramsey," Elijah said.

"Had you ever seen a tobacco plantation before?"

"No, suh."

"And how were the living arrangements there?"

"Elijah live with Ol' Joe and some other slaves. Ain't no floor in the hut, not like Mastuh Ramsey's. Dirt only, and when rains come, floor all turn to mud. Elijah sleep on a plank board only."

"How were you treated by this new master, Elijah?" Still asked, lowering his voice.

Elijah stared at his hands for several moments. The steely faces of Mastuh Fowler and Buckra exploded in front of him. He blinked his eyes to make their faces disappear.

"Take your time, son," Still said. "Remember, you're among friends here. You may say whatever you want. No harm will come to you for speaking freely. In fact, Elijah, it may help you put some painful memories to rest."

Elijah whirled in his chair and looked questioningly at Billy.

"Go on and tell 'em, Elijah," Billy whispered, leaning forward.

Turning back, his eyes focused on the floor, Elijah spoke. "Mastuh Fowler didn't let me say good-bye to my pappy. Whupped me right off."

He took another deep breath. His heart was beating hard against his chest.

"So he whipped you the first day he owned you?" Still asked. "In front of your pappy?"

"Yes, suh. Whupped me afore Elijah even get in the wagon. Pappy say run like the wind. But Elijah too scared to run then."

"Tell us about the work you did on the farm."

"Farm so big Mastuh have an overseer. Slaves call him Buckra. He a big-bellied white folk. He feedin' the slaves food in a trough, just like hogs. Buckra come to the hut first night, and he cussin' and sayin' he hear Elijah strongest nigguh in North Carolina—say he gonna break me.

"Then in the mornin' time when the farm bell ring, Elijah go to the field like he supposed to. Overseer, he right off collar Elijah. Buckra unhitch the wagon and he say Elijah got to pull it all day with the tobacco leaves. Sun real hot and Elijah didn't get no water 'til evenin'."

"Finally Elijah just fall down. Legs don't move no mo', so Elijah crawl on the ground. Buckra laugh and drink his rum while he watch Elijah crawl. He say maybe Elijah not so strong now."

Still wrung his hands. "Every muscle in your back must have been torn or strained," he asked. "Did things get any better after that? Did he leave you alone?"

"No, suh."

"Tell me."

"Elijah work hard in the tobacco fields, but Buckra, he keep on whuppin' for any little thing."

"How did he whip you?"

"Most times he tie me across a barrel and then lash me with the cowhide." Elijah stirred uncomfortably in his chair as if the pain were still raw on his back.

"Do you know how many lashings you received?"

"One time he say he count a hunnert and twenny times before he tire and take a rest. Ol' Joe, he put wet rags on Elijah's back."

"Tell me about Ol' Joe."

Elijah remembered lying on his stomach on his plank, the wet rags on his back, intense pain shooting through him, and Ol' Joe beside him playing his harmonica during the long suffering hours. His eyes brightened when he thought of his kind old friend. "Ol' Joe know a lot of things. He been at the farm a long time and he not afraid of the overseer 'cause he say Mastuh like Ol' Joe." Elijah smiled to himself. "Ol' Joe say Elijah just like his own chillun—his boy die when he fall from the rafters in the curin' barn when he tyin' tobacco leaves. Ol' Joe say overseer most like pushed him, and now he worry for me."

"What about the master? Did he know about this?"

"Mastuh didn't pay no mind to Buckra. He let him do what he want. Then Elijah get in trouble with the Mastuh."

"What kind of trouble?"

"One day in the field Buckra say stop plowing. But Elijah plow down one furrow and go on and furrow another one."

"So you ignored the overseer?"

"Yes, suh. Buckra jest all liquored up and Elijah know Mastuh want his field plowed. Mastuh say that morning, field got to be plowed good."

"But that only got you in trouble with Master Fowler?"

"Yes, suh. Last time only. Buckra tell Mastuh, and they take me to the curin' barn. Buckra strip me naked and tie rope around my wrists and hoist me up off the floor. Feet almost clear the floor. Whupped me good while I be hangin' from the rope. Then Mastuh tell Buckra to pour some rum he drinkin' over my back and cob me good."

"Tell us about the cobbing."

Elijah looked directly at the committee members. "With a corncob. Buckra pour liquor and make Elijah's back feel on fire. Then he scrape that husk all up and down Elijah's back. After a time, Elijah pass out."

One of the committee members mumbled under his breath. "How in the name of God . . ."

Still stood up from the table, paced the floor, turned back and paced again. Then he approached Elijah. Bending down on his knees, Still said, "Elijah I want to see what this evil man did to your back. Will you show it to me?"

Elijah shook his head. "No, suh. Ain't no one gon' see this back again."

Still placed his hand on Elijah's knees. "This committee has seen the scars of many slaves—slaves who have been badly beaten."

Elijah motioned for Still to come closer. "Why Elijah got to take off his shirt? Maybe white folk here tell Mastuh Fowler," he whispered.

"Oh, Elijah, you have my promise that no one here will tell Mr. Fowler anything. We are here to help you. You must believe me and trust us."

Elijah looked straight at Still for a long moment.

"All right then." He nodded.

"You have suffered greatly, Elijah," Still said as he stood. "It is a testimony to others to continue the fight for our freedom."

Elijah nodded and slowly unbuttoned his shirt. Slipping it off his shoulders, he tucked it against his waist. William Still placed a hand on his shoulder and turned him around. Elijah felt Still's fingers running over the jagged scars that began at the top of his neck and disappeared below his waist. He winced when Still's hand ran across his lower back. Ol' Joe had said there was barely enough flesh left there to reach the other side. For a long while, Ol' Joe had worried that the battered skin would never heal.

Placing his hands on Elijah's shirt, Still pulled it up over his shoulders. He walked to the hearth and stared at the flames. Finally, he turned away from the fire.

"Elijah," Still said, "you said it was the last time—is that when you decided to run?"

"After the cobbin', Buckra say Mastuh sell Elijah on the auction block. But Ol' Joe, he tell Elijah to run. He fear Elijah die like his son. He say ain't no white folk gon' buy Elijah with this back."

Still walked slowly back to the table. "So you ran like Ol' Joe told you to, in order to save your life?"

"Yes, suh. Then Mastuh send the slave catchers after me." Elijah started to shake.

Still placed a comforting hand on his shoulder.

"And where did you plan to run to?"

"Ol' Joe say go west and run the rails north. He say go to Sandy Spring 'cause the Underground Railroad take me to Canada."

"Quite a story, Elijah," Still said. "Son we're nearly finished here. I have just a few more questions. Questions we ask all of the runaway slaves we interview. Elijah, suppose your master was to appear before you and offer you the choice of returning to slavery or death on the spot. Which would be your choice?"

Elijah stared at William Still and the committee members. Without blinking his eyes, he spoke in a hushed tone. "Elijah cross the waters before he go back, Mistah Still."

"I understand," said Still.

"Even if it were with Master Ramsey?" asked Coates.

"Elijah ain't gon' be no slave again and be sold to 'nuther bad mastuh," he said angrily. "Mastuh Ramsey, he a good mastuh, but Elijah don' want to go back."

Still's eyes flashed. "There is no such thing as a good master or a bad one, Elijah. Because freedom does not exist under either."

"Elijah be free now, Mistah Still?"

"Tell me, what does freedom mean to you?" Still reached for his pen.

Elijah squirmed. He wasn't sure how to answer the question. The only life he had ever known was under watchful eyes while he worked in the fields. And Pappy, well, he'd worked in the same fields his whole life, too, and he'd probably die in them, like Mama. Some slaves, like the ones who worked in Mastuh's house, had better food to eat, and some even learned to read and write, but they still weren't free. Elijah fidgeted in his chair and stared at the floor. Then he remembered something Billy once asked him—early on, at the creek.

"Mistah Still? Elijah think he know what freedom be," he said finally.

"And what is that?"

"My friend Billy, suh, well, one time he ask Elijah if he ever been fishin'. Maybe freedom mean Elijah can go fishin' when he want."

"Yes, Elijah. Sometimes freedom is as simple as going fishing." He looked at him and smiled.

Still glanced at the other committee members. "Does anyone have any further questions?"

"If I may digress for a moment—about his first master," said Coates. "Did you go to church at Master Ramsey's?"

"Nigguhs only go to the preachin' place, suh, under the tree. Preacher, he come on Sunday." He heard his name whispered across the floor, turned quickly, and looked at Billy.

"You ain't supposed to say that word," Billy said.

"Elijah mean coloreds."

"Did you feel that the preaching you heard was the true word of God?" Coates continued.

"Oh yes, suh."

"Even with all the suffering you endured at the hands of the overseer, Elijah?" asked Depee. "You still believe the Lord takes care of you?"

"Preacher tell us nig—coloreds—Lord gonna help us. Just like he done when he bring Billy, suh, so Elijah don't die by the creek. Then he bring Billy, suh, and me to Missus Johanna and Missus Anna. They take care of us. Preacher say wicked folk spread out on the earth like branches on an oak tree. But the wicked gonna perish, he say. Then all little folk is gonna see the blessin's of the Lord. Preacher say we got to believe. So Elijah believe—yes, suh, even when the whuppin's come, Elijah believe."

"Amen to that, Elijah" said Still. "Nathaniel, I think we are finished with the interview. Perhaps you can explain to Elijah what happens next."

Nathaniel Depee nodded, cleared his throat, and talked about the general route on the Underground Railroad that would take Elijah through northern Pennsylvania, New York, and on to Canada. "If your father ever escapes, Elijah, or if we can learn some word of him, we will pass that on to you. That's one of the reasons we want to know so much about you, and know where you will be living."

Elijah rubbed his sweaty palms across his pant legs. "Can Elijah go see Billy, suh, in Maine?"

"Let's see how this war evolves, Elijah," Depee answered. "For now your freedom requires you to go to Canada. You will be leaving tomorrow." Nathaniel Depee glanced around the long table. "It's late in the evening and time for us to close."

Gathering his notes, Still said, "Gentlemen, it may be that Elijah, as one of the few field hands we have interviewed, is less articulate than the house slaves we have interviewed, but I will be the first to say that he speaks within the soul of every man." He closed the leather journal and smiled. "God willing, Elijah, you will be in Canada in less than a week's time."

"What gonna happen to Billy, suh, Mistah Still?"

"I have thought of a plan for Billy," said Anna as she approached the table, hands clutching her handkerchief. "I will talk to him about it this evening."

"Elijah," Still said, "when you are settled in Canada, I hope you will go to school, learn to read and write, and succeed from this day forward. Perhaps you might even end up a preacher." He led him across the worn floorboards.

"Elijah gonna write his name, Mistah Still, and learn to read. Then Elijah teach Billy, suh, too," he said, his spirits lighter.

Chapter 22

Cold water spewed from the kitchen pump, spilling over Billy's head as he leaned over the sink. Goose bumps rose on his skin when Anna dipped the bar of soap under the flow and then dug her fingers into his scalp, rubbing the soap into a frothy lather. Despite the fact that his head bobbed up and down from the push of her busy hands, and the soapy water dribbled into his nose and down the back of his neck, Anna's fingers soothed Billy's nerves, which were spinning like a whirligig.

Anna pumped the handle several more times, one hand tickling water and soap from his ears before the frigid water numbed his scalp. Relief washed over him when Anna splashed a kettle of warm water over his hair until it squeaked clean. His scalp was tingling as she wrapped the towel around his head, covering his face as she rubbed the towel back and forth in furious motion. He stumbled blindly as she backed him onto the stool, cheerfully giving him directions. Then she brushed and smoothed the dampened hair away from his face, and pouring more water into a pitcher, sent him to his room to finish washing. Clean clothes, she said, were laid out across the rocker.

Billy put on the homespun white shirt and black pants and attached a pair of suspenders to his waist before he pushed his arms through the sleeves of a long black coat. He stared at his reflection in the beveled mirror on the dresser and, smoothing back his shiny hair, placed the black broad-brim hat on his head. The clothes hung loosely on him; his face looked pale and gaunt against the darkness of his clothes.

He smoothed the wrinkles in the flannel sheets, pulled the pale green quilt over the single bed, and then picked the pillow up off the floor, stuffing it into the lacy cover slip leaning against the headboard. He scooped up his canteen and haversack from the top of the blanket chest and flung them over his shoulder. Using the heel of his boot, he straightened the rag rugs scattered across the floor, tucked his soiled clothes under his arm, and took one last glance around the room before he closed the door behind him.

Billy opened the French doors into the parlor and stood quietly in the entryway watching Anna tie back the muslin curtains. He thought it a beautiful room even though there wasn't much furniture, the largest piece a grandfather clock in the corner. Dark cherry wainscoting rose from oak floorboards, scrubbed worn and pale. A rocker sat near the hearth, and a pine drop-leaf table decorated with a small lace doily stood against the far wall. Billy stepped forward.

Anna turned at the sound of his footsteps. "Thee is handsome in a gentleman's suit!"

"Feel a might strange in these clothes," Billy said.

"Well, thee now looks like a Quaker. But Billy, thee must wear the coat over the canteen and haversack."

She waited as Billy shed his army issues, took off his coat, and looped the canteen and haversack straps over his neck. Then he put the coat back on. "The provost marshal will not so much as glance at thee now. With God's will, thee will have an uneventful journey from this day forward."

She wrapped a shawl around her shoulders, crossed her arms across her chest, and paced back and forth in front of the fire. "I think we should go over the trip one more time. Thee will be taking the Philadelphia and Trenton Railroad as far as New York.

And since there is no rail between New York and Boston, thee must take the steamship to Fall River, Massachusetts, to catch another train to Boston." She hesitated, her glance meeting him squarely in the eyes. "Does thee remember the name of that train?"

"No, ma'am," he said, frustrated. "You sore at me?"

"No, Billy, I'm not angry with thee, but I see I will need to write these things down. Thee will be able to ask someone kindly looking to read them for you if you forget. It is the Old Colony Railroad that runs right into Boston. Thee will change trains one more time, to the railroad that takes thee to Somersworth, New Hampshire."

Billy brightened. "Berwick's just across the river, like I was telling you. Me and my friends took the train out of Somersworth when we enlisted."

He followed Anna into the kitchen, clothes bundled under his arm until she reached for them and tossed them into an empty hogshead in the corner. "I ain't likin' these good-byes," he said, slumping against the wall, hands in his pockets.

The thought of facing the rest of his way home without Elijah frightened Billy, and he remained sullen throughout the morning and the long carriage ride across the city. Only when the horses pulled to a stop in front of the Anti-Slavery Society office did his mood brighten as he charged up the narrow staircase two steps at a time to William Still's office. Elijah stood at the top of the dimly lit stairwell to greet him.

"Billy, suh, you some fine-lookin' white folk this morning!" Elijah said, chuckling.

"Miss Anna went and washed my hair." Billy yanked off the wide-brimmed hat and glanced over his shoulder. Anna was halfway up the stairs; her bonneted head bowed as she raised her skirt, carefully maneuvering the narrow steps. Billy whispered. "Miss Anna and me's still married, seems like."

"Billy!" William Still stepped into the hallway with a surprised, appraising glance. "I almost didn't recognize you. You look dapper in Quaker dress."

Billy wondered if Mr. Still had heard him talking about Anna; he pinched his lips in embarrassment and then turned his head and glanced down the stairwell. "Miss Anna's comin' along, Mr. Still." Billy rushed to the top of the landing and waited for Anna. Once she'd joined him, they followed William Still and Elijah into the office.

"Miss Anna says I got to carry me a Bible, even if I can't read," Billy said to no one in particular. "Needin' to fool the provost marshal when I take the train to New York."

Anna smiled. "His clothes already served him well at the station this morning when we purchased his ticket," she said. "The provost marshal walked by and never gave him a glance."

"That is good news," Still said with a quick look at his pocket watch. "Well, Elijah will be on his way by sundown, so it seems you lads are on your final journeys. We need to be across town shortly, so I'm afraid you two don't have much time together. Perhaps, Anna, you and I could go downstairs for a short while."

Still walked across the floor and reached for his coat, turning to face Billy and Elijah. "I'm sorry your time together has been shortened." With a nod to Anna, Still led her out of his office, closing the door behind him.

Billy looked around the room, spotted a bench, and sat down. Staring at the floor, he twirled the wide-brimmed hat in his fingers. His initial excitement upon seeing Elijah faded with the reality of their parting.

Standing behind Mr. Still's desk, Elijah ran a finger back and forth along its edge.

"You goin' to school in Canada?" Billy finally asked, breaking the silence. His stomach churned with anxiety.

"Mistah Still say Elijah work and go to school. He say they lots of colored folk in Canada." Elijah didn't return his glance. "What you gonna be doin', Billy, suh?"

"Don't rightly know. Just stay on the farm, I reckon, unless the army finds me," he said. He paused and watched quietly for several moments as Elijah began pacing across the floor, stopped, turned and paced again, his hand rubbing his chin.

"Billy, suh, Maine got them provost marshals?"

"Well, there's lots of army folks there."

"They any colored folk in Maine?"

"I ain't never seen colored folks in Berwick. Thing is, I stay on the farm most times."

"They slave catchers there?"

"On the farm?"

"No, Billy, suh. In Maine."

"Naw, ain't never heard of no slave catchers." He crinkled his brow as he watched Elijah pace across the floor again. Finally Elijah turned and faced him.

"How Elijah gonna find this farm?"

"You comin'?" Billy let out a whoop, tossed the hat in the air, and yelped again as it fell to the floor.

"Yes, suh. Elijah come by summertime."

It was all Billy needed to hear. For several minutes he talked animatedly about the farm, his folks, and Jamie. "Then just before you cross the Little River, there's a lane gonna take you right to the farm." He hesitated, glanced at Elijah, and drew a big sigh. "Seems like a long time from now, summer and all. And you bein' so far away."

"Maybe not so far." Elijah raised his face to the ceiling, his eyes closed. "When night come, North Star be right up over both our heads."

"Ain't both of us seein' the North Star—you bein' so far away in Canada and all."

"Billy, suh, we both be under the same ol' sky—moon and stars, they all the same up there." Opening his eyes, he lowered his head and stared at Billy. "And every time Elijah stand under that star, he be thinkin' about Billy, suh."

"And I'm gonna lie me right down in the pasture and look at the star, too. And I'll know you're right there—just like we was talkin' and all." Billy crossed his arms over his chest, scrunching his nose. Another thought crossed his mind. "I been wantin' to whittle something for you," he said. "Come summertime, I'll have it ready. What you wantin' me to whittle?"

"You whittle Elijah a fish. Then Elijah think 'bout the creek."

"All right." Suddenly Billy jumped to his feet, uncrossed his arms, and sliced them wildly through the air in a wide arc. "And I'm gonna whittle me a spear right through the fish!"

"That right, Billy, suh. That the only fishin' Elijah know."

Billy froze in place. His excitement evaporated. "What if the army shoots me like Leighton says?"

"Billy, suh," Elijah said shaking his head, "it be like the army shootin' Elijah too—right in the heart. That where Elijah carry you, Billy, suh, right here—the thought of you, I means." Elijah poked a finger to his chest. "Just like Elijah carry his mama and pappy."

Billy reached down and picked his hat off the floor. "I'm wantin' you to make a promise."

"What promise you want?"

"If they shoot me—I'm wantin' you to take care of my little brother. Like you was in my place."

"Billy, suh, don't you go and talk like this no mo'!"

"Ain't you gonna promise?"

"How I gon' be a big brother? He white folk chile!"

"No matter. Jamie, he's a right good boy—besides, you can learn him things." He bit down on his lower lip, crossed his arms in a defiant stare. "You're needin' to promise."

"Billy, suh—"

"Friends gotta have promises."

"All right, Billy, suh, Elijah promise."

Billy turned his head at the sound of footsteps in the stairwell. Anna and William Still stood in the entryway, their faces somber. Billy did not want to believe it was time to go. "We needin' to go now, Miss Anna?" he asked in a halting voice.

She nodded.

Billy shot a glance at Elijah. No one spoke or moved.

Finally Anna walked over to Elijah. "Thee will be able to go to school and learn to read the letters that I write thee."

"Yes, missus," he said.

"And Billy," William Still said as he stepped forward and extended his hand, "I pray for your safety—for a just and fair ending to this unfortunate matter with the army."

Timidly Billy reached for Still's hand.

"In spite of your troubles, you were a soldier of freedom," Still said with a firm shake of his hand. "It is as if Elijah is your badge of honor—you saved his life and helped him find his way here. No matter what happens, may you always remember that, Billy."

Billy swallowed, but his throat felt dry. "Them's nice words, Mr. Still."

"Words you have earned, Billy."

Billy spun around and threw his arms around Elijah, holding him tight.

"Good-bye, Billy, suh," Elijah whispered.

On the train station platform, Anna repeated the instructions to Billy once again, and then passed him a folded piece of paper with travel instructions. "If thee is confused, ask a station agent to read this. And as I have said, thee has more than enough money for the train and steamer fares and food. I put some bread and cheese in your haversack. Thee should be in Boston in two days' time."

Anna pressed her hand against her bonnet to keep it from lifting in the wind. "My address is written on this paper. Thee can ask thy mother to write me and let me know how thee is doing. Does thee remember everything I have told thee?"

"Reckon," he said nodding his head.

"I do not know what train leaves from Boston—"

"Miss Anna," Billy said, "I ain't afeared. If I can't find the right train and all, I can walk home most like." For the moment he felt strong, pleased to see her breathe deeply and smile at him.

"Then thee must follow the rail bed north."

Over the hiss of steam and screeching wheels, the conductor shouted for final boarding.

Placing a hand under Anna's elbow, Billy gently turned her around. Her eyes were watery. Awkwardly, he pressed his face close to hers.

Anna leaned her head against his chest. "I will miss thee, Billy Laird. Go now; my heart is gladdened, knowing thee is going home," she said. He turned away from her, fearful that

Anna would see him cry again. Words dissolved on his tongue. He looked at the car. The conductor caught his glance and waved him forward.

"Needin' to go. 'Bye, now, Miss Anna. And thanks for all you done for Elijah and me."

"Godspeed, Billy."

Anna pressed the Bible into his hand. Holding it against his chest, he turned and ran as the car pulled from the station. He found an empty seat near the back, peered out the window, and spotted her, standing on the platform, bonneted head bowed against her chest. He wondered if she was sheltering her head from the cold wind or whispering a prayer. He tapped on the window, pressed his face against the glass, and waved. But Anna never raised her head. Still, he kept waving until the station platform at last faded behind him and city streets turned to empty meadows and gray, leafless forests.

Settling back in his seat, the Bible clutched tightly in his hand, Billy stared dreamily at the changing landscape that was bringing him closer to home. Soon he would see his folks. And sleep in his own bed. He smiled to himself, remembering how Jamie liked to sneak across the hall and crawl in beside him. He would wait through the long winter in eager anticipation for spring, the sap run, and the sugaring house filling with the sweet scent of boiling maple sugar. Then soon after it would be summertime—and Elijah would come. And maybe the war would be over and Harry, Leighton, and the others would all come home.

Chapter 23

Billy raced down the gangway and stood on the pier at Fall River, Massachusetts. He had slept little on the overnight run from New York harbor, having lain on a hard bench in the noisy, smoke-filled lower deck of the steamer. As soon as the *Bay State* was docked, he remembered Miss Anna's advice. He sought out the steward and inquired about the train to Boston. The steward scratched his stubbled chin. He told Billy the "boat train" was just across the street from the pier. Now, scanning the dock overcrowded with hordes of seamen and harried travelers, Billy spotted a man standing off to one side, holding a large straw basket and shouting "Meat pies for sale!"

Billy pushed his way through the throngs of people and stopped in front of the dark-haired man, his mouth watering at the sight of pies tucked in the folds of a red-and-white-checkered cloth. The coins jingled heavily in his trouser pocket. Unable to resist the pie, he decided to save the last of the bread and cheese Anna had put in his haversack. The pie man looked at Billy and held out an empty hand. Without a word, Billy handed him all of his change and anxiously watched as the pie man silently counted each coin.

"How many pies will you be wantin', kid?" the man grunted, his eyes still fixed on the handful of coins.

"One is all—if I got me enough money. You thinkin' them's enough coins for a pie?"

The pie man raised his eyebrows and gave Billy a long, curious stare from head to toe, and then chuckling under his breath, he quickly stashed the money into a leather pouch and handed Billy a pie.

"Sure, kid—just enough for one. Now git yourself out of here," he said.

Billy tucked the pie under his arm and hurried across the street to find the boat train. The rail car was filling quickly. He spotted an empty seat by the window, scooted in front of an elderly man, greeted him with a nod, and sat down. He bit hungrily into the golden-brown crust, enjoying the thick chunks of boiled meat covered in salty gravy.

Beside him, the elderly gentleman tapped him on the shoulder and, leaning over, pointed to the massive, iron-spanned bridge rising above the fast-flowing waterway.

"Slade's Ferry Bridge," the old man said. "Carries the southern-bound trains over the Taunton River." Moments later he pointed to the large granite mills dominating the riverbank. It was all so much like home.

Wiping his hands on the sides of his pants, Billy jingled his trouser pocket, heard not a single coin, and shook his head when he only now recalled that he had given the pie man all of his money. He had no money left for the next fare. I'll just hafta walk home, he thought. He would follow the rail bed north, like Miss Anna had said. And he was sure the rail tracks would take him to Portsmouth. From there he would cross the river into Maine. It didn't seem so far now. He wouldn't even have to go into a store and ask for directions. Billy yawned, and leaning his head against the window, drifted into a light sleep.

When the Old Colony Railroad train pulled into the Boston station, Billy felt a rush of renewed excitement. He leaped down the platform steps and stared at the massive rail yard. The mid-morning sun glinted off the steel roadways. Then it hit him. The rail yard's endless tracks ran in every direction. Which way north? He combed the platform, hoping to spot the friendly old man who had sat next to him, but the cars were emptied. Weary travelers rushed into and out of the station, but the old man was nowhere to be found.

Frustrated, Billy shaded his eyes with the palm of his hand and looked toward the street, finally spotting the old man heading down the brick sidewalk. He hurried after him. The old man told him to head for the harbor and follow the rail lines along the waterfront, all the while pointing his arm in a northerly direction. Feeling certain he had his bearings, Billy thanked the old man and hurried down a narrow cobbled street heading straight to the sea.

Hands in his pockets, his gaze down on the rails, his thoughts drifted to last summer and the 17th Maine, marching through the narrow streets across Boston in the stifling heat, suffocating in their new woolen uniforms and full packs. It was a happier time, laughing and joshing with his friends on that hot August day. This time the city was bitter cold, and he was alone.

The railroad tracks took him right into the inner harbor and a seemingly endless parade of tall ships, square-rigged brigs, sloops, and schooners all tethered to pilings that stretched far out into the bay.

Billy stepped off the tracks and hesitated, staring in fascination as he watched ships' crews slather pine tar over the standing riggings. Line after line of deckhands hauled sails, bolts of canvas, and coils of rigging up the gangway onto the ships. Billy watched until the cold penetrated his clothes. To stop his shivering, he walked briskly beside the tracks while gulls circled overhead.

He walked along the harbor for most of the morning, grateful when at last the procession of ships diminished from view and the landscape opened onto an endless stretch of coastal plains. He found himself on a strip of raised earth just wide enough to carry the rail bed across the gray, wet expanse.

The distant clacking of a train startled Billy, and he leaped from the rail bed onto the frozen marsh. He clapped his hands over his ears as the train roared past him, the ground shaking beneath his feet. In its wake the train left a deep silence, filling him with loneliness. He shuddered as the wind sliced through his wool suit coat. He climbed back onto the raised rail bed and hurried his pace to the northern side of the marsh and the distant forest, a welcome barrier against the wind.

Billy crossed a marsh as the last of the light disappeared behind the tall pines, and found a place to sleep not far from the tracks. He fumbled in the darkness for scraps of wood and lit a fire as the blackness engulfed him. He was scared, and he missed Elijah. He was also hungry again, but wanted to save the last of Miss Anna's bread and cheese. He lay down on the freezing ground to sleep.

When Billy awoke, the morning was raw and biting. Pain shot through his hips and shoulders as he sat up, and his hands stung from the cold. He quickly tucked them in his armpits for warmth as he stood and stretched his legs. He walked over to the tracks and combed the dull, gray landscape. Picking up his haversack, he struck out along the rails.

Later that morning, Billy stood beneath the twin towers of a white clapboard church atop a steep rise overlooking the bay. He shook his head at the boundless view of towering ship masts, the clustered timbers more like a leafless forest. This must be Gloucester. Reverend Snow once said the ships in Gloucester filled the harbor from end to end—like a long wooden bridge. Along the hillside, the cupolas of grand colonials towered above sprawling horse chestnut trees.

Billy followed the tracks down a gradual slope and through the bustling port city. Not wanting to face the gathering throngs of shoppers or rugged seamen loitering near tavern doors, he pulled the wide-brimmed hat low over his forehead and hastened along the tracks.

Billy walked tirelessly for the rest of the day. He had spoken to no one, and no one had spoken to him. When it got dark, he made his meager camp and settled in for the night. The wind howled through the trees, sharp and unfriendly, and he hurried to build his fire.

He wasn't sure what woke him later that night. The fire had dwindled to a pile of low-burning coals. Shivering, he got to his tired feet and scavenged in the dark for more wood. Away from the fire's faint glow, he gazed at the sky, its moon and stars brilliant in the clear night. He spotted the North Star low in the northern sky. Billy rekindled the fire and lay down just far enough away to stay warm and still keep his sights on the North Star. Comforted by the thought that Elijah might be looking at it and thinking of him, too, he fell at last into a soothing sleep, as if his friend were there beside him.

There was no wind the next morning, and it was eerily quiet as Billy lay on his back listening to the waves breaking. Frost blanketed the ground, and although he struggled to rebuild his fire, he was unsuccessful. Frustrated, Billy stalked off toward the rail bed, deciding to get an early start. Opening his canteen for a drink, he found that the water had frozen solid, and the last remnants of his bread and cheese crumbled in his hands. He pulled the wide-brimmed hat close to his ears, raised the collar on his coat, and started off, still hoping he was close to Portsmouth. He could smell the snow before it started to fall. The wind returned and blew heavy flakes sideways, stinging his face. He took a mouthful of snow to quench his thirst. Afraid of losing his way, he hunched his shoulders against the snow, searching with each careful step for the tracks beneath his feet. His hands froze as he gripped his hat, and snow ran down the sleeves of his coat, sending cold, wet shivers through his body.

Suddenly all was still. Without slowing in its intensity, the blowing snow just vanished, and a hazy sun slowly emerged. While walking in the blinding snow, Billy had lost all sense of time and distance, and now he wondered how far he had walked. Ahead he saw a church spire towering above the tree-tops, and spiraling tufts of smoke.

Billy broke into a run. He followed the tracks over the last tract of marsh, not stopping until he had reached a muddied road that curved around a ragged, rocky shore and spilled onto a working harbor of canneries and fishing vessels. He headed inland, toward the center of the town, where a bumpy cobbled street ran into the town square. It looked familiar . . . the square . . . the redbrick church. *It's Market Square, I'm thinkin'! It's Portsmouth—it is, it is!*

He spun around in the middle of the square, looking for the street that led to the inner harbor and the bridge to Kittery, Maine. Crossing Market Square, he headed for the winding street that ran downhill toward the river, and then followed it to the stone bridge that spanned the Piscataquis River separating

New Hampshire from Maine. He was fairly sure he knew the rest of the way home; he'd driven Ma back and forth to the big market a number of times over the years and if he hurried, he thought he might just make it to Cranberry Meadow Road that night.

Chapter 24

Much later, in the dimming light, Billy spotted Jamie walking toward the barn carrying a bucket. He cupped his hands. "Jamie! It's me! It's me—Billy!"

Jamie turned, dropped his bucket, and stood motionless in the middle of the barnyard. His head darted back and forth as he scanned the field.

Billy shouted again, "Jamie! Jamie!" He waved his arms over his head. This time he was sure Jamie saw him.

"Billeeeeee!" Screaming at the top of his lungs, Jamie raced through the gate and into the field, stumbling, tripping in the darkness until he jumped up into his brother's outstretched arms.

"Billy, it's really you!" Jamie's thin legs wrapped tightly around Billy's waist as he hugged him long and hard. When Billy at last lowered Jamie to the ground, Jamie still had his arms wrapped around Billy's waist, refusing to let go. Laughing, Billy just picked him up and carried him across the field.

The barn door flew open and Pa came out. "Billy—Lord, it's my son—" he said in a halting voice. His eyes filled with tears.

"I come home, Pa." Billy eased Jamie from his arms and stepped hesitantly toward his father. "I'm sorry, Pa. I know I done wrong to run." He lowered his head against his chest. "You sore at me?"

"It's all right, my boy," Pa said, pulling him close in a strong embrace. "Lord Almighty, after your ma and I heard what you done, I never expected I'd see you again." Pa sighed and offered a faint smile as he removed the wide-brimmed hat from Billy's head and ran his hand through the matted hair. "By the God, how did you find your way?"

"I remembered what you learned me, Pa." Billy raised his face to the sky, spun around, and pointed a finger. "The North Star . . ."

"Well, I'll be. I never—come, let's find your ma."

"Ma's in the kitchen," Jamie chimed in. "C'mon!" Pushing himself off Billy, he ran ahead to the farmhouse.

Ma's back was to the door, hands dusted with flour as she turned dough on the tabletop. The door opened and slammed shut.

"Ma . . ."

For a moment Ma did not move, and then she turned and stared, blinked her soft blue eyes, and calmly wiped her floured hands on her apron.

"Billy!" Hands clutched across her bosom, she took a step forward and fainted.

The old rooster crowed from his lofty barnyard perch, startling Billy from his peaceful sleep. Tossing his quilt aside, he stretched his arms and, yawning himself awake, rolled over on his back. With eyes half-closed, he glanced sleepily at the window. And then it hit him. *He was home.* In his own bed. He heard the bedroom door creak open and bare feet padding across the floorboards. He pretended to be asleep as Jamie tiptoed into his bed. Jamie scrambled beneath the covers, inched his way across the sheets, and burrowed against him.

"I ain't doin' your chores no more, Billy," said the tiny voice beside him.

"You're needin' to do all the chores, I'm thinkin'," Billy said, mocking the tone of the recruiting officer from months ago. He pulled his pillow out from under him, raised it above his shoulders, and with driving force smacked it against Jamie's head.

"Am not!"

"Are too!"

Jamie flipped over and armed himself with another pillow before Billy could whack him again. Arms and pillows dueled across the bed, mingling with shouts and hoots of laughter. Finally Jamie collapsed in defeat. "Billy, was you scared in the woods?" he asked, catching his breath as he dropped down on his back.

"Naw. Thing is, most times I was with Elijah." His face brightened, and flipping on his side, Billy leaned on his elbow, resting his face in his hands. "Did I tell you last night about them fellas chasing us?"

Jamie bolted into a sitting position. "Tell me, tell me!" He listened as his brother described the chase through the woods, the men on horses close at their heels.

"Then Elijah said we got to jump this here fence. We hunched down beside the cows—moved real quiet like 'til we got to the barn."

"And the horsemen chased you right to the barn?"

"Yeah. Elijah said we was needin' to hide."

Jamie clutched his pillow against his chest. "Where'd you hide—in the hay?"

"Elijah said they'd find us in the hayloft, so he helped me get into one of them hogsheads. Put the lid right over me. Them fellas came runnin' right into the barn."

Jamie burrowed under the quilt. "Did they look for you in the hogsheads?"

"One of the fellas went and poked the hay with a pitchfork. Never once looked in them barrels. Elijah's right smart." Billy leaned back on the pillow, his arms clasped under his head. "Me and him like brothers, seems like." Jamie made no response. Billy glanced at the lump under the quilt. There was no movement. He hesitated, then called out Jamie's name, but his brother did not answer. Billy raised the comforter to see Jamie's lips curled in a pout.

"Aw, Jamie, I told Elijah 'bout you and all."

"Don't care."

Billy reached under the quilt and with both hands pulled Jamie out and into his arms. "When Elijah comes to Maine, he can be your big brother, too."

"I don't want another big brother!"

"But Elijah ain't got family."

Jamie clasped his arms around Billy's neck. "You likin' Elijah more'n me?"

"It ain't about likin' someone more, I'm thinkin'. Reverend Snow says folks' hearts don't never fill up. Elijah bein' like a brother don't take nuthin' away from how I feel about you."

The bedroom door flew open. "Well, there you are, Jamie. And here I was thinkin' that you was doin' chores!"

Billy reveled in the grin on Pa's face.

"I'm goin', Pa, but I ain't doin' Billy's."

Tossing the covers aside, Jamie hopped out of bed and raced to his room across the hall.

"I ain't mindin' chores, Pa." Billy glanced in his closet and saw his old clothes: a winter jacket, a few pairs of worn trousers, and a handful of flannel shirts hung neatly on the wooden pegs. "Besides, I'm wantin' to be in my own clothes again."

"Hardly recognized you—what with you all dressed like one of them Quakers. Well, hurry on up. Your ma's fixing pancakes." Pa turned to walk away, hesitated, turned back, and grinned. "Still got us some maple syrup, Billy Boy."

Billy watched Pa head down the narrow staircase. The cold air penetrated his nightshirt, and he hurried to the dresser and grabbed a wool sweater. He glanced at the pipe lying on top of the dresser. It was the only thing he had of Grandfather Ephraim's, and the old man had carved it himself. Now he could whittle as well as his grandfather had. He was eager to begin a fish for Elijah and a three-masted schooner for Jamie.

Later that day, after Billy had helped Ma gather eggs, she told him to go find his father. "Pa's wanting to talk to you. He's out gathering the herd—near milking time."

He heard the clanging of harness bells before spotting the small dairy herd inching lazily across the field. It had been a long time since he'd last milked the cows with Pa. As the cows plodded slowly over the rise, he watched Pa behind them, swatting and goading them with a long stick. Billy called out to Pa and raced across the field.

Pa turned to Billy, a stern look on his face. "There's something I'm needing to tell you, son."

"Pa?"

"This business with the army ain't over." Pa rested his hands on his hips and looked out across the pasture, watching the cows move slowly to the barn. "It's likely the army will find out you're here."

"You gonna tell them, Pa?"

"No, I ain't telling the army, or nobody, Billy. But Lord knows it's gonna be plum hard keeping this secret—and make no mistake—they'll come looking for you."

Pa took a few steps forward, hesitated, and then started walking again. "Harry wrote us what you done."

Billy studied Pa's grim face.

"He wrote that they'd sent you on to another unit. Said he didn't think you would have deserted if you'd been able to stay with him." He took a deep breath and looked down at his son. "Is that why you run off, Billy?"

"You sore at me?"

"Billy, listen—"

"They gonna shoot me, Pa, for what I done? Leighton says they shoot fellas who run off."

"Don't you be talking like that—especially around your ma!" Pa broke in sharply. "We just need to figure things out—figure a way to keep the army and the folks around here from finding you."

"Pa," Billy said, his voice cracking. "These privates went and—"

"It was wrong that you run, Billy, but what's done is done. Folks in town all know you deserted. Most folks been real kind. Henry Kinsley, though—well, his two oldest boys are fighting, and he about took a fit when he heard you run off."

"I can't go back, Pa. Sergeant Noyes, he—"

Pa grabbed Billy by the shoulders, pressed his fingers firmly into his jacket. "You ain't going back. I never should have let you go from the start. I let that fool recruiting officer take you without a fight. Too late for that. I'm wanting to let you know right now, Billy, that some folks ain't to be trusted. It's important you understand what I'm telling you. You hear me?"

Billy nodded.

"Can't even let you ride Daisy 'til all this is settled, until we figure out what to do with you or where to send you."

"I got to go away again, Pa? I don't—"

"I don't know, Billy. There's a lot to think about. For now, you got to stay plum out of sight when folks come around here." He looked at Billy. "Your ma's talked to Jamie about this. He ain't to say nothing to his teacher at the schoolhouse, or to his friends."

"You think the army's gonna come lookin'?"

"Reckon I can't answer that." Pa spit on the ground. Leaning over, he picked up a stick and drove the herd across the field.

The days rolled quickly into December. Except for helping Pa in the barn, Billy spent most of his hours by the parlor window, whittling and watching for Jamie to come down the lane, grateful the school day was finally over. In the half-light of the evening, he and Jamie would cross the pastures to the edge of the forest, gathering branches of hemlock, pine, birch, maple, and oak. Billy chose the white birch for Elijah's fish and the harder red oak for the spear. On the nights Billy carved, Jamie rarely left his side, delighted when at last the fish, perfectly arced, its belly pierced with a long thin spear, was placed in his hands. Promising its safekeeping for Elijah, Jamie begged Billy to let him keep it in his room.

One evening Billy asked Ma to write a letter for him, handing her the crumpled slip of paper Anna had given him at the station. With a curious smile, Ma sat at the table and penned Billy's words to the young Quaker woman.

"The Seventeenth Regiment's camped in Fredericksburg," said Pa as he peered at his family over the top of the newspaper.

"Says they're readying for their first engagement since going south."

"Harry still writin' you?"

"Harry writes us when he can," answered Ma. Pa looked over and nodded at her. "Billy," she said in a quavering voice, "Jeb Hall took a fever some weeks back—got left behind at sick call while the rest of the regiment marched on to Richmond." She hesitated.

"They send him on home?"

"No. Jeb . . . well, he didn't make it, Billy. Jeb's gone to the Lord."

Billy laid his head on his arms.

"His folks took the train down to Virginia. They're wanting to bring his body back, bury him on the farm," Pa added.

Eager to be alone, Billy grabbed his jacket from the kitchen hallway and left the house. He ran behind the barn, out of view of the farmhouse, never stopping until he reached the middle of the pasture. A thin layer of fresh snow dusted the ground. For a long while he stood, staring at nothing and shaking his head in disbelief. "Why did Jeb have to die?" he said out loud. "He never hurt anyone."

Billy stomped the snow around him and kicked the drifts that piled against the fence posts. Finally he made his way to the barn, still angry.

Daisy's stall was in the far corner, but when he lit the lantern and called out to her, the old mare nickered in response. Holding the lantern in front of him, he watched Daisy stretch her long neck over the stall. He raised an arm and stroked her dappled face, his voice only a whisper as he bared his soul to his old friend. It felt good to talk to her as he rubbed his hands in the thick winter fur of her neck. Daisy nuzzled against his chest and, still nickering, moved her mouth up and down the front of his jacket.

"Sure enough, Daisy, I got me some candy." Billy reached into his pocket and pulled out a piece of candied ginger and, laying it flat in his palm, smiled as Daisy curled her lips around it. He patted her neck again and then sat down on the barn floor in front of the stall.

His anger diminished, he was left with a profound sadness—for Jeb. For Harry, Leighton, Charlie, and Josh somewhere south, in a place called Fredericksburg. Shootin' them Johnnies, like Harry had said. He thought of the long drills along the Potomac in the blazing heat—loading muskets—fixing bayonets—charging and firing. A voice echoed in his ear. Leighton's voice. In the tent at Camp King. *Truth is, we ain't all comin' back, Billy Boy.*

Billy turned and rolled over on his knees in the soft straw, bowed his head, and prayed for his friends.

Chapter 25

In the foggy predawn, the sharp crack of musketry startled Leighton from his sleep. He glanced at Harry, Josh, and Charlie, already awake and listening as nearly two hundred cannons belched forth deadly fire across the Rappahannock River.

"The pontoons must've arrived." Harry said. "Three weeks of sitting in sleet and snow waiting for them pontoons. We're finally moving on Fredericksburg."

"I hope some rations arrived with them. Been nearly starved for three weeks," Leighton mumbled.

The four privates scrambled from their tent. By roll call the cannonading was a ceaseless roar. Throughout the day muzzles flashed from cobbled streets and riverfront houses as Confederate sharpshooters thwarted the Federal army's attempts to complete the pontoon bridges and secure their crossing.

"I can't even see the city for all this smoke in the air," said Josh. "Don't even know what's going on!"

"Don't think I wanna know," said Leighton as he scratched his back against the trunk of a white pine.

Hoping for a sight of the battle, Harry was perched high in a pine above Leighton and Josh. Along the riverbank trees were filled with hundreds of other men from the regiment, all clamoring for a better view.

Through the dense smoke, they could see chimneys and entire brick buildings crumbling to the ground. The city was burning. Suddenly, the faint sound of cheers erupted from the distant Federal ranks. "No guns. We must've crossed the river!" shouted Harry.

"Sure enough. Look-a-here! I can see the ol' Stars and Stripes flying above the town," said Charlie as he climbed higher up the tree.

"Did we win? That mean we ain't gotta fight?" Josh squinted and peered up the wide trunk of the knotty pine. The overly laden branches swayed from the weight of the soldiers, who were busy echoing the cheers of their victorious comrades, their blue caps waving wildly in the air.

"Can't say," Harry called down. "Gonna be dark soon. Reckon there won't be any more fighting today, leastways." He leaned his body over the branch and cupped his hands. "Climb on up, Josh, and take a look."

At sunset the regiment moved downriver and bivouacked in a stand of pine. Under the dark canopy of trees, the ground was still sprinkled with patches of snow. Feeling the cold and with their nerves frayed, Harry, Leighton, Charlie, and Josh gathered pine boughs to cushion themselves from the snow before they spread their bedrolls under the starry December sky.

"We ain't heard one thing since morning," said Charlie angrily. "Why'd they march us two miles down the river?"

"Harry," asked Leighton, as he unrolled his blanket, "you think we'll see fightin' tomorrow?"

"Seems like. Not sure what to expect, though. We're way south of the city now. Maybe the Rebs are planning on moving this way come morning."

"I'm gonna fight and all, but I ain't got much stomach for this. I'm just plumb scared." Leighton stomped his boots to shake off the snow and walked back to the small fire. "Gonna warm my feet and make some coffee. Can't sleep."

"Make me a cup, too," said Josh, his blanket wrapped tightly around him. "If this is gonna be my last night on earth, then I ain't sleeping yet neither."

Harry let out a deep sigh. "Josh, we're all scared 'cause we ain't seen our first battle yet. That don't mean we're gonna die. Someday we'll all be sitting at Frog Pond again, remembering this night and laughing—you'll see."

Charlie rolled over and pushed the damp, sticky needles off his blanket. "Hope that means Billy, too," he said quietly.

"I'm gonna keep thinkin' that Billy Boy will be with us at the pond," Leighton said as he leaned over and handed Josh a tin mug of boiled coffee. "Where in tarnation could he be all this time? We woulda heard if he'd been caught."

"Still hiding in the woods, I reckon. I just hope the good Lord's watching over him," answered Harry. "Just as well he ain't here. I reckon Billy wouldn't fire off his musket even if some Reb was on him like fleas on a dog."

"Leastways, we don't have to worry about that now," Leighton said, sipping his coffee. He sat back and grinned at Josh. "We don't have to worry about Josh, neither. He's so puny, Rebs ain't even gonna see him out there on the battlefield."

"Let's try and get some sleep, fellas," said Harry wearily.

"Yeah, well, somethin' happens to me, you fellas get my fat bones back to Maine." Shifting his weight onto the ground, Leighton quickly buried his head in the sparse comfort of his blanket. Seeking warmth, Josh settled on the pine boughs, his back curled against Leighton.

The regiment turned out at 4:00 A.M. and waited impatiently throughout an agonizing day; no word to move was given. From what they could tell, there had been no advances or organized attack all day. By darkness, General Birney had moved the division to a new camp, nearly a mile from the river. Although small campfires were allowed, orders came down to make as little noise as possible. At last, word spread quickly that the enemy was close by.

Anxious troops awakened early to bitter cold and the welcome surprise of salt pork sizzling on the fires. By mid-morning, under a lifting fog, they heard the call to arms. "This is it, fellas," said Harry as he slung his knapsack over his shoulder. "We're marching to the Rappahannock."

A frightening scene greeted them. Across the river, the Army of the Potomac's left wing, under the command of General Franklin, was heavily engaged with the enemy on the old stage road to Richmond. "By the God! I heard the corps pushed the Confederates back into hills," said a stunned Charlie.

"Look at all them Rebel reserves! They keep running right out of those woods. We're outnumbered," said Harry, his eyes darting back and forth in every direction.

"They're slamming into the Federal lines."

"Looks like the Thirteenth Pennsylvania is falling back."

"No wonder! They must be nearly out of ammo, fighting all morning."

"Seventeenth! Across the bridge! Advance!" Under a curtain of fire, they rushed across the swaying plank bridges and scrambled up the riverbank.

"Form your lines across the road! Fix bayonets!" shouted company officers. The 17th unslung their knapsacks, adrenaline surging as they fixed their bayonets and formed their columns.

"Return fire!"

The guns of the 17th Maine exploded, volley upon volley; the air thickened with billowing, white sulfurous smoke. Cross showers of shot and shell pierced the air, and mingled with the shrill yells of the Rebels in a dramatic charge across the plowed fields.

"Advance your columns! Charge!" shouted Colonel Roberts to regiment commanders as he galloped down the lines. "Charge!"

The 17th Maine, over six hundred strong and larger than many battle-tested brigades, rushed down the turnpike, tearing huge gaps in the Rebel ranks. The Georgia regiment, in the fore-front, dropped like flies as the barrage of shells blazed through its lines, quelling their offensive. The Union batteries unleashed a relentless siege, and the Rebels withdrew into the hills.

"A gallant job, men," praised General Berry, commander of the 1st Division.

"We did it! By thunder, we did it!" screamed a jubilant Leighton, wiping the sweat on his face against the sleeve of his sack coat.

"We showed them Johnnies that two can play this charging game." Harry smacked his big friend on the shoulder and turned around. "Hey, you okay, Josh?"

"Weren't nothing," he answered in a hollow voice, nearly col-lapsing to the ground. "Guess it's just my knees still shaking."

Suddenly artillery shells rained over the hundreds of cheering soldiers as they stood openly in the middle of the old stage road.

"Lie down, men! Lie down!" roared General Berry as he paced back and forth in the rear of the line. "Stay out of range!"

Harry dropped quickly into the mud, pulling Leighton down with him. The road exploded in front of them, splatter-ing mud into the air. A shell fragment ripped Harry's pants, just barely grazing his leg.

"Oh, God, Harry," Leighton cried. "Ain't this day over yet?"

For several hours the troops lay in the miserable mud. Each movement attracted a barrage of artillery and musketry fire from the crest of the wooded hill as the Rebels refused to give up. During the long afternoon, the pitiful moans and cries of the wounded haunted the wretched men as they lay still, unable to help.

"You hear that?" Josh nodded his head in the direction of the pleas for help. "It ain't right to be left out there to die. Just ain't right."

At 4:00 P.M., the Rebel lines began to move again, unleashing a firestorm of masked artillery on the front lines. Impressed with the 17th Maine's first round of fighting, General Berry ordered the regiment to the front to support the left flank.

Dodging shells and artillery, the Maine regiment scrambled across the road, advancing left in front of the batteries.

"Prone positions! Return fire!" shouted Captain West as Livingston's battery unleashed hundreds of shells over their heads into the advancing rebel lines.

Harry dropped down again, into the mud. He fired his last musket ball and turned his head to check on Leighton, lying on his back near him. Blood oozed from a gaping hole in Leighton's blue jacket. A few seconds too slow hitting the ground, he had been shot.

"Leighton!" Harry crawled to his side. Frantically Harry pressed his hands on the open wound.

Leighton's fingers touched Harry's blood-soaked hands. "Ah, Harry," he whispered. "It hurts . . ." He grimaced in pain and looked around, his eyes blinking with tears. "I don't want to die here. Get me home, Harry, promise me . . ."

"I promise, Leighton, I promise. But you ain't gonna die—don't give up!" he yelled. He slipped his arms under Leighton's chest and rocked him gently, holding him close.

"Tell . . . Josh . . ." Leighton's eyes, vacant like a hollowed log, stared blankly at the sky.

"Leighton! Leighton!" cried Harry.

Leighton's eyes blinked, resting on Harry's pale, anguished face, and his lips parted slowly. "Tell Josh—"

"I'll tell him, I'll tell him—just hang on!" Harry's voice cracked.

"Without you fellas, I weren't nuthin' . . ." Leighton's head fell limply into Harry's chest. Harry felt the life leave Leighton's body. He touched his face. "No!"

"Private Warren! Move out!" Captain West started across the road. "Now!"

The front lines were still under heavy fire, but as the battery continued its incessant reply with deadly force, the Rebel lines pulled back, disappearing into the woods.

Harry looked around quickly and saw that he was alone. He grabbed Leighton's body by the shoulders and began dragging him across the field to the embankment by the road. Captain West shouted at him once more.

"Warren! Leave him be. Move!"

Releasing his grip on the heavy body, Harry leaned over and whispered, "Don't you worry none, Leighton. I'll be back for you." With a last look at his friend, Harry ran low across the field.

"What's happened to Leighton? Where is he? There's blood all over you!" screamed a terrified Josh as Harry leaped into the ditch. Harry nodded solemnly to Charlie, who wrapped his arms around Josh and held him tight against his chest.

"He's gone," sobbed Harry.

"Let me go! No, no, he can't die!" Josh wailed and kicked his legs wildly, desperate to free himself from Charlie. "He's out there alone! Let me go!" But his body crumpled, wracked with sobs. Exhausted, he collapsed in Charlie's arms.

"I got to reload," gulped Harry. "Stay alert. We'll both keep an eye on Josh."

"Harry—the shooting's stopped," said Charlie in a hoarse whisper as he released one arm, placing it firmly on Harry's taut shoulder. "It's over."

The clatter of musketry grew faint, and the rumble of the cannons' booms faded in the distance like a dying thunderstorm. Harry leaned his head against his rifle.

Harry awoke during the night and stretched his arm out from under his sodden blanket, reaching for Josh. They had bedded down on broken cornstalks gathered earlier to shield them from the dampness and huddled together to generate warmth. His blanket was empty. Frightened, Harry called out. "Charlie? Wake up! Josh is gone."

"I know," he answered sleepily.

"Where is he?"

"He's okay—let him be—he's with Leighton." Charlie pulled the blanket over his head, shivering from the dampness. "We'll fetch him in the morning."

Harry lay back down and stared at the starlit night. "By the God!" He raised himself up, leaning on his elbows. "Charlie, look at the sky!"

The northern lights, luminous arches of yellow light, streamed brilliantly above them. Charlie sat up and stared wide-eyed at the brilliant sky.

"Them's northern lights!" said Harry in a shrill voice. "Heaven's lighting up the sky for Leighton, make no mistake."

"Leighton and the thousands of other northern boys lying out there on the plain."

"Ain't no northern lights supposed to be this far south. What do you think it means?"

Charlie scanned the sky and shook his head. "I reckon it's a northern dawn . . ." He paused and rubbed a hand across his eyes. "Leighton—and all the others—have gone home."

In the early hours of a gray morning, a two-hour truce was declared to protect the men on either side who went out into the trampled plains to bury the dead and bring in the wounded. Harry and Charlie walked across the crimson-stained fields in silent bewilderment. Around them, stretcher bearers in blue and gray hastened by in search of the living. Shovels tore at the crusted ground as both sides tried futilely to bury their dead before the short truce was over. As they approached the ground where Leighton lay, they stared sadly at Josh, asleep on his stomach, one arm stretched across Leighton's chest.

Charlie leaned over and eased Josh up into his arms, turning his back to the scarred ground. "It's time, Josh," he whispered.

Chapter 26

As the townspeople of Berwick gathered to grieve the death of Leighton Tasker, Billy lay in his bed, his pillow soaked from crying. He curled into a ball, burying his head under his quilt to block the sunlight.

Billy rolled on his stomach and sobbed more into his pillow, wondering if God was sore with him for deserting, punishing him by taking away his friends.

By mid-January snowdrifts had piled up against the barn. Icicles hung from the eaves, and an empty water trough lay buried in tufts of white. Inside the barn, Pa wielded his ax on a thick log while nosy hens clucked and scratched the floor and a small black goat nibbled at pieces of splintered wood. Beside him, Billy stacked a load of split wood in Jamie's outstretched arms and watched as his brother weighed each step over the icy barnyard. On his way back into the barn, Jamie stopped suddenly and turned around. Then, he turned a panicked face back to the barn and with a wave of his hand motioned Billy to hide.

"Pa!" he shouted. "It's Mr. Kinsley!"

Henry Kinsley slid off his saddle and pulled the reins over his mare's neck. "What's got you so all fired up, young'un?" Shaking his head, he hitched the horse to the fence post and headed into the barn. A thud caught his attention, and he glanced in the direction of the noise, the empty stalls under the main loft.

Crouched on his knees and holding his breath, Billy peeked between the slats of Daisy's stall. Sure enough, Mr. Kinsley was staring right at the pen. Not even daring to breathe, Billy sunk into the shadows.

"Henry." John Laird lowered the ax to his side. "What brings you here? Needing more wood this early in the winter?"

"Ayuh." Henry nodded, eyes fixed on the horse stall. A brown hen pecked at his boots, snapping his concentration, and he turned to John, spitting a wad of tobacco on the straw-covered floor. "Too much pastureland and not enough standing timber. What little I cut's too green for this year. That pile of timber in your back field—would you be willing to trade straight out for one of my calves this spring?"

John Laird sighed and blew out his cheeks. "Fair enough."

"Thank you kindly, John. Dang lumber mills stripped the forests so I can't even scavenge for wood. Thought I had enough to last the winter, but we've not had a January thaw this time—cold spell's left me plum short. I'll send my boys over come Saturday with the wood sled." He hesitated, pushing at scattered straw and chips of wood with the toe of his boot. The goat bleated and scampered to the other side of the barn.

"Damn shame 'bout Leighton."

"Ayuh. He was a good lad." Pa wielded his ax and tossed the split halves off to the side. With the sleeve of his shirt he wiped the beads of sweat that dripped along his forehead and took a deep breath.

"Heard from your boy since he run off?" Mr. Kinsley stole a lingering glance at Daisy's stall.

Billy stiffened at Mr. Kinsley's words. Leaning into the slats, he saw Pa's jaw tighten in anger. Moments passed; the silence hung in the air like thick fog. All of a sudden Jamie rushed up to Mr. Kinsley, pulling furiously on the sleeve of his coat.

"Mr. Kinsley? Mr. Kinsley? Can I name the calf when she's born?"

With barely a nod, Kinsley brushed the small hand from his coat, his eyes steadfast on Pa. But Jamie darted in front of him like a pesky fly, still tugging on his coat.

"Whaddya think I should be callin' her?" Jamie asked.

"I don't give a tinker's damn. Now, Billy, he—"

"Then I'll be naming her Nellie." Jamie yanked again on Kinsley's coat sleeve. "Come with me, Mr. Kinsley—I'm wantin' to show you where I'll build Nellie a pen."

Kinsley elbowed the purposefully annoying Jamie aside, sending him sprawling to the floor. The hens squawked and scattered, flapping their feathers in frenzied confusion.

The ax dropped from Pa's hand as he rushed over to help Jamie up. He pointed his finger in anger. "There's no need of that, Henry! I'm asking you to leave."

"Tarnation!" Kinsley held his palms up in the air and hurriedly retreated from the barn onto the icy footpath. His boots slipped beneath him, lifting his legs over his head and flinging him onto the frozen ground. For a moment he lay still, groaning and cursing under his breath before he shot a miserable glance in their direction.

"Mr. Kinsley," said Jamie. "I'll help you—"

"Stay away from me, you dang little . . ." He stopped short of finishing his sentence, and, still muttering to himself, rolled on his side before crawling back onto his feet. Without a backward glance, he untied his horse, guiding him cautiously down the icy lane.

"All clear, Billy." Jamie climbed up the slats to greet him.

223

"Some mighty fast thinking there, son," Pa said as he leaned over the stall and placed an arm over Jamie's shoulder. He was visibly shaken.

"Pa?" Billy's voice was barely a whisper. "You thinkin' Mr. Kinsley saw me?"

"He did," Jamie said. "I could tell."

Across the barnyard Ma's voice called for supper. A heavy silence fell as they stacked the uncut timber. Pa pulled the barn door along its tracks, and the three headed for the farmhouse.

After supper, Pa wiped his hands on his napkin and leaned back in his chair. "We're needing to find some place for you to go, Billy," he said. "Reckon it ain't safe for you to stay here now, what with Henry Kinsley snooping around."

"Billy ain't leaving home this time, John Laird," Ma snapped. "He'll not leave my side again." Billy glanced at his brother before he lowered his eyes.

"Martha, we've no choice in the matter." His chair scraped across the floor as Pa pushed away from the table. He walked to the mantel and grabbed his pipe. For several anxious moments he paced the floor. Finally he hesitated and struck a match, inhaled, and blew tufts of smoke. "Billy can't stay—"

"Then hear me out," Ma said. "I guess I knew this day was coming. We can't expect all folks to be taking kindly to Billy's running off, what with the deaths of Leighton and Jeb." She paused, watching her husband renew his rigid pacing across the floorboards. "I'm willing to ask Mary Rogers if Billy can stay at her farm; it's close enough to home. She's fixing to marry Harry after the war, and knowing how Harry feels about Billy—well, Mary ain't gonna tell no one."

Billy's gaze darted back and forth between his ma and pa. "Mary Rogers?"

Jamie started to giggle. "She's my teacher!"

"But she lives with her ma. We can't ask Elizabeth to take him in. Ain't proper for a widow."

"Elizabeth is in New York and will be for a time, taking care of her ailing father. Billy could stay there during the day and come home after dark. Sleep in his own bed." She folded her hands, nervously playing with her fingers, and waited. "I won't have my boy any farther away than that, John Laird."

Pa was quiet. Slowing his pace, he hesitated, removed the pipe from his mouth, and set it back on the mantel. "I reckon that will do for now. Don't figure the army will be looking for him at the Rogers farm—got no reason." He turned to his wife. "But we'll have to figure something else out real soon. A place where he can stay for a long while."

With a heavy sigh, Billy pushed the ruffled curtain across its rod and sat down in the rocker. He pushed his long legs against the floorboards, rocking and brooding in sullen silence. It had snowed all day, and the stretch of fields back to his own farm would be impassable. Each evening for the past three weeks he had darted across the shadowy pastures for home, returning to the Rogers farm in the gray light of dawn

"You're looking right sad this evening," Mary said, entering the living room. "Here, I brewed some coffee."

"Wantin' to go home is all." Billy reached for a mug of the steaming coffee.

"You're to stay here tonight. Snow's too deep to cross the field, and you surely can't take the roads." She took a sip from

her mug and then smiled. "I'm thinking about fixing some biscuits. Still got a jar of last June's strawberry jam."

"Yes, ma'am." His pinched lips collapsed into a smile. He
liked Mary. It had been hard at first, spending his days at the
Rogers farm. Mary was shy like him, and mostly they just
smiled at each other, their words few and awkward. After a
while, they began to talk more easily, and Mary would ask him
questions or explain things to him in a way that he could
understand. He wished Miss Dame had been more like Mary.
Maybe things would have been different for him somehow.
Sipping his coffee, he slowed his anxious rocking.

"And here's something that will cheer you up even more. I
got a letter today," Mary said, her eyes sparkling.

Billy almost spilled the coffee over his trousers. "From
Harry?"

She nodded, set her mug on the side table, and pulled the
letter from her pocket, unfolding it tenderly as if it were fine
lace. "I'll read some of what he has to say," she said shyly. He
saw the pink flush of her cheeks as she leaned closer to the
kerosene lamp. "Listen good."

*We're back at our winter quarters, Camp Pitcher, after General
Burnside's miserable attempt to have us cross the Rappahannock again
and attack General Lee. It rained so hard the ground turned into a sea
of mud. Horses and artillery were so mired as not to move an inch. I
never dreamed winter in Virginia could be so cold. All the fellas got
coughing fits, it's so damp. Now we spend most of our days building
corduroy roads and our evenings building fires to dry us out. Last night
the Union bands massed together and gave a concert along the riverbank, being it wasn't so cold for a change. There must have been*

thousands of us singing songs. Even the Rebs gathered on their side of the river to listen. After a time, some Reb shouted from the banks for the bands to play one of their songs. So the band played "Dixie" for them. Then "Home Sweet Home." Seems like quite a few of us got pretty choked up before the song was near over. Things got real quiet. Then the Rebs just up and walked away from the river, without a sound. And we all went back to our tents, not a one of us saying a word.

Mary paused and looked at Billy.

Billy's eyelids lowered as he stared absently at the floor. Mary leaned over and touched his arm. "Billy?" she asked softly. "I know it's sad."

He nodded his head. "It ain't that kind of sad, Mary."

"Whatever do you mean?"

Billy hesitated before he spoke. "Fellas all singin' together. Folks ain't hurtful when they got something to sing."

"No?"

"I'm thinkin' of them times—before Harry, when I didn't have no friends. When I tried to be friends with the other fellas, they just poked fun, and sometimes they was real mean. Then come Sunday we was all in church standin' there, side by side, singin' like we was friends and all. Not a one pokin' fun." He hesitated for a moment and then said, "Figure music just makes things right."

Mary let out a sigh. "My gracious, Billy, you surely did understand what Harry was writing about. You surely did," she repeated once more under her breath.

Her eyes scanned the next few lines, and then she quickly folded the letter in half. "I guess that's about all he says . . ."

Billy saw the color deepen on her cheeks. "You sure like Harry. In the evenings, at camp, Harry most always fingered that pink ribbon you give him."

Mary smiled warmly. Placing the letter on the side table, she stood. "How about we fix those biscuits now?"

Billy followed her and watched eagerly as Mary lifted the barrel's lid, leaned over, and opened the sack of flour. "I wish it wouldn't snow no more. I ain't seen the stars for a long time, what with it being so cloudy and all. Mary, does it snow in Canada?"

"Yes, it snows, and even more there, I reckon," she said, carefully sifting a cup of flour into a yellow bowl. "You thinking of Elijah again?"

"Yes, ma'am."

"Well, I'm sure he can't see the North Star tonight either."

"Elijah says we're both right under it, just the same."

Mary smiled. "He's right, Billy. Even when you can't see it, that old North Star's still up there, shining down on the both of you."

Chapter 27

The commanding general scowled as he read the letter. He shouted to his aide in the outer office.

"Sir?" responded the young lieutenant as he raced into the room. He had been working in Maine as General Deering's aide at Augusta headquarters since the onset of the war, and he could easily recognize the general's moods by the tone of his voice. This time the mood was urgent and filled with loathing.

General Deering waved the letter in his hand. "Seems a deserter, a private from the Seventeenth, was spotted at his home, in Berwick." He shook his head. "We have a record on him?"

"What's his name, sir?"

"Laird. Private William Laird."

The aide stared vacantly at the tin ceiling, his razor-sharp memory searching, sifting through countless reports from the field. "Yes, I remember the name from one of Colonel Robert's reports. Laird deserted last October, from Edward's Ferry, this side of the Potomac, if I'm not mistaken."

"Potomac in early fall? Hell, it was still warm and the soldiers' bellies were still full. Not even a skirmish with the enemy," he said with disgust.

"Who saw him, sir?"

"A neighbor, Lieutenant. Kinsley's his name. Has two sons in the war. One was wounded but remains with his unit."

He handed the letter to the aide. "Send this on to Major Andrews at Fort Preble down in Cape Elizabeth. I want this private captured. Major Andrews can detach an officer and whoever else he needs to take with him to Berwick."

The lieutenant hesitated at the door. "Not an easy feat to make it all the way back from Maryland, I would imagine."

General Deering nodded. "Tell the major to have his men exercise caution. We don't know what this private's like. You're right; if he worked his way back to Berwick, I suspect he will likely resist arrest."

"I'll contact Major Andrews, sir."

"Lieutenant!" shouted the general before the aide disappeared through the doorway. "This may be our first deserter to face a court-martial in Maine."

"And if he's found guilty, sir?"

"He's guilty, Lieutenant. Make no mistake."

The general got up from his desk and walked to the window, staring down at the Kennebec River, the large chunks of ice along its banks breaking away in the early spring runoff. From all the reports it appeared that the 17th Maine had endured an unusually cold, wet winter in Virginia. General Burnside had been removed from command of the Army of the Potomac. The infamous Mud March was a complete disaster. Soldiers stalled for thirty hours in ceaseless rain, slipping and sliding in greasy mud as entire regiments pulled lines of coiled rope to loosen mired artillery. Cold, sickened, and desperately hungry, hundreds of soldiers deserted on a daily basis. Given the miserable conditions, he mused that one could almost have a modicum of understanding for the desertions at Camp Pitcher. He fumed over this Private Laird, sitting at home while his comrades endured such misery. He turned away from the window, staring grimly at the lieutenant.

"Fort Preble may need to assemble a firing squad."

May 21 dawned bright and warm, the air offering a faint promise of spring. Billy's ma smoothed the folds of his bed and scooped the dirty clothes off the floor. In the early darkness Billy had headed out across the fields to the Rogers farm. The arrangement with Mary was working out well, Ma thought. Mary and Billy were becoming good friends, and Billy seemed to thrive on the attention she lavished on him. Downstairs, the heavy stomping of boots interrupted her thoughts and, taking a last glance around the room, satisfied that it looked undisturbed, she closed the door and headed down the back staircase to the kitchen.

Pa and Jamie ate hungrily, sopping thick slices of bread in the rich gravy, sausage heaped on their forks. Ma leaned against the counter by the window, warming herself in the sunlight. She spotted a movement in the lane. Squinting against the glare, she shaded her eyes and leaned closer to the windowsill. She watched in stunned silence, straining to identify the three men approaching on horses. As the sharp blueness of an army uniform came into view, Ma gasped.

"John!" she cried. "It's them! The army!"

Pa pushed his chair back, the thrust knocking it on its side as he ran to the window. He turned to his son, a look of fear flashing across his pale face. "Get your books and be off to the schoolhouse, Jamie."

"Are they gonna take Billy?"

"Hush, Jamie," said Ma. "Not a word, do you hear? Now do as you're told," she whispered, twisting her hands in the folds of her apron.

Pa hurried to the entryway, pushed open the door, and stood in the threshold, his jaw tight, knuckles white from the pressure of his clenched fists. He stared in silence as the three men, only one wearing a uniform, stopped in front of the doorway.

"Mr. Laird?" asked the man in the officer's uniform as he slid off his saddle.

John Laird nodded, his eyes fixed on the officer.

"Mind if we come inside, Mr. Laird?" The officer hitched his horse to the post and waited for his civilian companions before he entered the house.

The strangers stepped confidently into the kitchen, their eyes darting around the large room. Removing his gloves, the officer stepped forward and extended his hand to Pa. "Lieutenant Nathan Walker. Attached to the Fifth Regiment, Maine Volunteers, at Fort Preble." He glanced at Ma and nodded his head. "Ma'am."

Ma did not move. She stood rigid, not returning his greeting. Pa looked directly into the lieutenant's eyes but said nothing.

"Mr. Laird, headquarters in Augusta received word that your son William arrived back in Berwick. He's under court-martial for desertion and, sir, it's my duty to take him into custody."

"What do you mean, you've received word that my son is here?"

"Ma'am, Major Andrews was informed by headquarters, that's all I know. Most likely someone here in town reported it."

"I don't believe you, Lieutenant. No one's reported anything," Ma said, breathing heavily. "Billy ain't here."

"Ma'am, I know this must be hard for you—"

"Hard for me? My son never belonged in your army."

Pa reached for his wife's arm. "Lieutenant, I tried to tell the army about our boy. He ain't smart like most other folks."

"He volunteered, Mr. Laird," said Walker, "and he's over eighteen."

"Oh, he mustered on his own, all right—against our wishes. He only wanted to be with his friends. Billy knows he done wrong, Lieutenant. But he ain't got the ability to figure out the why."

"So you have spoken to him?"

Pa bristled at his obvious mistake and lashed out at the lieutenant. "You're just like the recruiting officer. Don't want to hear what I got to say about my boy. Like the wife said, he ain't here."

Pa marched over to the back door. "It's time you left now."

"Mr. Laird, I understand your desire to protect your son. But as an officer of the army, it is my duty to arrest Private Laird for desertion. And I will find him," said Lieutenant Walker.

"How can you expect a mother to turn her son in?" Ma fell against Pa's shoulders and sobbed into his chest.

"Lieutenant Walker, you're upsetting my wife. My boy ain't here. Now I'm asking you again to leave my farm."

The young lieutenant stiffened. "Don't make this more difficult than it already is, Mr. Laird. I intend to find your son, with or without your help. If he's on this farm, you need to turn him over to us now."

"He ain't on the farm, Lieutenant, as God is my witness."

"We'll have to take a look around. Mr. Hanson and Mr. Waterhouse will check the barn. I assume you'll want to accompany them. Mrs. Laird, ma'am, why don't you walk me through the house."

Without a word, John Laird gently released his wife from his arms, grabbed his jacket, and followed the other men out the back door.

Holding his schoolbooks, his face frozen in fear, Jamie stood on the front hall staircase as the man in the blue uniform entered the room. The officer appeared startled but said nothing as he hurried up the staircase. He entered the first room. A pile of clothing lay heaped on the seat of a caned chair, and Walker quickly rifled through it, acknowledging to himself that the clothing belonged to the young child downstairs. He scanned the single shelf that ran across the inside wall, examined the casing of a small pocketknife, and glanced briefly at the books. His eyes rested on the unusual carving of a fish with a spear pierced through its belly.

"Your boy whittle this?"

"Yes. His pa taught him," Ma said.

He walked to the bedroom across the hall.

"This is Billy's room," Ma said harshly.

The room was tidy; a worn comforter lay smoothly across the undisturbed bed. The lieutenant walked immediately to the closet and looked closely at the clothes, finding only a few flannel shirts, a pair of tow-cloth trousers, and a light jacket. He poked around the dark corners of the narrow closet but found nothing. His right hand brushed across a pair of boots, half-laced and cold to the touch. His fingers slid along the toes and soles. He yanked them out of the closet and held them to the light. The soles of the boots were damp. He peered into the closet again. There was a pool of muddy water on the closet floor. "Are these his boots?"

Ma nodded.

"They're wet." Walker stood and hurriedly walked to the dresser, yanked opened the drawers, tossing socks and underwear aside. Finding nothing else, he closed the bottom drawer and headed for the last bedroom.

Hanson, Waterhouse, and Pa stood uneasily next to the horses, no one choosing to speak. As Lieutenant Walker came out of the kitchen door, he stopped directly in front of Pa and said firmly, "I know you're hiding him, Mr. Laird. And the three of us will stay in Berwick for as long as it takes to find him."

Nodding to his partners, the lieutenant mounted his horse. John Laird remained silent as the three men turned their horses and headed back down the lane.

"I heard what he said." Jamie's eyes were red and swollen as he met his folks in the kitchen.

Ma pulled a handkerchief from her apron pocket. "The lieutenant found Billy's old boots, the ones he wears in the snow. He wore them over here last night. They were still wet."

"Then he knows. Just a matter of time, I reckon," said Pa as he slumped into a chair.

"Jamie, you need to tell Mary that the army's in town looking for Billy," said Ma. "You think anyone to school knows Billy's hiding out at the Rogers farm?"

"I don't know, Ma."

She hugged him tight. "I prayed this would never happen."

"Billy didn't do nuthin' wrong, Pa," said Jamie.

Pa shook his head and sat down at the table. "It ain't right what Billy done. He broke the rules, son. And now the army says he got to pay. He made a mistake, and even though he didn't mean to do nothing bad, he still done wrong just the same."

"You think Mr. Kinsely told them?" Ma asked.

"Can't think of anyone else," said Pa. "Don't much matter now. We've got to keep the army from finding Billy is all."

Jamie looked at his parents. "After dark, can I go to Miss Rogers's house and fetch Billy?"

"Ain't a good idea for Billy to come back home tonight, but we're needing to talk to him right away and work out another plan," said Pa. "Cut through the fields and stay off the roads. There's a full moon out tonight, and the fields are more passable now. I'll wait up for you both, son."

Jamie silently put on his jacket and picked up his schoolbooks.

"You tell Billy we'll do what we can," Pa continued. "Tell him the good Lord must have a reason for this here to be happening."

Sniffling, Jamie walked out the door, his small shoulders braced against the morning sun.

Chapter 28

Lieutenant Nathan Walker walked into Blaisdell's Store, his stride heavy and purposeful. After talking to Laird's parents, he was convinced that the private was hiding in town. Colin Elkins, Freddie Biggs, and Tom Piper were sitting in chairs around the unlit potbellied stove, pipes fixed in their hands. They exchanged curious glances when the imposing man in the dark blue uniform entered the store. The lieutenant rested his gaze on a plump, gray-haired woman who was busy stacking loaves of warm bread. Aware of his penetrating stare, Harriet Blaisdell nervously wiped her hands across her gingham apron and hurried behind the counter.

"Ma'am." Walker tipped his hat, his face unsmiling. "I'm Lieutenant Walker, Fifth Maine Regiment, attached to Fort Preble. I'm looking for Private William Laird. I understand he's a Berwick boy, and, well, I'm wondering if you might know him, or where I might find him."

Harriet's eyes widened. She looked at the men around the stove, each exchanging glances. "Why, no!" she heard herself say. "I mean, I know Billy run off from the army some time ago, but he ain't been back here . . ."

"Well, now, ma'am, it seems someone from this town notified headquarters in Augusta that he was back home." He turned and faced the men at the stove. "I'm asking each of you for information that might help me find Private Laird," he said, using a more official tone.

"What's gonna happen to Billy, Mr., ah . . ." Harriet stumbled.

"Lieutenant Walker, ma'am," he repeated, raising his eyebrows. "Who were his friends?"

Harriet trembled. "Lieutenant Walker, I don't know much about the army and all, but I've a mind to tell you that Billy ought not to have been in the army in the first place. Never could understand why John Laird didn't keep him from going. Why, Billy can't even make change by himself. He's a real nice boy, but simple, if you know what I mean."

"No disrespect, ma'am, but this simpleton also figured out how to find his way back from Maryland."

Tom Piper stirred in his chair. "Well, you're wrong about that, Lieutenant. Billy ain't smart enough to find his way home." Elkins and Biggs nodded their heads in agreement.

"I'm not looking to argue Private Laird's intelligence. I'd appreciate you folks telling me about his friends," Walker asked again, placing his hands on his hips. "I don't wish to conduct needless searches of every home in Berwick, but if I have to . . ."

Elkins leaned over his chair and spit in the cuspidor next to him. "His only friends were going to war. That's why he mustered." He wiped his mouth on the sleeve of his shirt.

"And their names?" asked the lieutenant.

Elkins glanced at Harriet, who sighed and lowered her head. "Harry Warren—that was his best friend. More like his keeper. There was Leighton Tasker, he was killed at Fredericksburg. Then there's Josh Ricker, Charlie Marston, and Jeb Hall. Jeb's dead too, poor fella. Just took sick and died. Town's right shook up over these boys' deaths coming so close together and all."

"Their families live in Berwick?"

"Ayuh, but that's all we got to say," said Elkins, and puffing slowly on his pipe, he turned his gaze away from the lieutenant. Harriet and the other two remained silent.

Lieutenant Walker turned his attention to Biggs and Piper, staring directly at them. He watched as one of the men leaned over in his chair, struck a match against the stove, and lit his pipe. Neither glanced his way. Turning his head, Walker looked at Harriet. Averting his gaze, she picked up a rag and ran it over the countertop. Silence hung in the air. The lieutenant turned and headed to the door.

"Lieutenant Walker," Harriet said in a pleading voice as he reached for the latch. "Just remember what I said about Billy."

The lieutenant hesitated and looked back over his shoulder. "Ma'am, if what you say about Private Laird is true, it will come out at the court-martial. And for his sake, he'd better pray that it does." He turned and walked out the door.

Hanson and Waterhouse were standing by the horses as Walker emerged from Blaisdell's Store. "How'd you both make out?" Walker asked.

"Folks aren't talking much," said Hanson. "Seem right surprised, though, about Private Laird being back. Didn't seem to think he could make it on his own. Only lead I picked up was about his friend, Harry Warren. Talk is he's a fine soldier, even catching the attention of his regiment officers. Folks live over to Pine Hill."

"Yes, we'll need to visit them and some families by the names of Tasker and Hall. Their sons mustered too—friends of the private's. No one wanted to tell me where they live. Both boys are dead." He looked directly at Hanson. "Perhaps they won't feel too kindly toward a deserter, friend or no."

"I'll go back and ask the town clerk about their whereabouts. At least she's friendly enough," said Waterhouse chuckling. "I think the ol' gal even took a fancy to me."

Walker, Waterhouse, and Hanson were greeted warmly by the Taskers, who insisted they sit for tea in the steamy warmth of their kitchen. Any intrusion in their lives was a distraction from their grief, and they eagerly tried to please the strangers. Mabel Tasker brought out her best china, poured tea, and placed a plate of fresh raisin muffins on the table as she listened to the lieutenant speak about Billy.

Excusing himself, Leonard Tasker stepped into the front parlor and returned with a small daguerreotype in his hand. "This here's our boy, Leighton," he said, his hands shaking.

Lieutenant Walker sipped the hot tea. "I'm truly sorry about your son. If we win this war, Mr. Tasker, it will be because of brave men like him who gave his life for his country. I hope you can understand why the army feels it's necessary to find Private Laird. Unlike your son, he turned his back on his sworn duty. That's why I'm here, Mr. and Mrs. Tasker, to honor the duty your son unselfishly believed in."

Leonard Tasker set the daguerreotype down gently on the table and folded his arms across his chest. "Lieutenant, I understand what you're tryin' to say about duty and all. But Leighton most likely mustered for the same reason as Billy. I'll wager he was more interested in being with his friends than setting his mind to some sworn duty. I'm not sure he knew just why we're fighting this war. Don't judge young Billy so harshly. He probably don't even know he done wrong when he ran," he said.

The lieutenant tried to soften his words. "I'm hearing from folks that Private Laird may be simple, Mr. Tasker, but nevertheless, he committed a serious violation of the Articles of War. And, well, sir, the army just can't afford to let people walk away from their obligation. We have to win this fight, and the president needs every soldier the towns can give us."

Lieutenant Walker leaned closer to the couple and asked softly, "Do you have any idea where he might be hiding?"

Mabel Tasker wrung her hands. "Why, no . . . I didn't even know about Billy being back home 'til you spoke of it."

"Will they bring my boy's body back to Maine, Lieutenant?" asked Leonard as he stared at the photograph.

Lieutenant Walker bit his lip and stirred uncomfortably in his chair. Any further chance to learn more about Private Laird was lost. He stole a glance at Hanson and Waterhouse and, shrugging his shoulders, tilted his head toward the door.

"Mr. Tasker, I'm afraid it won't happen until after the war. Someone will have to go down south and look for his grave. Perhaps one of his friends marked the site. I'm sorry. I wish I could be more helpful."

Mabel Tasker slumped against her husband. Whatever hope they had held for retrieving their son's body withered in front of them, and they cried openly. Lieutenant Walker pushed his chair back and stood up from the table.

"You gonna be takin' a look in my barn and outbuildings?" Leonard asked feebly.

Lieutenant Walker shook his head. "No, sir, I don't think that will be necessary."

The three men rode silently up the winding road to Pine Hill, its timbered sides now planted in fields of apple trees. The wind was strong at the crest, but through the budding trees the view was spectacular. At the top of the hill was a red Cape with black shuttered windows. A center chimney loomed against the clear blue sky.

"Must be the Warren farm," said Hanson. "Right where Frances Porter said it would be."

The lieutenant nodded and leaned forward on his saddle. "Keep your eyes open; if you can't hide in the home of your best friend, then where else?"

A handsome middle-aged woman looked up from the porch and felt her heart leap in her chest when she noticed the man in uniform. Florence Warren called out to her husband and walked away from the basket of laundry. Her hand over her mouth, she approached the men as they dismounted from their horses. Hank Warren ran out of the barn.

"Oh, Lord! Has something happened to my boy?" she said, barely able to utter the words.

"Ma'am," Walker interrupted, "far as we know, your son is fine. I'm sorry to give you such a fright."

The Warrens shook their heads when Lieutenant Walker talked to them about Private Laird. It was simply not possible, they told him, for Billy to have found his way home from Maryland.

The lieutenant pursued his questioning, and as with the Taskers, he found the Warrens' responses sincere. "So what you're saying, then, Mr. Warren, is that Laird's only friends mustered? There's no one else here who might hide him that you know of?"

"That's what I'm saying to you, Lieutenant," Hank Warren glanced at his wife. "Billy's a fine, God-fearing boy. Just plain simple is all. As far as the missus and I are concerned, we don't want to see Billy arrested. Reckon I'm glad I don't know his whereabouts. Don't take kindly to lying, and I don't want to be untruthful to the army. Thank the good Lord, I don't have to make that choice."

"I hear your son is a mighty fine soldier, Mr. Warren. You and Mrs. Warren should be proud," offered Hanson.

"Oh, we've always been proud of Harry. He's a good boy. We just want him home safe and sound, so he and Mary can get married and settle down."

"Who's this Mary?" the lieutenant asked.

"Mary Rogers," chimed in Mrs. Warren. "She and Harry are promised to each other. She's a lovely girl—the schoolteacher in town, you know."

"So she must know Private Laird?"

"Well, yes. Everyone in Berwick knows everyone else. And young Jamie Laird is one of her students."

Hank Warren stepped forward and asked, "Will you be needing to search our farm?"

"Yes, sir, my partners and I want to take a look around. We'll be quick about it," said the lieutenant.

"Do what you must. We've nothing to hide."

Lieutenant Walker walked the farmyard while Hanson and Waterhouse scoured the large barn, opening doors, checking stalls and haystacks. Again, they found nothing. The afternoon sun was fading as the three mounted their horses and headed down the long, steep hill. Anxious to reach the schoolhouse, Walker pressed his legs into his horse and moved quickly down the lane, hoping to beat the dark.

Chapter 29

In the chilly twilight, Jamie raced across the muddy fields. The light at the Rogers farm was faintly visible, the night air serene; the sting of winter was at last fading into early spring. In spite of Pa's admonitions, Jamie dashed onto the road to shorten the distance, replaying his secret plan in his mind.

"Billeeee!" he cried as Mary opened the front door to his heavy knocking. "Billeeee!" Jamie leaped into his brother's out-stretched arms, burying his cold, reddened cheeks against his chest.

"Pa said you're to come home with me tonight. Said he and Ma are needin' to talk about a new plan, what with the army in town."

"It's been a frightful afternoon," Mary said, her face ashen. At school, Jamie had told her about the people looking for Billy. "I'm not sure you should go home tonight, Billy, but we'll do whatever your Pa says."

Billy led Jamie into the living room and Mary followed. Billy sat down on the braided rug, fidgeting nervously. "Tell me more about this morning."

"Pa made me leave the room when they came, but I listened behind the door," Jamie said. "They said they're gonna arrest you for desertion. Then Ma got real upset. Talked sharp with the lieutenant. And Pa asked them to leave." Jamie glanced at Billy. "The lieutenant said he was under orders to find you. They went and searched the house and barn. They found your boots."

Billy lowered his head and stared vacantly at his hands, his eyes wide with fear. "They're gonna shoot me. Leighton said—"

"No, Billy! I got a secret plan! They ain't never gonna find you." Jamie plopped down on the floor beside his brother. "We'll build us a hiding place in the woods. We can stay there forever. Just you and me, like you done with Elijah. You said it ain't so bad, remember?" Jamie's earnest blue eyes clouded at the look of fear on Billy's face.

Billy got back up on his feet and walked to the hearth, leaning his head against the mantel. He felt the touch of cold metal against his forehead and jerked back. His eyes fell on the pistol, which had belonged to Mr. Rogers. Mrs. Rogers had set her late husband's gun there before leaving for New York, telling Mary she was worried about her daughter being there alone, without protection. Billy ran his fingers along the barrel. Mary had scolded him when he'd picked up the gun that first day he stayed at the farm. She didn't want him holding it, said it scared her even having it there, but she had promised her ma. While Mary was at the schoolhouse one day, Billy had opened the chamber. It was loaded.

"You likin' my plan?" asked Jamie, shaking Billy from his thoughts.

Abruptly, Billy turned and nodded, forcing a smile he didn't feel. "Likin' it fine. We'll talk to Pa about it."

"Wantin' to play checkers, Billy?"

"I don't think that's a good idea, Jamie," cautioned Mary. "Your pa will be watching for you."

"One game is all—it ain't so late yet, Miss Rogers."

"Well, one game won't delay you too much, I reckon," she answered. "Might be nice to take your minds off the army."

Billy and Jamie set up the board, and Mary sat down with her needlepoint.

The wick in the kerosene lamp flickered across the trestle table. Jamie leaned closer to the board, scrunched his nose, and jumped his black checker over three red.

"Why'd you go and jump all them checkers like that?" Billy asked, biting his thumbnail in frustration.

"I already told you. When you go and leave your checkers all spaced in a row like that, I get to jump them is all."

"But then I ain't got many checkers left. Ain't fair, seems like."

"Is too. Someone's got to win."

"Ain't never me."

"Then don't move your checkers in front of mine. Your turn."

"I'm gonna jump all them black checkers."

"No you ain't."

"Am too. You just went and done it."

"Your checkers was all lined up is why."

"Then you put yours in a line."

"I ain't!" Jamie was shouting.

"Boys!" called Mary as she dropped her needlepoint in her lap. "It's late; I think it's time you headed over the fields."

"We ain't finished the game, Miss Rogers," Jamie said as he turned his head and looked her way.

With Jamie distracted, Billy hurriedly reached for a red checker and jumped over several black ones, crisscrossing the board in a haphazard pattern. Satisfied, he tossed the jumped checkers beside the board. "Your turn," he announced.

"Billeeee!" Jamie picked up a red checker and threw it. "Not fair."

"Do your checker games usually end like this?" Mary asked, shaking her head.

"Yes. Jamie always wins," Billy said glumly. "It's them black checkers is why."

Mary placed her hands on her hips and glanced at Jamie as he gathered the checkers. "Might be real nice of you, young man, if you helped your brother understand this game a bit more."

"Yes, ma'am." Sulking, Jamie moved away from the table and walked to the front hall. He turned to his brother, resignation in his small voice. "I'll learn you checkers better when we get to the hiding place."

Billy grabbed their jackets and glanced affectionately at his brother, the tufts of sandy brown hair, the impish blue eyes, the lanky body so much like his own. Without thinking, he leaned over and kissed the top of Jamie's head.

"You only do that to Ma."

"Just wanted to is all."

Mary checked the buttons on Jamie's coat, wrapped the wool scarf snugly around his neck, and kissed him lightly on top of his head. "That one's from me, Jamie," she said. "And don't be telling your friends at school tomorrow," she admonished.

"I'm tellin' Harry for sure when he gets home."

Billy took his brother's hand and, opening the door, walked out with him across the moonlit fields.

Finding the schoolhouse dark when they finally arrived, Lieutenant Walker, Hanson, and Waterhouse decided to find themselves a hot meal and a place to stay for the night. Later, over bowls of hot stew at the inn, Hanson stirred uncomfortably and groaned. "I don't reckon we're wanting to hear your answer, but are you figuring on some kind of watch tonight?"

Walker shook his head. "Before first light. There's a ridge overlooking the Laird farm. I'll wager it offers a clear shot of the house, and it's no more than a few hundred yards off the road.

We'll keep watch just until the little fella goes to school. Follow him in—talk with Mary Rogers then. If nothing pans out, we'll ride out and talk with the Rickers and the Halls after that."

The morning sun lifted, spilling a thin yellow line along the crest of the surrounding hills, the valleys still gray. Hanson and Waterhouse hunched over their saddles. The lieutenant, invigorated by the crisp air, sat upright, eyes fixed solidly on the Laird farmhouse, waiting.

A door slammed, echoing against the hillside. Then voices. Faint. Walker leaned forward. Waterhouse jerked his reins, stilling his mare as she stomped her hooves on the rocky ledge. In the dim light a solitary figure, tall and lean, moved away from the farmhouse, past the barn, walking east over the fields.

"Think it's the father?" whispered Hanson, straining for a better look.

"Can't say. Still too dark. Depends on where he's heading, I'm guessing," said Walker.

The lone figure crossed one pasture, opened a gate, and continued walking, each step taking him farther away from the farm. Minutes later a light glowed in the kitchen windows. The door opened. Another man, similarly tall, moved swiftly toward the barn.

"I'll be damned!" murmured Walker. "I bet that's the father." He turned excitedly to his companions. "I think we found our deserter."

"We going after him, Lieutenant?"

"Not yet. As soon as he hears us, he'll make a run for the woods. Forest's so damn thick, we won't be able to push the horses through." Walker jerked his obedient bay sideways, changing his viewpoint on the sweeping outcrop. "I'm not about to risk losing him. We'll follow this ridge until we spot wherever it is he's heading for, then take the road. Wherever he's going, he'll likely stay put until dark."

"Explains the wet boots, all right. He tracks across the fields after dark, sleeps at home, and heads out before dawn. Not a bad plan." Waterhouse grunted and rubbed his glove across his beard. "I'm wagering that for a simpleton, he's a pretty smart fellow."

"Let's go. He'll disappear over that slope soon."

Billy trudged across the field, tired from not enough sleep. He and his folks had talked well into the night. Jamie was excited about the hiding place, but Pa just kept shaking his head. Billy wished Ma wouldn't cry so much. He was glad he had tiptoed into her bedroom this morning. She was still asleep when he leaned over and kissed her on top of her head. Then Ma opened her eyes, still red and puffy, and smiled at him. Right then he decided to whittle something special, just for her. Most likely a flower; maybe Sweet William, her favorite. Besides, the name would make her think of him. Things was real bad. He wished he'd never signed up for the army. And while Mary was real nice to him, he still missed his friends.

Billy raced the last few yards to the farmhouse and, careful not to waken Mary, quietly opened the door. The kitchen was dark and barn cold. He filled the stove with kindling, struck a match across its surface, tossed it in, and latched the door. He added a few split pieces of wood to the fire, waited until he was satisfied it was burning well, then left the kitchen and headed toward the barn.

The barn door creaked and groaned as Billy pushed its bulk along the track, latching the hook on the outside wall. Sunlight rushed in ahead of him, and the scent of hay filled his nostrils. The pigs squealed and scampered across the floor. He picked up a pitchfork and walked to the haystack.

"Private Laird!"

Lieutenant Walker stood in the barn's doorway, a towering outline against the morning sun.

Air sucked from Billy's lungs. Cold, raw fear devoured him.

The officer's eyes bore down on him like a hawk ready to strike. Then the officer moved slowly toward him.

Billy's hands tightened around the handle of the fork.

Walker took another step closer. "Private Laird, I'm an officer in the discharge of my duty. I'm here to arrest you as a deserter. Drop the pitchfork—that's an order!"

Billy heard the stern command, but he couldn't move. His body felt locked, fastened to the floorboards. He swallowed, but his throat was dry. He looked down at the fork, its prongs now pointed squarely at the officer. His knuckles ached as he squeezed the handle.

Suddenly there was a different voice. Billy jerked his head and saw two other men enter the barn. They weren't wearing uniforms.

"Son," said Hanson as he stepped forward. His tone was low, almost friendly. "Do as he says: drop the fork."

Billy stared at the stranger, perplexed. Lieutenant Walker lifted the pistol slowly from his holster.

"Drop it, son. Go ahead, it's all right," Hanson repeated with a shake of his head at the lieutenant.

Billy loosened his grip, and suddenly the officer lurched forward, yanking the pitchfork from his hands.

Cold, heavy, iron shackles snapped around his wrists. The men were on top of him, grabbing him, pushing him across the yard. His legs weakened. He stumbled. He was jerked back onto his feet. *Pa! Help me. I'm scared.*

"We'll watch the prisoner while you get the horses," Walker said to Waterhouse.

"Can I-I-I see Mary?" Billy heard himself ask as he was dragged across the barnyard.

"Mary who? Does she live here?"

"Mary Rogers. This is her farm."

"The teacher?" Walker stole a glance at Hanson. "No, you can't see her. Now get moving."

"Ah, let him see her, Lieutenant. He's ironed," said Hanson. "He's not going anywhere."

Lieutenant Walker tugged at the shackles. "All right, Private, you can go inside—but be quick about it. And leave the door open so we can see you." Billy tried to slow his breathing, stop the trembling in his knees. Slowly, he walked to the farmhouse steps, dazed. Inside, he stood before the mantel. The pistol. It was still lying there, shiny and bright.

Footsteps clattered down the staircase, startling him.

Frightened, Billy picked the pistol up with his shackled hands.

"Billy, whatever is happening? What's wrong?" cried Mary as she ran into the room, pulling the sash of her robe around her. He saw her eyes widen, heard her gasp in shock. "Oh, Lord, Billy, put that thing down!" Mary screamed.

"I-I-I . . . Mary—the army . . ."

He saw her turn and run from the room and out onto the porch. He thought he heard her voice shouting in panic, then footsteps loud, heavy, racing up the steps.

251

He tried to cock the pistol, tried to place his thumb on the hammer.

"Put the gun down, Private Laird." Lieutenant Walker moved cautiously into the room, his eyes fixed on the barrel.

Billy stared at the gun in his hand. It looked so shiny against the heavy irons around his wrists. He tossed the pistol from his hand, heard it crash against the chair.

Then pushing, shoving. Sunlight. He was hoisted in the air, legs lifted over a saddle, boots pushed into a stirrup. Where was he going? He blinked, but everything was still blurry. His horse lurched forward. Billy closed his eyes and slumped forward.

It was all over now.

Chapter 30

"Major Gardiner, sir?" said the lieutenant as he knocked on the door to the provost marshal's office. Provost marshal John Gardiner glanced up from his desk. "Come in," he said briskly. "Have we finally received word from the Department of the East about the disposition of our prisoner?"

"Yes, sir." Lieutenant Libby flashed the letter in his hand. "General Wool's adjutant, Christensen, dispatched the orders." He looked at his superior officer. "Would you like me to read it to you?"

"Go ahead."

"Special order, number seventy-five," he began, clearing his throat. "A general court-martial is hereby appointed to meet at Augusta, Maine, on the third day of June next at ten A.M. for the trial of such persons as may be brought before it by authority from these headquarters—"

"Three June?" the major interrupted. "We've been waiting for over a month to hear anything, and suddenly we have orders to hold this court-martial in a matter of days?" The provost marshal pushed away from his desk and paced heavily across the floor. "Is there a detail of the court?"

"Yes, sir, the representatives have been named. All from different regiments. And First Lieutenant Frederic E. Shaw of the Seventh Maine, Artillery, is the judge advocate." The aide continued reading. "No other officers than these named can be assembled without manifest injury to the service. Should any of the officers named in the detail be unable to attend, the court will nevertheless proceed to and continue the business before it, provided the names present be not less than the minimum prescribed by law." He folded the letter in half. "That's it, sir."

Major Gardiner turned back to his desk. "Notify this adjutant that we have received the special order. Tell him, however, that it will be impossible to assemble the names listed on the detail of the court by June third, and that I will forward the earliest date for the court-martial thereafter."

"Yes, sir."

"Private Laird's been held here for a long enough time as it is. How is the prisoner doing?" asked Gardiner.

"Lonely—pretty low since his folks' last visit. Doesn't talk much. But he is slow, after all."

"I'm not sure they'll be back in Augusta again. Quite a scene we had with them. I told the father the matter was out of my hands. Suggested they write the president—had to give the old farmer some hope."

"Shall I start contacting the names listed for the detail of the court?"

"Absolutely; but with the troop and supply movements toward Gettysburg, we'll be lucky if this is over and done with in a month's time."

The court-martial convened on July 2.

"Having the case of George W. Kimball, Fifth Battery, Maine Volunteers, disposed of, the court will now proceed to the trial of Private William H. Laird of Company G, Seventeenth Maine Regiment, Maine Volunteers," said the clerk of the court as he read the special order.

First Lieutenant Frederic Shaw, 1st Maine Volunteers, Artillery, leaned forward in his chair. "The court will excuse

Lieutenant Nathan Walker from serving as a member of the court in the case of William H. Laird, being that he serves as a witness to this case," he said. "The clerk may call Private Laird into the court at this time."

Billy walked beside his attending guard and stood alone before the table of men in blue. It was just like Pa had told him it would be. He sat alone, facing a table of officers. Pa said the officers would hear him out, and then decide if Billy was guilty or not. Pa said he could ask for something, so he wouldn't be alone, but in his nervousness, Billy couldn't remember what to ask for. He lowered his head when the judge peered over his half-rim glasses and looked at him. The judge spoke in a heavy, slow voice as he read the special order, and the names of the men who sat at the long table in front of him.

"This court is now convened," Judge Shaw said. "Private Laird, do you have any objections to any member named therein?"

"No, sir," Billy answered, his voice wavering with uncertainty.

Judge Shaw turned to the members of the court and duly swore each one in, then called on John Freese as president of the court, to duly swear in the judge advocate.

Judge Shaw announced he would read the charges and specifications.

"Charge First: Desertion, Specification First: In this that the said Private William H. Laird of Company G, Seventeenth Regiment, Maine Volunteers, being duly enlisted on or about August fifth, 1862, and mustered into the service of the United States, on or about August eighteenth, 1862, at Portland, Maine, did desert the said service on or about the fifteenth day of October, 1862, at or near White Oak Church, Virginia, and was arrested as a deserter on or about the twenty-third day of May, 1863, at or near Berwick, Maine."

The judge coughed lightly and cleared his throat.

"Charge Second: Violation of the Ninth Article of War, Specification First: In this that the said Private William H. Laird of Company G, Seventeenth Regiment, Maine Volunteers, did with a weapon in his hands, known as a manure fork, forcibly resist and offer violence against his superior officer, Lieutenant Nathan Walker of the Fifth Regiment, Maine Volunteers, he being then and there in the execution of his office. All this on or about the twenty-third day of May, 1863, at or near Berwick, Maine.

"Specification Second: In this that the said Private William H. Laird, Company G, Seventeenth Regiment, Maine Volunteers, did after having been arrested as a deserter and placed in irons succeed in drawing a pistol and did attempt and try to shoot his superior officer, Lieutenant Nathan Walker of the Fifth Regiment, Maine Volunteers, he being then and there in the execution of his office. All this at or near Berwick, Maine, on or about May twenty-third, 1863."

Judge Shaw let the paper slip from his fingers and, peering over his glasses, asked in a brisk voice, "How does the accused plead to Charge First, Specification First?"

Billy shook his head in confusion and frowned at the judge. "Desertion?" he asked.

The judge nodded.

"Guilty." Billy's voice was barely audible. He tried to swallow. He wanted to speak, to say he was sorry for deserting, but the judge held up a hand to silence him.

"And how does the accused plead to the Specification First, Charge Second?" No expression marked the judge's face. He glanced down at his papers in his hand. "Resist arrest with a manure fork," he quickly added.

Billy stiffened his shoulders. *I was holding it is all.* "Not guilty."

"And to the Charge Second, Specification Second?"

Billy looked questioningly at the judge.

"Drawing a pistol at your superior officer."

"Not guilty." Billy shook his head wildly. *Counsel! That's what he was supposed to ask for!*

"Sir?"

"What is your question, Private?"

"I'm wantin' counsel."

Judge Shaw grunted and glanced at the members of the court. "This court will close for deliberation of the accused's request for the privilege of counsel. The clerk will escort the accused from the room and remain with the prisoner until the court reconvenes."

Billy stood in the hallway. He wasn't sure he could walk back into the courtroom and face the men at the table alone. It didn't seem fair that Pa couldn't be there to help him. He bit at his fingernails and tried to breathe evenly. The sun was beating in the bare windows, the heat almost unbearable. Already Billy's shirt was soaked in sweat. When the clerk came for him, he stood, wiped his sweaty palms down the sides of his trousers, and followed him into the room.

"After mature deliberation, the court has granted the accused the privilege of counsel," said Judge Shaw. "The court has appointed Lieutenant Parker as the accused's defense for the duration of this trial."

Billy stared at the young man in uniform who walked over to his table and sat down beside him. The officer was short, and had fine, brown hair that hung limply over his ears. Billy waited for his counsel to turn and speak to him, but the man stared directly ahead with not so much as a glance in Billy's direction.

"Lieutenant Nathan Walker will come forward as a witness for the prosecution," announced Judge Shaw.

Billy stole a glance at the lieutenant who had arrested him, watched him stand before the members of the court.

The judge began. "Please state your name and rank."

"Nathan Walker, First Lieutenant, Fifth Maine Volunteers."

"State the particulars of the arrest of the prisoner William H. Laird about the twenty-third of May, 1863, at Berwick," the judge advocate asked.

"I was sent from headquarters at Augusta to arrest the prisoner before the twenty-third of May; I'd been after him for two or three days. I arrested him at Berwick between eleven and twelve o'clock at a house by the name of Rogers, I think. He was hauling hay in the barn. I was concealed in the woods. He was a hard man to find, as he was in hiding. I approached him and told him I was an officer in the discharge of my duty and had come to arrest him as a deserter. He had the manure fork in his hands. I told him to lay the fork down, but he was not inclined to put it down. I took hold of it and tried to get it away. He held the fork in an attitude of defense and resistance. I held my pistol in my hand and took hold of the fork and twitched it away from him and threw it down. I then ironed him.

"He then wanted the privilege of seeing a lady in the house as the folks had gone away. He went into the house, to the parlor or living room. I stood on the steps talking with Mr. Waterhouse and Mr. Hanson of Great Falls. The lady of the house suddenly rushed by me, looking pale and gasping. I rushed in the door, and as I went in, he changed his position and had a pistol in his hand which he was trying to cock with his hands—as well as he could, with them handcuffed. I ran toward him, and before I got to him, he threw the pistol to a chair. I took the pistol and led him outdoors. I took him to Augusta. The pistol was loaded and half-cocked and cupped when I took it. I took the cup off in the car. It appeared good. Cyrus Waterhouse and Mr. Hanson went with me."

Billy startled as his counsel pushed back his chair and stood, nervously tapping a pencil on the edge of the table. After what seemed to Billy a long hesitation, his counsel spoke. "Are you positive that the prisoner pointed the pistol at you?"

Lieutenant Walker averted the counsel's eyes, as if speaking directly to the judge. "He stood at an angle, quartering, at work cocking the pistol."

"Can you say that the prisoner attempted to cock the pistol?"

"He had the pistol in his hands, and I saw his thumb on the hammer, working it."

"After you clinched him, did Laird show any further resistance?"

"He did not."

"No further questions." The counsel sat down.

Billy stared at his counsel. Tugged at his arm. "You wantin' to ask me questions, sir?" he asked.

The counsel turned his face to the members of the court.

Billy wasn't sure what was happening. The clerk of the court once again escorted him out of the room. His counsel was right behind him, but when they reached the hallway, the officer walked away, disappearing into another room. Only when the clerk told him the court was making its decision did Billy understand that his court-martial was nearly over. He wished desperately he could talk to his folks. *If only Harry were here.* Harry always made things right.

In minutes the door was pushed open, and the clerk escorted Billy back into the courtroom. Billy stood alone before the court, head slightly bowed, hands trembling, not wanting to see the faces of the men in front of him.

Judge Shaw called out his name. "Private William Laird. With regard to the following charges, the court finds the following verdicts: Charge First, guilty. Charge First, Specification First, guilty. Charge Second, Specification First, guilty. Charge Second, Specification Second, guilty."

Silence. Billy did not raise his head.

"I do therefore sentence you, Private William H. Laird, of Company G, Seventeenth Regiment, Maine Volunteers, to be shot to death with musketry. The execution will take place no later than July fifteenth, 1863, on the grounds of Fort Preble, Maine."

Chapter 31

Gulls circled overhead as a platoon of construction workers toiled in the hot July sun on the clamorous grounds of Fort Preble. The old revolutionary fort was under expansion, and its redbrick buildings above the beach offered a striking contrast against the backdrop of blue water and islands of towering pine. Garrison sentinels paced the perimeter of the open fort, guarding the entrance to the Fore River and the strategic waterfront of Portland Harbor.

From his office in Cates Hall, Major George Andrews gazed out at the bay and then turned to Provost Marshal Gardiner. "Any problems I need to know about with regard to the prisoner?"

Gardiner shook his head. "No, Major. He's pretty subdued. Didn't say a word on the train down from Camp Keyes."

"I'll report to headquarters in New York that the prisoner has arrived at the post."

"General Wool requests that the proceedings of the execution be as private as possible, sir."

The veins on Andrews's neck bulged, and his face reddened in anger. "Keep the execution private? Nearly impossible!" he shouted. "Need I remind the general that the security of the Rebel prisoners now here requires one-half of my force for guard each day? Look out the window! The post is under expansion. I have several engineers at work, as well as a hundred and fifty civilian employees out there. There are as many entrances to the fort as there are individuals desiring to enter. And I have nothing but a chain of sentinels encircling the garrison to keep them out!" Andrews stormed back to his desk and picked up two newspapers. "And if that isn't enough to illustrate how news circulates around here, look! Already the morning and evening editions have articles about Private Laird. The public is well aware we are about to execute one of their own boys."

Gardiner threw Andrews a puzzled look. "What are you suggesting, Major?"

Andrews tossed the papers onto his desk. "Perhaps General Wool could decide to send the prisoner to Fort Independence or some other isolated or enclosed post if he desires this execution to be private. He would have to detail his own guard, however. I have neither officers nor men sufficient to furnish such a guard without jeopardizing the safekeeping of the prisoners of war."

"I do not think the general will transfer the prisoner. Perhaps you have no stomach for this, Major?"

Major Andrews shrugged his shoulders. "I know of no other Maine soldier who has been shot for desertion—and God knows, there are hundreds of Maine deserters!"

"I have no quarrel with his sentence."

"The orders will be carried out, Provost, but perhaps you are right—I have no stomach for this execution." He turned sharply and walked to the office door. "Good day."

Billy clutched an unopened paper bag as he sat on his hard wooden cot, leaning his head against the cool slab wall of the tiny cell. He sniffled and rubbed his runny nose against the sleeve of his shirt, his loneliness greater since the visit with his family had ended just minutes ago. He agonized about his ma, how she cried the moment she saw him, pressing her fingers gently on his cheeks, fussing over the darkened circles beneath his eyes. No one talked much, except about the pardon they hoped would still come from President Lincoln, late as it was. Pa said not to give up hope, and then he read from the Bible, but that just made Ma cry even more. Leastways Jamie brought the checkerboard. It took Billy's mind off things. And for the first time ever Jamie let him play with the black checkers. Billy shook his head slowly from side to side, wondering if he won because he got to play with the black ones. Best of all, Jamie didn't even take a fit when he jumped all them red checkers clear across the board.

The silence was heavy in his small cell. Patting his shirt pocket, Billy pulled out a letter, unfolded it, and stared at the words, even though he could not read them. He knew what the letter said, having asked Ma to read it over and over again. He glanced at the signatures scrawled across the bottom, knowing they belonged to Harry, Josh, and Charlie. He replayed the thoughts again in his mind. His friends coming home, promising to take him fishing; swimming at Frog Pond. Said they would all go back to Virginia some day after the war, find Leighton's grave, and bring him back to Maine. Then Harry went and thanked him for helping Mary while she was alone. Billy smiled, comforted by the last few lines, insisting Ma read them until he knew them all by heart: *You've been a real good friend, Billy Boy. We know how much you tried to be a good soldier. And in our hearts we know how brave your efforts were.* He carefully folded the letter and placed it back in his pocket.

Billy glanced at the paper bag on his cot, reached in, and grabbed a piece of ginger candy. He had no appetite for his supper, but the sugary ginger tasted sweet on his tongue. In spite of the heat, he shivered and crossed his arms over his chest, his hands cupping his elbows. There was nothing else to do but wait for the darkness.

"Private Laird." Major Andrews peered at him from outside his cell.

Billy blinked and rubbed his eyes. He must have been dozing; a half-eaten piece of candy lay crushed in his hand. He stared at the officer, only vaguely remembering him from when he'd first arrived at Fort Preble.

"I understand you didn't eat any supper tonight. Is there anything you'd like now?"

Billy glanced at the window high over his bed. It was dark outside. "Yes, sir—I'm wantin' to see the stars," he said, surprised by the strange expression on the officer's face.

"You mean, you want to go outside?"

"Yes, sir."

"Nothing to eat?"

"No, sir."

"All right, Private. I'll send one of the guards in here. He can take you to the parade ground."

"Thank you kindly, sir."

Andrews lowered his head and stepped back from the cell, turned, and walked away. Then he stopped and turned around. "You'll have to be shackled, Private," he said before he disappeared through the doorway.

I'm gonna see the stars! His heart racing with excitement, Billy leaped to the floor, pushed the blanket aside, and reached under the cot. With trembling hands he slipped his stocking feet into his boots and leaned impatiently against the cell bars.

Unsullied by clouds, the sky was profuse with stars. Billy stood in the middle of the parade ground, the far end of the lush green field rolling into the bay, the moonlight cutting a wavy golden path over the ocean swells. A lighthouse beacon shot through the darkness. He breathed deeply of the ocean air. It felt good to stand beneath the night sky again. He turned his head and glanced at the guard, briefly watched him pull a thin slip of paper from his jacket, open a pouch, and roll a cigarette. The guard didn't seem to be in a hurry.

Billy studied the millions of stars, searching for the large cluster shaped like a ladle. He turned in all directions, anxious nerves pulsing through him. He followed a shooting star as it fell below an island in the bay. *That ol' star's all used up—she's gonna splash right into the sea, I'm thinkin'.*

"You seen enough, Private?" shouted the guard through the dark as he flicked his cigarette to the ground, stubbing it into the grass with the toe of his boot.

"No, sir. Please, I'm needin' more time, if it's all right."

"Sure. What are you looking for anyway?"

"Shooting stars is all." He didn't want to tell the guard about the North Star, and Elijah, and carefully moved a few steps away from him. The iron irritated his hands. Again, he searched, worried he would run out of time before he found the North Star.

A faint voice whispered in his head.

Billy, suh, the North Star, she right over there! She low in the sky now.

Elijah? Had he heard him call? Instinctively, Billy took a few steps forward, lowered his gaze, and stared straight out into the bay. *I see the Big Dipper. I see her!* He raised his shackled hands and, using his forefinger, traced the dipper's ladle down until it crossed the bowl. From there he stretched his neck and looked a little higher. The North Star sparkled. He felt his skin tingle; his lips formed silent words. *Elijah? I'm right here—under the*

North Star. They're gonna shoot me tomorrow. Just like Leighton said. Elijah, I ain't ever gonna see you again. I know you'll be comin' soon. For sure Ma and Pa will take you in. I told them all about you. And Jamie, well, you remember our promise? He won't have a big brother no more. Will you take him fishin'? I went and whittled you a fish—put a spear right through it. Jamie's keepin' it for you. Oh, if you play checkers with him, you have to jump all his checkers before he—

"Let's go, Private," the guard called out in the darkness. He walked over and yanked at Billy's irons.

Billy walked slowly behind him. At the edge of the parade ground he turned and looked back up at the sky. *Good-bye, Elijah.* He raised his shackled hands and tapped his fists against his chest. *Right there, Elijah, right there.*

"You find yourself a shooting star, Laird?"

"Yes, sir. Yes I did."

Major Andrews sipped his coffee and paced across the floor while the anxious lieutenant sorted through the mail pouch.

"No word from General Wool about my request to transfer the prisoner to Fort Independence?"

"No, sir, strange in fact—there's nothing at all from head-quarters," answered the lieutenant as he hurriedly sifted through the mail. "Hmmm . . . Here's something interesting." He handed the paper to the major.

Major Andrews put his cup down and quickly read the letter. "Draft riots? There are reports of draft riots in New York. The rioters have control of the trains and omnibuses at the moment. General Wool obviously has his hands full if that's the case."

"That explains why nothing is coming through—not even telegraphs if they have control of the stations," said the lieutenant.

266

"Yes, it would seem so. Well, I'm sure the general will have this quelled in short order." Andrews sighed deeply and stared out the window at the bright blue morning. "Everything's in order for the execution?" he asked with a hint of sadness.

"Yes, sir. As you directed, there will be a volley of twelve—one blank will be fired. And the ramparts have been secured, Major."

"Good. I don't want any citizens trying to witness this. That Reverend Snow will accompany Private Laird. He has convinced the family to remain at the train station and await the arrival of the coffin. We can't afford to have a scene. It's already affected the morale of the soldiers here; some are even sympathetic, and grieving parents are not something we need to deal with."

The lieutenant nodded. "The coffin's assembled. One of the workers completed it yesterday. Any chance for a pardon from the president, sir?"

Andrews shook his head. "The fields of Gettysburg are not yet cold, Lieutenant. It would seem impossible that the president has had anything else on his mind these past weeks. And we have heard nothing." He turned and stared intensely at his aide. "Tell the firing squad to pierce the heart. I don't want to see a wounded soldier slumped over his own coffin."

"Billy."

Hearing his name, Billy rolled over on the cot and rubbed his eyes. He glanced up, pleased it was Reverend Snow, his wavy white hair brushed neatly away from his face. Billy swung his legs over the side of the bed as the guard opened the cell and let the reverend in. Then the door clanged shut, and the guard stepped away.

"Did I get me a pardon, Reverend?"

Reverend Snow sat down beside him and slowly shook his head. "We have heard nothing, my son." He placed his hand on Billy's knee and forced a smile.

"Where are my folks?"

"They are waiting just a short distance from here, and still hoping, Billy. They are with you in spirit and love this morning. I will be by your side—that we may pray together."

"Then I'm gonna die?"

The reverend nodded slowly. "But you will see God today, my son."

"You said we ought not to fear death, Reverend Snow. But God is angry with me, I'm thinkin'—what with me desertin' and all."

Reverend Snow leaned his back against the cold wall. "That is not the God I know, Billy. God loves you. God is not angry with you. He is very forgiving—especially when we own up to our mistakes."

"But I didn't hurt Lieutenant Walker! I was holdin' the pitchfork before he came is all."

"Yes, I know."

"And the gun—I ain't even rememberin' holdin' that." He wiped the back of his hand across his eyes. "Does God know that?"

"Oh, yes, Billy, God knows that very well, and I'm sure you were very frightened. Our mind has a way of protecting us from remembering fearful things."

"Why did God make me this way? Why ain't I smart? Why ain't I like Harry?" He turned his face to the ceiling, ran his fingers through his hair.

Reverend Snow cast a long look at the opposite wall. He hesitated for several moments before he spoke. "God makes people in all kinds of ways—tall, handsome, short, not pretty, strong, weak. We don't all have the same collection of gifts. But each of us has a gift of God's work." He turned and placed his arm around Billy's shoulders, hugging him close to his chest. "God gave you a good soul, Billy. And a very brave one. I remember how you saved Josh from almost drowning at Frog Pond. The others, including Harry, did not see what you saw. And you rushed into the water without regard for yourself, pulling Josh to safety."

"Like I done with Elijah."

"Elijah was drowning?"

"Yes, sir. In Goose Creek. I pulled him out."

Reverend Snow smiled. "There, you see, Billy. God made you very special indeed."

"Why did God make Elijah a slave?"

"The real Elijah is much more than a slave, Billy. That was the work of men, not God."

"Elijah says God's gonna help the little people." His eyes widened and he turned to face the reverend. "I saw the North Star last night!"

"You were outside?" The old man's eyebrows arched in surprise.

Billy nodded. "Guard came and took me to the parade ground."

"The North Star is very important to you, isn't it, son?"

"Yes, sir. Elijah and me, we followed it when we was in the woods."

The reverend smiled and folded his hands in front of his robe. "A very long time ago, others followed a star. Do you remember what star that was?"

"No, sir."

"It was the Bethlehem Star. The Wise Men followed the star to find Jesus, in much the same way that you and Elijah followed the North Star. The star was a gift from God." Reverend Snow sighed deeply and placed his hand over Billy's. "Today, Billy, you must follow the star again. You must follow its perfect light to see God."

"What's it gonna be like—I mean, dyin' and all?"

"I don't really know; the Bible does not tell us. But it does promise us that there is something more. Jesus said that he who believeth in God will have eternal life."

"I ain't understandin' so good."

The reverend chose his words more carefully. "Jesus tells us there is something after this life for us. And those who have gone before us are now in heaven. You must take comfort in knowing that there are friends in heaven who are waiting for you."

"You mean Leighton? And Jeb? Am I gonna see them, Reverend?"

"Yes, Billy, you will see them."

They sat together, huddled on the cot throughout the long morning. Billy refused his lunch, choosing instead his last pieces of ginger candy. Just before two o'clock, guards entered the cell. Behind them Major Andrews stood silent. As they latched his hands in the irons, Billy turned to Reverend Snow, hesitating to move in spite of a nudge from one of the guards. Not until Reverend Snow moved in beside him did he walk away from the cell.

Tufts of clouds drifted across the warm summer sky. Billy stepped down the porch stairs and onto the dirt pathway, one guard in front of him and one behind. Ahead, Major Andrews and Dr. Tewksbury, the post surgeon, walked briskly over a long green rise, past hedges of wild roses and down steps of flattened stone to the ramparts overlooking the sea and a sweeping rocky shore.

"May God comfort you, Billy, and wrap his arms around you," Reverend Snow prayed as he clutched his Bible to his chest.

Major Andrews walked to the center of the ramparts and stopped beside a lone pine coffin. Against the seawall, a line of twelve men stood motionless, muskets at their side.

"Private Laird, you will kneel beside the coffin," said Major Andrews. Billy froze.

The guards moved forward, escorted Billy to the center of the green, and eased him to his knees.

Billy raised his face to Reverend Snow before the blindfold wrapped over his eyes.

Darkness. "Reverend Snow—"

"When thou passest through the waters, I will be with thee; and through the rivers, they shall not overflow thee; when thou walkest through the fire, thou shalt not be burned; neither shall the flame kindle upon thee." The reverend's voice was tremulous.

"God is close, Billy. He asks you to have courage, to die with love."

"Reverend—"

"Look for the star, Billy. Follow its light. Your friends are waiting—go with love, my son."

Then it was silent.

He thought he heard a crack, the sharp crack of musketry.

271

Billy Boy

Dr. Tewksbury leaned over and examined the lifeless body slumped over the coffin. "Put him in, boys." Turning to Major Andrews, he spoke in a low tone. "Five, Major. Five to the heart."

Chapter 32

Cranberry Meadow Road wound through rock-strewn pastures, and fields of ripened corn rose gently over the granite hillside. Brightened by the early morning rain,
blue-stemmed goldenrod bloomed in the meadows.

The endless rows of corn triggered painful memories for
Elijah. A year ago he was on his belly, crawling through wither-
ing stalks and feeding on rotting corn, worried that bloodhounds hard on his scent would plunge across the field and tear
his body to shreds. Now he had his own room, a real bed with
crisp white sheets, and a goose-down pillow. Had Billy not
found him on the banks of the creek—he shook the cobwebs
from his mind, squinted as sunlight streamed on his face. He
still reveled in his hard-won freedom. *Billy, suh! Elijah almost
there, just like he promise.*

It had not been easy to keep his promise. His new friends in
Canada had warned him it would be a dangerous journey,
pleaded with him not to go. Only Molly, the missus of the
boardinghouse, understood his unflappable promise to Billy.
She watched Elijah on cloudless nights walk into the field
behind the boardinghouse, lie on the grass, and gaze at the stars
for hours at a time.

His new home in Canada was not far from the New York
border, and only a three- or four-day walk to Burlington,
Vermont, where he was told he could find refuge at the
Wheeler farm, a station still active in harboring runaways.

Elijah rested at the Wheelers' for two days before he set out for Littleton, New Hampshire, a small town along the Ammonoosuc River in the middle of the White Mountains. Mr. Wheeler said the Carleton house there was the only known station along the careful route he had sketched for him.

Elijah was awestruck by the emerald green countryside, its pastures marked by endless walls of piled stone, abundant dairy farms so unlike the plantations of his southern fields. At night he slept on the cool grass, content to share the meadows with the grazing herds, comforted by the occasional clanging of their harness bells. To Elijah's delight, on the morning of his departure from Littleton, old Edmund Carleton hitched his horses to his buckboard and the two set out for Crawford Notch. For several miles they plodded over forested hills before the road opened onto sprawling alpine meadows against a backdrop of ragged mountains. Carleton slowed his wagon before the road disappeared through a narrow pass that dropped sharply through the mountains. "This here's the Notch," he told Elijah as he pointed his finger. "See them red and yellow tips on the leaves below? Starting in to change already. Another few weeks and the whole pass will look like she's on fire. Mostly oak, birch, and maple down through the ravine."

Elijah had never seen a sight more beautiful, and he tried to imagine the green forest ablaze with color. He listened to the sound of water rushing below.

"You'll pick up the Saco River near the bottom of the Notch. Follow her like your best friend," Carleton had cautioned. "She gets her water from the mountains and flows nice and easy to the sea. Reckon it's about a three-day walk from here. Once you see that blue Atlantic, you'll find the railroad nearby—follow the tracks south. Berwick's not but a day's walk from where the Saco River ends her run."

The cool forests offered Elijah comfort against the late summer warmth, and the old man, who seemed to enjoy fussing over him, had packed his knapsack full of dried meat and carrots and tomatoes fresh picked from his garden. Elijah drank from the clear mountain-fed river and rested under the shade of the birches leaning delicately over its banks. Slowly the White Mountains faded behind him, and he watched with fascination the river cutting through tall and flowering grasslands, flattening at last into an expanse of sand and marsh rolling into the sea. It was his first look at the ocean. He wanted to stay and study it longer, but he didn't want to delay. Maybe Billy would take him back here to see it some more. He found the railway tracks easily, and hurried off on the last leg of his journey. Children playing on the tracks told him he was in Berwick. Giggling and staring, the children gave him directions to Cranberry Meadow Road.

The road climbed a long hill. Stone walls edged the roadside, and leafy maple trees cooled the way from the heat of the summer sun. When he reached the crest, Elijah stopped to catch his breath and, wiping the sweat from his brow, scanned the forested valley below. He saw the Little River; Billy had described it well. A small lane, almost hidden by the pines, branched off the main road just before the bridge. Elijah's heart thumped rapidly, his legs pulsed as he raced down the hill. The lane cut a path to a white clapboard farmhouse.

Before he reached the house, Elijah brushed the dust from his trousers and tucked his shirt into his waist. He heard a door slam shut, then footsteps racing down the porch steps. Above a hedge of rosebushes, Elijah glimpsed a sandy brown head moving his way.

"Billy, suh!" he shouted. "Elijah here!"

A blue-eyed child peeked slowly around the bush and then took a cautious step forward, one hand clutching a wooden toy.

Elijah gasped at the child's striking resemblance to Billy. "You must be Jamie, suh?"

With a frightened look, the boy drew back. He said nothing.

Elijah glanced at the toy clutched in the boy's hands. A fish. With a spear in its belly.

"Billy, suh, go and whittle that fish you got in your hand?"

Blue eyes flashed back at him. The child grimaced; looking down at the carving, he hastily whisked it behind his back.

Across the farmyard a door opened and slammed. Jamie turned and ran.

Elijah looked away. A sense of unease welled inside him. He stared out across the fields. Finally, Elijah got up his nerve to walk to the porch. Standing in a patch of sunlight, Elijah stood at the foot of the steps.

From the porch railing, John Laird stared down at him, his eyes hard and piercing.

"Mistah Laird?"

"Who are you?"

"Elijah, Mistah Laird."

"Elijah? Billy's—I'll be damned!" Calling out to his wife, John Laird nearly stumbled as he hurried down the steps.

"Never thought—Elijah—well, I'm mighty glad to see you," John said, extending his hand. "You come all this way—from Canada?"

"Yes, suh. Elijah keep his promise to Billy, suh."

The smile vanished from John's face.

Nothing was as Elijah expected. And where was Billy?

Then the missus came down the steps and smiled. "I'm Billy's ma. It's good to finally meet you, Elijah," she said. "Come, sit with us." Elijah turned to Billy's pa, relieved to see him nod and motion him up the steps. But Jamie darted past him and out of sight, disappearing behind a pile of wood stacked on the porch.

"Don't pay no mind to Jamie—he ain't doing so good right now," John Laird said as he reached for a matchbox from his shirt pocket. With a trembling hand he lit the match against the heel of his boot. "Thing is, we're all having a hard time right now. Elijah, have a seat."

Elijah sat down on a rocker and stirred nervously while Billy's pa took a long draw on his pipe.

"Billy's gone from us," said John Laird, his voice cracking.

"Gone, Mistah Laird?"

"Army shot him—near a month ago."

"Oh, no, suh!" Elijah leaped from the rocker, stumbled across the porch, and ran down the steps. Instinct told him to run, but fear and shock overcame him, and he found himself unable to move. Bile churned in his stomach. He didn't know how long he stood there, his mind blurring with images of Billy. Finally he pressed his fingertips hard against his temples.

Elijah felt an arm across his back, and he knew it was Billy's ma. He felt her softness as she pulled him close. He stiffened but did not pull away.

"Billy talked about you often, Elijah. Said you would come here someday." Martha Laird patted him gently on his back before she released her hold and stared into his face. "Come, let me show you something."

Unsure of what to do or say, yet warmed by her softness, Elijah followed Billy's ma across the barnyard. Stopping at the fence, she pointed to the sweeping meadow beyond. Elijah stared at the field sprinkled with patches of clover. What was it she wanted him to see?

"On clear nights Billy would lie down on his back, even on the snow, and stare up at those stars—near an hour sometimes. Said that was his way of talking to you."

Elijah swallowed hard and stared at the empty meadow. He turned his head and looked at Billy's ma. Grief was etched in deep lines across her otherwise pretty face.

"When night come, Elijah go into the fields, missus. Just like Billy, suh. Elijah talk to him just the same."

She offered a wan smile, and he thought he saw a sparkle in the paleness of her blue eyes. Billy's eyes. "He my friend, missus."

"I'm not sure Billy could have made it home if he hadn't met up with you. Billy thought you was mighty special."

"He first white folk ever nice to Elijah."

The sun dipped behind a bank of clouds and painted the meadowland black, mirroring the darkness Elijah felt in his soul as he stepped back onto the porch and sat on the edge of the rocking chair. He glanced up at Billy's pa as he started telling Elijah what had happened to Billy.

"We wrote to President Lincoln while Billy was in jail, asking for a pardon—well, what with Billy's learning problems . . . ," said Martha Laird.

"Oh, Billy, suh, he act more like a chile sometime, yes, missus. Elijah have to tell him what to do after a while."

Billy's ma nodded. "His friend Harry also wrote a letter to Mr. Lincoln," she said, clutching her chest. "We hear that Mr. Lincoln granted Billy a pardon, only word didn't arrive in time to save him."

"Why that, missus?"

"We understand the Irish rioted in New York against the draft—seized all the telegraph lines. Nothing got through," said John Laird as he leaned over in his rocker and tapped his pipe against the railing. "Riots only lasted three days, but they cost my son his life."

Elijah leaned his elbows on his knees, rested his head in his hands, and let out a huge sigh. "Mistah Still, he say Billy wear the badge of honor—from the colored folks. And now he dead."

"Whatever do you mean?" asked Martha Laird with a puzzled look.

"Elijah running from the slave catchers a long time. Then Elijah can't run no mo'. God almost take Elijah home. But Billy, suh, he come along. Elijah think he a slave catcher and fall in the creek. But Billy, suh, he save me, and then he go and build a fire and keep Elijah warm. Elijah wake and find Billy, suh's, jacket over him."

Billy's pa leaned forward in his chair. "He did tell us he took care of you." Elijah nodded. "Billy, suh, he take care of me good." He heard a low cry from behind the woodpile and turned as Jamie crept into sight.

Martha Laird buried her face in her hands.

"Well, now, Elijah," said John Laird as he stared vacantly into the sky. "I guess you just made us mighty proud today." Leaning over in his chair, he glanced at Jamie. "Son, did you hear what your big brother done?"

With a quick nod, Jamie stole a glance at Elijah before he plopped to the floor, turned his head, and began rocking back and forth.

"Elijah," said Billy's ma, "would you like to see where he's buried?"

"Yes, missus. Elijah want to see where Billy, suh, sleep now." Rising from the chair he walked slowly toward Jamie and, bending down, hands on his knees, spoke in a near whisper.

"Jamie, suh, want to go with Elijah?"

For an instant Jamie stilled, this time studying Elijah's face with curious innocence. Elijah could almost hear the questions rising in the child's throat and, feeling encouraged, waited for a response. But none came.

"Mebbe Elijah come and talk later."

The garden was still lush with late summer flowers sprouting among the dry stalks of earlier blooms, their pods withered and empty of seeds. Elijah watched the missus pick only a single red-and-white flower. As if reading his mind, she turned to him and smiled. "Sweet William. Billy always liked this flower."

"Elijah thinkin' he gone an' upset Jamie, suh," he said finally, out of sight of the child.

"No, Elijah," responded Billy's pa. "Jamie ain't been right since Billy died. Ain't said but a dozen words this past month. Doc says we got to be patient. Says he'll come around when he's ready."

"Jamie loved his big brother," said Martha Laird, twirling the Sweet William in her hand. "They had so much fun together. Like you said, Billy was more like a child at times. Then, when I hear you tell about what happened at the creek, I know there was a grown man inside him, too."

At the crest of the hill, they walked into a grove of birch trees that arched like a green-and-white canopy bed over a mound of earth. Billy's grave was marked with a wooden cross.

Raising the hem of her skirt and bending down to her knees, Billy's ma gently placed the sprig of Sweet William on the grave. Twigs scattered by the wind littered the site, and leaning over,

John Laird gathered them and tossed them aside. Then he turned back, straightened the cross, and patted the earth.

"Elijah, son, you stay here long as you please," he said. "I'm needing to take a walk now, along the riverbank, before we head on back to the farm."

He fidgeted at his pocket for his pipe. "Mrs. Laird will be fixing a good supper before long. We'd both be right pleased if you'd stay on at the farm for a while. It's what Billy would have wanted." Looping a hand through his wife's arm, John Laird helped her to her feet. "You think on it, Elijah."

Elijah nodded and offered a slight smile before he sat down on the ground beside the grave. Under the birches, finally, he cried. *Oh, Billy, suh. Here we be by a river again. Elijah don't know what to do, Billy, suh. Elijah wanted to stay with you for a time, and maybe Elijah think you come to Canada with him. Now what Elijah do?* Through the long winter and spring of his new life, Elijah had longed for summer, so he could go to Maine and find Billy, and maybe, just maybe, become part of a family. Never had he wanted anything more. Now he was all alone again.

He sat unmoving by the grave through the rest of the afternoon, watching the fields turn pink and yellow as the sun lowered. Perhaps he would stay for supper. Finally, he raised himself from the ground and stretched. He stared at the grave one last time. His head bowed, he uttered a simple prayer and whispered good-bye. He decided to walk to the river.

Maidenhair ferns flanked the riverbank. Picking up a stone, he tossed it into the middle, lost in his memories.

"What'd you do that for?" A child's voice called out behind him.

Elijah froze, wondered if he should turn around, afraid that the skittish child might retreat from him. He hesitated, then leaned over, and without glancing over his shoulder, picked up another stone and fingered it in his hands.

"See how far it go," he finally answered.

Moments passed in awkward silence.

"I can throw one far as I want."

Elijah stood still and from the corner of his eye, noticed the child's arms held behind his back, hiding something. He hesitated, then rolled back his arm and hurled the stone, listening to the hollow thump as it landed on a log floating in the middle of the river.

"Ain't so far," Jamie said. "I can throw one clear across."

"That so?"

"Yeah."

Elijah offered a slight glance and a nod of his head. "Mebbe you show Elijah how far you throw." He reached for a stone on the forest floor, turned, and held it out to him.

"Ain't wantin' to right now."

Elijah nodded, all the while rolling the stone in his palm.

"Billy could throw it clear across the river and then some," said Jamie. "I seen him do it. Threw it so far it went right through them trees and clear past that stone wall."

"Yes, suh, that be far, all right." Elijah let the stone fall through his fingers and drop to the ground, and then he placed his hands in his pockets. He stepped closer to the riverbank and hesitated. "Billy, suh, he talk a lot about you. He say Jamie, suh, right smart."

He heard the child take a step forward. A twig snapped beneath his feet.

"Billy said that?"

Jamie came up beside him and, placing a hand firmly on his trouser leg, squeezed the cloth. "What else did my brother say?"

"Billy, suh, he tell Elijah lots of things, like you playin' checkers. He say one time you go and turn all the hay for him when he run off to town. He say Jamie, suh, do his chores from time to time so he don't get no whuppin'.'"

Jamie's lips curled into a smile. "Yeah, I remember." He turned an eager face to Elijah. "Pa says you're stayin' for supper."

"Oh, now, Jamie, suh, Elijah just don't know." He shrugged his shoulders.

"Ma's fixin' a place for you."

"You want Elijah to stay?"

Jamie fixed his gaze to the ground. "Reckon. You like carrots?"

Elijah only nodded.

"Not me. Cooked ones that is. Billy liked 'em, so I used to sneak my carrots to him when Ma wasn't looking."

"Mebbe your ma be fixin' carrots today?" said Elijah.

"Yeah." Jamie kicked the golden needles, scattering them in heaps along the bank.

"Mebbe Jamie, suh, sneak his carrots to Elijah. But don't you be gettin' Elijah in trouble with the missus."

"I won't, I won't!" A streak of color flushed Jamie's cheeks and he ran to the water's edge, peering into the water. "Hey, did you really spear a fish?"

"Oh, Elijah done spear two fish—one for Billy, suh, and one for Elijah."

"How come you went and speared a fish for Billy?"

"Oh, Billy, suh, he didn't spear so good—he, well—he go and tell Elijah how to do it. But he sure move real good in the water."

Jamie shot a dogged glance, his eyes resolute. "My brother can swim better'n anyone."

283

"Yes, suh. Billy, suh, he swim real good. Mebbe you want to fish with Elijah and we use the spear only?" He winked at Jamie, but the child seemed not to have heard him.

A bird chirped overhead and swooped low over the river, landing on the stone wall. Hands clasped behind his back, Elijah stared at the dull brown bird as it pecked its way along the top of the wall. Suddenly something sharp jabbed his palm. Startled, he spun around.

Jamie had thrust the whittling into his hand.

"Billy made this for you. This here's the spear you caught them fish with."

"Yes, suh, it look just like that," he said as he turned the carving over and over and fingered the smooth wood. "This real nice whittlin'. But you keep it if you want."

Jamie's head shook back and forth. "Unh-unh. Billy wanted you to have it. He was gonna make me a three-masted schooner before he—" Suddenly Jamie plopped to the ground and stuck his thumb in his mouth. The child began to rock back and forth.

Elijah panicked. "Billy, suh, he say you learn me checkers."

"Billy said that?"

"Oh, yes, suh."

"Me and Billy, we was always playing checkers," he said.

Elijah dropped down on his knees. He pressed both hands gently on Jamie's shoulders but the rocking continued.

"One time Billy, suh, hold Elijah and we rock just like you. He hold me until Elijah stop. Just like Elijah gon' do for you, Jamie, suh. Then Elijah let go."

Jamie rocked for a long time, all the while feeling the pressure of Elijah's hands resting firmly on his shoulders. Finally, he yanked his thumb from his mouth and rubbed it dry against his trousers.

"I guess I can learn you checkers."

"Elijah like that." Slipping his arm from Jamie's shoulder, he reached for his hand. Small fingers wrapped tightly around his. Elijah eased them both up from the ground. "We go eat them carrots now, Jamie, suh."

Jamie giggled. Pointing the way, one hand clutched tightly in Elijah's, he led him along the river path until it turned abruptly away and into the forest.

"Billy, suh, he tell Elijah he got to use them black checkers."

"Them black checkers is mine. My brother didn't know how to play checkers so good." He turned to Elijah. "Billy thought it was them red checkers is why he couldn't win a game."

Elijah smiled in understanding, finding comfort in the child's uncanny likeness to Billy.

"Elijah?"

"Yes, Jamie, suh?"

"Billy said you was like his big brother."

"He say that?"

"Yeah." Jamie squeezed Elijah's hand. "You thinkin' maybe you would be my big brother now?"

A sharp ache passed through Elijah's chest. He stopped and squatted on the ground, cupping his hand under Jamie's lowered chin, raising his face until fragile blue eyes met brown.

"Elijah be wantin' that too—oh, yes, suh."

The path opened to the farm fields beyond, and Elijah turned his gaze to the top of the rise and the forest's edge where Billy lay.

Oh, Billy, suh, Elijah keep his promise. Look like Elijah go and help Jamie, suh, eat his carrots.

Billy Boy

A breeze had come up and Elijah turned his back to it, tucking the child close. His eyes watered, and using his free arm, he rubbed his moistened lids against his shirtsleeve. He raised his face to the river, his blurred vision catching a flower, withered red and white, lifting by him in the wind.

Elijah tapped a fisted hand against his chest as the sprig of Sweet William swirled past him into the lofty pines and drifted quietly into the river.

Afterword

In 1996, my husband, Bill, attended the funeral of one of his former U.S. Army Reserve commanders, Colonel Richard Stillings, a World War II veteran from Berwick, Maine. At the funeral Bill learned that Stillings had chronicled all of the town's veterans and during the course of his research, came across the unusual story of William H. "Billy" Laird, a private who served briefly in the 17th Regiment Infantry, Maine Volunteers, during the U.S. Civil War. My husband, who knows of my love of history and the U.S. Civil War, guessed correctly that this story would become my first book.

Over the next two years, I worked to uncover Billy's story. Intending at first to write a nonfiction account of his life, I conducted research and interviews in Maine, at the National Archives in Washington, D.C., and in Maryland. It soon became clear, however, that the only facts I could find about Billy's story were just the beginning and the end of it. I then set out to write a fictional account, while striving to keep it as factual as possible.

Here are the facts.

Billy Laird mustered with 1,370 other men in the 17th Regiment Infantry, Maine Volunteers, on August 18, 1862, at Camp King in Cape Elizabeth, Maine, according to Regimental Histories, Maine State Archives. For the next two months, Private Laird served with Company G along the Potomac River and then, according to his military service records held at the National Archives, he was reassigned to Livingston's Battery in

Edward's Ferry, Maryland. Historian William B. Jordan Jr., in his book, *The Red Diamond Regiment*, states that Laird "had been enlisted 'lacking in common intelligence' and illiterate." Berwick historians, including Robert Stillings (the brother of the late Colonel Stillings), say it was likely that Laird, found intellectually unfit for infantry, would be sent instead to work with horses. While Jordan cites that Laird was unhappy with his transfer, articles written about Laird by the late Colonel Stillings state that he was unhappy largely as a result of ridicule and his being the constant butt of jokes.

Private Laird deserted on October 15, 1862, two days after his transfer to Livingston's Battery. There the facts of this story come to an end until Laird is captured and arrested in Berwick, Maine, sometime on or about May 23, 1863.

The original transcript of Laird's court-martial, which convened at Camp Keyes in Augusta, Maine, on July 2, 1863, is held at the National Archives. The transcript notes that Laird had a gun in his hand when confronted by Lieutenant Walker but that he threw it down. Found guilty of desertion and sentenced to death by firing squad, he was transferred to Fort Preble, located in what is now South Portland, Maine.

In their writings, Jordan and Colonel Stillings suggest that Major General John E. Wool, Department of the East, issued a stay of execution for Laird pending an appeal to President Lincoln for clemency. Town lore also alludes to a presidential pardon. Ultimately, I found no documentation for a pardon from President Lincoln. However, during the Draft Riots in New York City, which began on July 13, 1863, and continued for over three days, rioters seized military and governmental buildings, including telegraph offices. It is conceivable that during these few riotous days the alleged pardon became irretrievably lost.

Billy Laird was executed on July 15, 1863, and is buried just east of Cranberry Meadow Road in a small wooded plot near the Little River in Berwick, Maine.

Billy Laird was one of approximately 73,000 from Maine who enlisted to fight in the Civil War, and the state suffered over 18,000 casualties. According to Colonel Stillings's research, Laird was the only Maine soldier in the Civil War to be executed for desertion. With regard to the 17th Maine Regiment, Jordan writes in *The Red Diamond Regiment*, "The 17th Maine may not have always fought the most effectively nor the most savagely, but they frequently stood where the fighting was the fiercest and faced the heaviest fire. They suffered more casualties than any other infantry regiment from Maine. The 17th easily laid claim to the honor of being one of the best combat units in the Union army." Of the 1,371 soldiers of the 17th Maine Regiment, 207 were killed, 552 wounded, and 163 died of disease.

For information specifically dealing with the 17th Maine Regiment, beginning at Camp King and then through their movements along the Potomac River, I relied extensively on the day-to-day accounts of Private John Haly in his published diary, *The Rebel Yell and the Yankee Hurrah: A Civil War Journal of a Maine Volunteer*. For accuracy of the battles referenced in my novel, I relied on numerous authenicated historical records. Haley's diary, however, was a wonderful source for the 17th's role in the Battle of Fredericksburg as seen through the eyes of a private.

In my novel, the slave runaway, Elijah, is fictitious. However, I wanted to balance Elijah's story with perhaps some lesser-known historical facts about William Still and the Underground Railroad. I've had a lifelong fascination with

Billy Boy

William Still, a free black man who has often been called the
Father of the Underground Railroad. Elijah was the means
through which I could offer an authentic glimpse of
Philadelphia's Anti-Slavery Society's Vigilance Committee, in
which William Still was chairman and recording secretary.
Many of the questions asked of Elijah by the members of the
Vigilance Committee were taken directly from Still's book, *The
Underground Railroad*, in which Still recorded interviews of so
many fugitives from slavery before they were assisted to
Canada.

My husband and I tracked Billy's and Elijah's escape route
beginning at Edward's Ferry, Maryland, the site of Billy's desertion. From there we traveled to Sandy Spring, Maryland, and
gathered information on the early Quaker settlers at the Sandy
Spring Museum, some of whom are mentioned in my novel,
and on to the train station at Ellicotts Mills, Maryland. The
train route that Billy traveled from Ellicotts Mills and ultimately to Boston, Massachusetts, was authenticated with assistance from the National Railroad Historical Society.

The U.S. Civil War is only the backdrop to this story, which
explores the reccurring themes of duty, loyalty, injustice, and
the human condition. Throughout the history of warfare, we
have been witness to man's inhumanity against man, and yet we
are also touched by the better angels of human nature. The
Quakers in my novel are examples of those angels. While
Johanna Samson is fictitious, Anna Dickinson was a young
Quaker from Philadelphia who spoke publicly against the evils
of slavery. Her relationship with Billy and Elijah is my creation.

A few final notes: In developing this story, the symbiotic
relationship between Billy and Elijah became an important
theme; when one stumbled, the other carried. Both young men

are challenged mentally; Billy, by his simplemindedness, and Elijah, by his view of the world shaped by the brutality and confinements of slavery. Finally, it is important to recognize that Billy's Laird's desertion was not unique in and of itself. It was a tragedy played out at home. For me, the collective belief that Laird was of limited intelligence only made his story more poignant.

About the Author

Jean Mary Flahive has always had a keen interest in American history. Born in Maine to a military family, she grew up all over the United States, lived for a while in Canada, and spent her childhood summers in New England.

She received a degree in political science from the University of New Hampshire and a master's degree in public administration from Pepperdine University. Her career includes owning a store in Albuquerque, New Mexico, teaching at the college level as well as serving as a dean of student services, and working as a grant writer, fundraiser, and project developer. She has worked closely with the Passamaquoddy Tribe in Maine. She is a member of the Board of Trustees of the University of Maine System and has won numerous awards for her work and community service.

She enjoys hiking, kayaking, orienteering, reading, and writing. She and her husband live in Falmouth and Eastport, Maine.

Billy Boy is her first novel.